Patchwork

Ila Yount

Rutledge Hill Press
Nashville, Tennessee

Published in Nashville, Tennessee, by Rutledge Hill Press, Inc., 513 Third Avenue South, Nashville, Tennessee 37210

The ballad on pages 86 and 87 is from *The Serpent Slips into a Modern Eden*, by James A. Turpin, Edwards & Broughton Printing Company, 1923. It is based on a murder that occurred in 1831.

Library of Congress Cataloging-in-Publication Data

Yount, Ila, 1928-
  Patchwork.

  I. Title.
PS3575.088P3   1987   813'.54   87-9197
ISBN 0-934395-45-4

1 2 3 4 5 6 7 — 92 91 90 89 88 87
Manufactured in the United States of America

To
Nola Willis Evans,
  for the inspiration of her life
Oliver A. Yount,
  for his love and support
Lewis W. Green,
  for giving me the courage to try

Patchwork

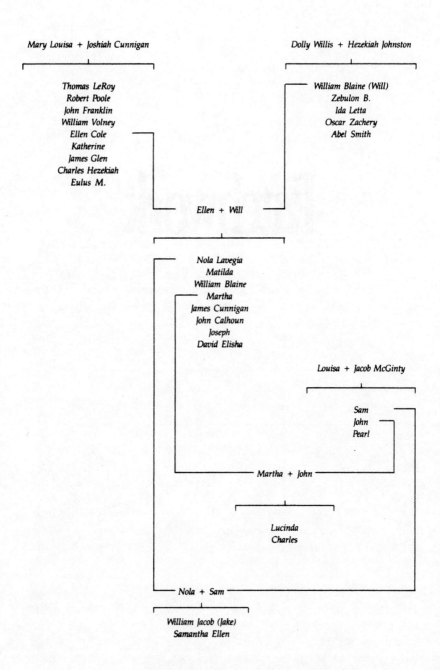

Mary Louisa + Joshiah Cunnigan

Thomas LeRoy
Robert Poole
John Franklin
William Volney
Ellen Cole
Katherine
James Glen
Charles Hezekiah
Eulus M.

Dolly Willis + Hezekiah Johnston

William Blaine (Will)
Zebulon B.
Ida Letta
Oscar Zachery
Abel Smith

Ellen + Will

Nola Lavegia
Matilda
William Blaine
Martha
James Cunnigan
John Calhoun
Joseph
David Elisha

Louisa + Jacob McGinty

Sam
John
Pearl

Martha + John

Lucinda
Charles

Nola + Sam

William Jacob (Jake)
Samantha Ellen

*T*he old woman raised an eyelid as the voice interrupted her dreams. *"Grandma. Grandma! Wake up! Do you know what day this is?"*

Oh Lord! Must I play the game with them again?

"No, I don't know. Guess it's Sunday," she answered, wondering what earthly difference it made.

"It's your birthday," the voice informed her. "Do you know how old you are?"

Of course she knew. Did they think she was senile? She was—she was. . . . Confusion swept over her as she struggled for an answer.

"You're one hundred years old today, Grandma. Happy birthday!"

She lifted a bony, gnarled hand in protest. "Who said that? Why, I'm no such thing! Who told that lie on me?"

The people crowded around her bed smiled, casting tolerant glances at each other. Suddenly it was too much for her, so she closed her eyes, willing her mind to shut them out. She wished Papa would come and take her back home.

Guess it'll be rough riding in the wagon, *she thought.* But anything would be better than lying here with all these strangers staring at me. Wish I could be rid of them! This pain in my hip, too. How did I hurt it? Was it when I was hurrying home to churn the butter and take the milk to the springhouse before suppertime?

I knew I shouldn't have stayed in the meadow, so late, but the violets were so pretty and the trillium and the ladyslippers are just beginning to bloom in the high places. I don't often get to just sit and look at things the way I wish I could. By the time I help Mama with the chores and help tend to the young ones, there isn't much time for mooning over flowers.

1

Again the voice interrupted her thoughts. "Grandma. Look at your cake. See the pretty roses and the candles?"

Something about the girl stirred her memory.

Maybe it's her dark eyes or that dark brown hair. Hair's almost as dark as mine, but not as long. Papa says mine looks like a brown river flowing down my back. Mama says I shouldn't be so vain about it, but I do love to brush it out at night and feel it spreading over my shoulders.

"Are you kinfolk?" she asked the girl abruptly. The name Cindy *flitted through her mind, and she spoke it tentatively.*

"Yes, Grandma. *it's me.*" *the girl laughed.* "Wake up and look at all your company. They've come to help you celebrate your birthday. Your grandchildren and great-grandchildren are all here, and there's more nieces and nephews than you can count. Sit up and see if you can tell who they all belong to. The whole family came just to let you know how much we love you and how proud we are of you."

No, *she thought.* Grandchildren? Great-grandchildren? Why, how could that be? Her mind groped frantically for something familiar to hold on to.

Cindy? Cindy? *she thought.* Oh yes, Sam's tune last night! "Git along home, Cindy, Cindy, git along home." *She saw the skirts swirling and the feet flying as the dancers circled the floor to the chant of the caller. She could smell the hay in the barn and see the bows flying over the strings of the fiddles as the music makers patted their feet to the beat of the tune. If her hip wasn't paining her so, she'd show them all a thing or two.*

The noise around the old woman rose and fell as kin visited with each other. Soon she was oblivious to it and gave herself over to her dreaming, plucking fitfully at the patchwork quilt on her bed.

Alma stood behind her daughter Cindy and gazed at her grandmother, recognizing the old woman's withdrawal. She had cared for her the last ten years, and it had not been an easy task.

"She's got a sharp tongue when she's a' mind to use it," Alma told her daughter, "but I don't know if I'd be any better if I was in her place. It's hard for her to be beholden to others."

"The hard life she's led, you'd think she'd be glad for somebody to wait on her for a change."

"Humph, not her," Alma laughed. "A day don't pass that she ain't fretting because she can't be up and doin'. Bet I'll never be able to say I kept my own house till I was ninety!"

"Did you hear her tell me yesterday to get her basket so she could gather the eggs?"

Alma nodded. "I just go along with her when she's like that. It upsets her so when I remind her she ain't livin' on the farm anymore."

"It's sad, in a way, to think she outlived both her children. She told me once the worst thing about growing old was not having anyone of her generation to talk to."

"I know. Sometimes when she's talking to me she calls me Samantha. It makes me feel funny—sometimes she has me wondering who I am!"

"The way she slips back into her girlhood is what gets me. I just can't imagine Grandma courting and flirting with the boys."

"Well, that's not too hard for me to imagine," Alma said drily. "I remember how she used to flit around like a bird before she fell and broke her hip. She could always charm any man in the room when she turned those big brown eyes on them."

One after another, the visitors slipped in to speak to the old woman as she lay in her bed.

Nola sank as far into the bedclothes as she could, trying to shut out all the confusing thoughts and the people milling around her. Her head spun dizzily, and she closed her eyes, retreating deep within herself and willing herself back to a time forever lost.

Faces and events whirled about her—the faces of loved ones long gone and events long forgotten. She drifted back to a time of happiness and childhood innocence, feeling the warm sun on her freckled nose and the heat from the ground warming the soles of her bare feet. Again she felt the broom sage tickling her legs as she ran through the pasture. Her breath quickened as she inhaled the clear, sharp air of the mountains. Her heart raced as she thought of Mama and Papa, and she felt as secure as the night her mother wrapped her in the first quilt she pieced for her.

"Now, your papa, Will Johnston, immigrated from England over the ocean to Charleston, South Carolina, with his ma and pa and his five brothers and three sisters. They didn't take to the flatlands, so they went on up the coast and met up with a train of settlers headin' across the Carolinas over into the mountains in Tennessee. It took them the better part of a year to make the trip, but finally they got there. That's where me and your papa met. My family had been there for some time. Mama and Papa come over from Ireland right after they got married. They lived in Virginny for a spell, but Papa said they was too many folks there for his taste, so they worked thir way down to Tennessee. Once he laid eyes on these mountains, he 'lowed as how he'd gone as far as he wanted to."

At this point in her story, Ellen always paused. She smiled at
the memory, then recounted Will's courtship. "Your papa said he
was curious to see who went with them blue eyes he seen peekin'
out from under that poke bonnet. Claims he knew right away
we'd marry, and sure enough about six months later we was married and a' farmin' the back acres of my papa's land."

Willie's eager voice urged Ellen on. "Then what happened,
Mama? Tell about the drummer and how you come to settle on
the Carolina side of the mountain."

"Hush, Willie," admonished Ellen, "I'm tellin' it as fast as I can.
Well, one day this drummer come around with his wares and all
he wanted to talk about was how beautiful it was on the other side
of the mountain range, and how black and rich the soil was. He
went on and on about it 'til yore papa got plumb curious about
why he thought it was so much better than Tennessee. Before I
knew what he was about, he packed up me and Nola, who was
just a baby less than a year old, tied the cow to the back of the
wagon and hitched up the two mules. We traveled better than a
hundred miles—took us nearly a month to make it. Wasn't much
of a trail to follow, and most of it was uphill. Sometimes it took me
and Will both a' pushin' and a' pullin' with the mules to get that
wagon over some of the boulders. Sometimes the trail just plumb
petered out, and we had to follow creeks and hope we was goin'
in the right direction. We just kept our eyes on that sun every
mornin' when it come up though, and headed straight towards
it."

"Did Papa find out what was better about the Carolina side
Mama?" asked Willie.

"Well, I reckon he did. You never heard a man take on so. He
vowed he'd never seen as many different kinds of trees as we
come across—and the big balsams! I reckon they's no prettier
sight on earth than them big evergreens etched out against the
sky. They put me in mind of soldiers the way they stood so
straight and tall a' guardin' them mountain tops. Now Tennessee
was pretty too, but some places the hills is as red as copper, and
when we come into these mountains, it was so green it almost
hurt yore eyes to look at it."

"How come you picked this place to stop, Mama," asked Nola.

"Well, yore Papa knowed we was in Carolina by now, and when
we come up to the top of that ridge up yonder and looked down
into this cove about sunset one evenin', yore Papa said, 'Ellen,

we've come home!' Guess I felt the same way too, so this is where we lit. I ain't never been sorry, and I don't reckon he has either."

"What do you think she's dreaming about, Mother?" asked Cindy. *"She's smiling in her sleep."*

"I don't know, but I know it must be something that made her happy."

Cindy watched her great-grandmother as she stirred restlessly under her covers. She looked at the thin hands, the skin so transparent you could see the network of blue veins thread through it. She touched the brown age spots and stared thoughtfully at the strong profile of the old woman.

"Grandma," she murmured softly,

> *Where do you go when you close your eyes?*
> *Do you run in the fields again?*
> *Do you cook and sew and churn and tend,*
> *or do you laugh and love and cry?*
> *What do you do in the endless hours*
> *that you lie in your bed and dream?*

Nola stirred and then settled back into her pillows.

ONE

Will paused at his work long enough to mop the sweat off his brow. He was grubbing up stumps from a newly cleared field. With the help of the mules, he had snaked out the larger stumps, but the smaller ones had to be grubbed out one by one. As he rested, Will gazed at the cabin he and Ellen had built. It was a rough, one room shelter utilizing a bank of earth for the back wall. Basic shelter was all he had time for. He had to get the fields cleared so they could plant crops.

There were few settlers in the cove, but one by one they had come by to give what help they could. Once the hickorys were felled, the cabin quickly took shape. Ellen helped him as best she could, dividing her time between baby Nola and the building.

"I've got to get a door hung," Will muttered as he watched Ellen push aside the quilt that hung over the opening.

His eyes wandered over the area he was clearing, looking for herbs. He was delighted at the abundance of medicinal plants he had found in the woods around them.

"Wish I had time to locate more of them," he thought as he pulled a dog-eared tablet out of the bib of his overalls. He flipped through it, remembering the granny woman who had helped him compile his diary of herbs.

A sharp bark from the dog brought him out of his reverie, and he looked up to see a boy stepping out of the woods into the clearing. As he drew near, Will recognized Jesse Cole's oldest son, Caleb. The Coles were their nearest neighbors, but lived far enough away to make a mid-morning visit unusual.

The boy called to him, "Say, Mr. Johnston, my pa says to ask can you come over to our place? He heard you do some doctorin' and we shore do need some help. My Ma's having a hard time birthin' the new baby, and Pa's awful scared she ain't gonna make it. He sent for Aunt Addie Carver, but she's over at the Hoopers a' helpin' out with them twin babies Mrs. Hooper had. I reckon we'd shore be much obliged if you could come help us."

"Well son, I'll be glad to do what I can. Let me get my things, and I'll be right with you."

Will dropped his axe and hurried to the house where Ellen helped him get his things together.

"At least it ain't a cow you're doctorin' this time," she said. "I'll bet that doctor you was apprenticed to in England didn't know you'd be doctorin' man and beast alike."

"Guess not. Now Ellen, I'll do my best to get back before dark, but if it's bad, I may have to stay the night. You bring old Shep in and make him lay by the door if I don't get back. I don't like the way that painter has been comin' so near lately. I don't think there's any danger, or I wouldn't leave you. I'd sure feel a lot better if I'd got that door hung."

"Don't worry, Will, we'll take care. Me and Shep will look after things."

Ellen watched Will and Caleb disappear over the ridge with a sinking sensation in the pit of her stomach. Her bold words hid her real feelings. As she turned back to her chores, she uttered a prayer.

"Please help Mrs. Cole have that baby in a hurry, Lord, so Will can get back home before nighttime. I couldn't let him know how scared I am to stay by myself."

Ellen kept busy all day, trying not to look up the mountain trail. In spite of her good intentions, she frequently caught herself straining to catch a glimpse of Will through the trees. The sun seemed to be in a hurry to set that day, and nightfall came too soon to suit her. The lengthening shadows took on ominous shapes as she hurriedly brought in her evening's supply of wood and finished up the outside chores.

Too soon the sun sank below the mountain peaks, and darkness descended on the valley. She had never noticed how total the darkness was when the sun disappeared. The trees surrounding the cabin formed a canopy that hid the sky, and she did not even have the starlight to break the still, heavy dark. The fire on the hearth did little to penetrate the gloom of the cabin, and every corner brooded darkly at her. She found herself jumping nervously at every sound.

Still hoping that Will would be home that evening, Ellen began preparations for supper. She patted out stiff corn dough and placed it on the sizzling embers she pulled onto the hearth rock. She covered the dough with more hot embers and live coals and left the ash cake to bake while she put some side meat in to fry.

The baby began fretting, and Ellen stopped her preparations and put her to her breast—taking some comfort from the feel of the tiny body against her own. After she settled the baby in the cradle, Ellen took up the ash cake, carefully brushed the ashes off and reluctantly sat down to a lonely meal. When she bowed her head to give thanks for her food, she added a special plea— "Please, Lord, don't let that painter come a' prowlin' around tonight with Will gone. I'm not very brave, you know, and I might not be able to stand up and pertect little Nola."

For several nights they had heard the snarls and cries of the mountain lion near the cabin. Will said it probably smelled the pig he had slaughtered, but Ellen could only think of the old wives' tales about wild animals sensing the presence of babies. One night when the painter had come too close, Will had fired his gun into the dark woods. For several nights now, they had heard nothing.

Ellen fed the big brown collie the rest of the food scraps and then led him to the doorway. "Now Shep, you stay! Stay right there, and don't let nothin' come through that door!"

She turned the wick up on the lamp and took up her bag of scraps. With neat, short stitches she began joining the pieces she had cut out for her quilt. As the fireplace burned bravely against the chill of the mountain evening, Shep watched her and began to doze.

As she bent over her work, words came almost unbidden to her mind:

> Life is like a patchwork quilt
> With pieces of every color, shape, and hue.
> Some are light and airy,
> Others sober and blue.
>
> Here's a piece of Mama's skirt,
> A patch of sister's Sunday best,
> And there's a strip from brother's shirt,
> Next to Papa's old grey vest

On and on the story goes
In each quilt pattern's design.
A life of joys and woes,
God's plan, not mine.

The panther's first scream came as Ellen reached to turn the lamp wick down. She froze in fright. Shep raised his head and tensed where he lay, the hackles on his back rising. He laid his ears back and bared his teeth in a deep-throated snarl.

With trembling hands, Ellen reached for Will's gun hanging over the fireplace. She breathed a prayer of thanks that he had primed and loaded it before leaving and that her pa had made her learn to shoot. When the pigs began squealing, she almost dropped the gun. Shep, now standing stiff-legged facing the doorway, began to bark. Ellen hastily laid her hand on his shoulder. "Stay now, Shep," she commanded as firmly as she could manage. "We can't do nothin' about them pore critters now."

She thought of how proud of those pigs Will was. Mr. Phillips had given him the sow for his doctoring. It was the most pay he'd ever received. *Guess the painter'll get all her babies 'fore it's over,* she thought.

Just when she began to hope the cat had left, the screams began again. This time the cries came from the clearing around the house. Desperately searching her mind for a plan to stave the creature off, she remembered Will telling how he had kept a pair of wolves at bay one night by keeping his campfire burning. She picked up a log and threw it on the fire, poked at the coals, and took heart as they flared up.

The cat was closer now, and its screams sent chills through her. Her desperation gave her the strength to shove the heavy plank table across the doorway and she turned it on its side, blocking the lower part of the opening.

"Well, Shep, at least we don't have to watch our backs," she said. "It's a good thing Will built this cabin against a bank."

No sooner were the words out of her mouth, than something landed on the roof with a thud. She froze as the animal began scratching at the roof, trying to find a crevice for its claws. The clawing seemed to go on for an eternity before the cat gave up and jumped off the roof.

She followed the panther's progress around the cabin by its screams. When it was almost on the stoop, she turned her large washtub over Nola's cradle and resolutely faced the door with the gun. With trembling fingers, she drew back the hammer and muttered a prayer. Shep backed up in front of her and braced himself for the battle.

With a loud scream, the panther tore through the quilt. Ellen tried to hold the rifle steady as she retreated from the door. She squeezed the trigger and felt the explosion as she fell over Nola's cradle and sat down hard on the floor. Stunned, she closed her eyes, expecting the cat's attack.

Ellen awakened to the feel of Shep's rough tongue on her face. In the eerie silence she became aware of the panther lying half in and half out of the cabin, draped across the table where it had fallen. When she found the strength to stand, Ellen took her broom and pushed the animal off the table, back into the yard. Then she turned to Nola, sleeping peacefully under the washpot. Picking her up, Ellen began laughing and crying at the same time and sat back in her rocker, clasping her to her bosom as Shep pushed against her legs. She alternately stroked the baby and patted the dog until her body stopped trembling.

When Will returned home early the next morning, he was stunned to see a dead panther lying across the doorstep and Ellen sitting at the table mending her torn quilt. The floor was wet where she had tried to scrub the animal's blood away. She dropped the quilt and threw her arms around him.

"Ellen, what on earth has gone on here? Are you all right? Nola—where's Nola?"

"Oh, Will, we're both fine. I'm fine and Nola's fine and Shep's fine. Everything's fine, now that you're home. I've never been so scared in all my life. Did you help Mrs. Cole get that baby borned? Is she all right?"

"Yes. Yes to both questions," Will answered. "It was a difficult birth, and I thought I'd had a right busy night, but nothing like what's gone on around here. What happened? I nearly fainted when I saw the way the pigs were scattered all over the place. Looks like only one of them's hurt bad. The rest must have run and hid."

"Well," she said shakily, "I reckon we've had a right busy night. Guess I wouldn't want to spend another one like it."

Then looking at him with a half smile, she said in mock severity, "Will Johnston, you'd best get busy on that door today. I've put too many stitches and too much hard work into my quilts to get them all tore up like this! It's a good thing it wasn't my wedding ring quilt. You'd be in a heap of trouble if it was."

Will could only hold her and stare at her in amazement. By nightfall he had completed the door and hung it securely in place. He also made a stout bar to fasten it.

TWO

The little garden they planted that first year flourished in the rich mountain soil. Will grubbed out the stumps and turned the ground behind the mule. When the rows were laid off, Ellen took out the seeds, packed so carefully when they left Tennessee. They planted their beans, corn, potatoes, and onions first. Ellen was careful to plant by the signs as her mother had taught her: underground vegetables in the dark of the moon, the others in the waning moon. Later they added pumpkins, squash, peppers, and turnips. After the garden was planted, Ellen dug her flower beds in front of the cabin and planted hollyhocks, zinnias, and pretty-by-nights.

The first spring in their new home was a time of anticipation and wonder. Each new day became a time of discovery. Ellen saw Will in a new light as he took responsibility for his family and emerged as his own man, respected by his neighbors and looked up to as one who stood ready to help anyone.

She wrote to her mother:

> Will is always surprisin me with his hungerin for knowin everything there is to know about medicine. His mind is so quick and there never seems to be an end to his questions when he hears about a new herb or a better way to grow crops. He works from sunup on past sundown with never a word of complaint. He takes all the burdens on himself and is always thinkin up ways to make things better for us. He's already busy makin things for us to lay up against the day we can raise anuther bigger cabin. He's done finished me a pie cabinet to hold my dishes and now he's workin on a new bedstead. I wrote you how the one we

brought with us fell off the wagon when we was a fordin that river and broke one of the legs off. It's as fine as any I've ever seen. Seems like when he gits a piece of wood in his hands, he just sorta feels the shape of what ought to come out of it. He's promised to make me a stout chest to put my quilts in soons he finishes the bedstead—and the quiltin frames he made me are the finest ones in the cove.

He's a good Papa to Nola too. He's so good and patient with her—more than I am sometimes, cause she shore tries my patience these days. She's walkin and just as curious as her Papa is and into everything. Will's always carvin her out some clever little critter from his wood scraps and then teachin her to say their names.

Course, her best words are Mama and Papa. She can near melt yore heart when she looks at you with them big brown eyes—they're so like Will's. Ah, I do love this cove where we live! The only thing I wish I could change would be to move it closer to you and Papa. I do miss you so!

Will was making discoveries of his own about this girl he had married. Although not one to boast, in a rare burst of candor he recounted Ellen's virtues to Jesse Cole one morning while they melted lead and poured it into their bullet molds.

"That Ellen never ceases to amaze me," he told Jesse.

"How's that, Will?"

"She'll work side by side with me in the field as hard as any man, and then go home and set a meal on the table that's fit for a king."

"Do tell? Well, you're shore a lucky man, Will."

"I don't see how she does it and tends to Nola too," Will continued. "What with her a' walking and into everything she can reach the minute your back's turned. And even after she's cleaned up the supper dishes and put Nola to bed, she don't stop. It's always an apron for Nola or else piecing on one of her quilts."

"Yeah, beats all how them women loves to get together at their quiltin's." Jesse laughed.

"What's so grand though, is she's always a'singing while she works," Will went on as if Jesse had not interrupted. "Usually she's singing one of them poems she's forever making up. It sure was a lucky day for me when I looked under that poke bonnet at them blue eyes! Yes sir, I'm a man twice blessed. A woman that works and helps me and that little girl a' coming along so like her Ma."

Jesse laughed heartily at Will's sudden eloquence, causing him to grin sheepishly. Jesse slapped him on his back and said, "Don't you fret none, Will. Just be glad you feel that way about your missus. I reckon I feel the same, but I just don't know the words to say it like you do. This is a hard old life, and it takes two a'pullin' together to make it, and that's for shore!"

Ellen's homemaking skills were complemented by her practical common sense, which made for a good balance to Will's sometimes impractical dreaming. He was apt to go off on a tangent when he heard about an herb that had some special curative quality to it. Many times Ellen had to remind him that the day-to-day needs had to be seen to first. He was often lured by the stories of the medicine man in the Cherokee village, but after the incident with the panther, he learned to content himself with brief trips that allowed him to get home by dark. Steadily his herb diary grew, and he spent many evenings poring over it by the dim lamplight.

One morning as they toiled together in their garden, Will paused to wipe his brow and, looking up, gazed at Ellen as she tended to Nola. He watched as Ellen tenderly wiped the dirt from the child's face and hands, teasing her out of the tears caused by her sudden tumble.

Bending again to his hoe, he smiled at her and said, "Strong and wise you are, woman!"

Then tossing aside the hoe, he picked her up in his arms and looked her full in the face, "Right comely, too," he added with a grin.

Ellen blushed, pushing the bonnet back from her face, then flashed blue eyes at him flirtatiously. The question she read in his eyes cause her to lower her head modestly, then laughing, answered his unspoken question with a quick kiss on his lips. He clasped her to him tightly, and they clung together there in the midst of the garden, feet planted firmly in the rich black earth. After he released her and they went back to their hoeing, he still felt her firm young body pressed against him.

A few days later her wisdom as well as her composure was tested when she had some unexpected visitors. Will had gone to help Jesse Cole fence in his new ground, and Ellen was sitting in the cabin door almost lulled to sleep by the rhythm of the churn dasher. Little Nola was napping in the cradle near by, and Ellen almost tipped over her chair when she looked up and saw two Indians staring at her.

Cautioning herself not to scream, she rose, and in her most charming manner she said, "Why, howdy, neighbors. Won't you just come right in and set a spell? My man's over to the spring-house and will be home directly."

Before the startled men could react, she pulled out chairs and seated them at the table. Then moving as fast as she could, she set two places, drew off the cloth protecting the food from the flies, and served each with generous helpings of beans, cornbread, potatoes and fried apple pies. She poured cups of sweet milk and stood back while they looked questioningly at each other. Finally they cautiously tasted the food, grunted at each other, and began to eat hungrily.

All the time she kept up a steady stream of talk. It soon became apparent that neither of them understood a word she was saying, so she talked as much to herself as to them.

"Why shore enough, you're a strange lookin' sight a' settin' in my clean kitchen, a' eatin' my victuals and thinkin' the good Lord knows what. Wonder what all that funny lookin' colorin' on your skin means. Hope it don't mean you're on no war party. I ain't a' goin' to bother you just as long as you don't bother me and mine. If you'll just eat these victuals and go on your merry way, we'll get along just fine. I'm a' watchin' though, and if you make one move toward my baby, I'll snatch up that butcher knife and cut your ugly heads off."

The men looked at her in puzzlement, then exchanged a glance that spoke volumes about this crazy, talkative white woman. When she saw they had eaten everything on the table, she gestured to the door and urged them out as charmingly as she had invited them in. They stood uncertainly on the stoop as she began waving to them and calling, "Goodbye, goodbye, go on home to your squaws and don't come back here again, you heathens!"

Finally, they raised their hands haltingly and imitated her waves, timidly at first and then with great enthusiasm, as they left the clearing around the house, speaking their first words to each other as they entered the woods.

"Probably wondering at the strange antics of the crazy white woman," Will chuckled when she recounted the event. "They probably went home and treated their squaws a little kinder when they realized how much white women talk!"

Before cold weather moved into the mountains again, Will built them a sturdier log cabin with the help of the few neighbors.

"There's something to be said about having lots of folks around you like we did in Tennessee," Will told Ellen, "but I don't think you'd find any better or harder working ones than we've found here. Every man of them has worked just as hard as I have."

Their new home not only had four solid walls, it had a loft for the children they hoped to have one day. After the hard dirt floor of the first cabin, Ellen rejoiced in the real wood floors Will laid. The great room seemed more spacious to them after the cramped space of the tiny room they had been used to. Since this was where most of their time was spent, Ellen was delighted with the extra space.

"I don't regret leaving this little old cabin," Ellen told Will, "but I'll always feel special about it 'cause it was our first home."

The furnishings were simple, but practical, pieces Will had made during the late evening hours, usually by lamplight. Ellen had saved every feather she could find and made them a soft feather tick for their bed to replace the cornshuck one they had been using.

"I feel as fine as any king in the world," Will declared the first night they slept on it.

The morning they packed the last of their belongings, she lingered with Will for one last look around the rough shelter that had been their home.

"You know, Will," she said softly, as she tied the strings of her blue bonnet firmly under her chin, "we must be mindful of the importance of this first home of ours. It's been nice here in this little cove, and we've had times here I'll never forget. Just think, someday maybe our grandchildren might play here just like little Nola has. Promise me you'll keep it up."

The little cabin became a place where Ellen could come when she needed time to be alone, to gather her thoughts. She often hiked up the mountain trail and sat on the stoop of the little cabin and drank in the solitude and peaceful quiet.

It was here she came when she received word that her mother had died some two weeks earlier, heartbroken that even the comfort of attending her funeral had been denied her. She wept bitter tears and cried out at the injustice of it, demanding an answer that she knew would not be forthcoming. It was here also that she came when she found that she was with child again. This time she sang out her joy and gave thanks for a new life.

"*Can you believe that first little cabin Great-great grandfather Johnston built is still standing?*" Cindy asked her mother as they sat by Nola's bed. "*Ever since I can remember, we climbed that hill and played house in that small room. I can't believe three people lived in that tiny space. It's just like a doll house. I used to pretend I was my great-great grandmother Ellen taking care of my family there. Some of the flowers she planted still come back every spring. I still like to go up there and write. I feel like they're all there around me sometimes—Grandmother in her calico dress with the snow-white apron over it. Can't you just see Grandma Nola in her long aprons trailing after her father?*"

THREE

The needles flew in and out as the six women bent over the quilting frame. Each was engrossed in the pattern she was weaving with her needle. The quilting frame Will had made during the long winter months was suspended from the cabin's rafters, so that it could be let down and pulled back up as they found time to work on the quilt.

Ellen had pieced this quilt from the bits and pieces of cloth painstakingly saved from dresses and clothing of her sisters and brothers. Each scrap had a special meaning to her, and as she pieced she thought wistfully of her family back in Tennessee. They had not been able to make the trip back since moving to North Carolina.

"Seven brothers and two sisters is a nice big family," she thought. "Mama always said that was just right for her. I wonder if me and Will are a' gonna have a big family."

Nola was nearly three years old, and finally Will and Ellen were expecting another child. She paused in her quilting frequently to stretch her back.

"I reckon we're mighty lucky to have such good neighbors," she thought as she looked at the women seated around the quilting frame.

Sarah Cole, wife of Jesse Cole, was their closest neighbor, living over the ridge to the east of their cabin. Sarah was a little woman who had borne her husband four strapping sons and one daughter. She had fiery red hair, which she wore in a tight bun on top of her head.

Will had remarked to Ellen, "That Sarah Cole may be little, but she sure rules those big boys of hers with an iron hand. Could be that she gets some help from that red hair."

Nellie Mann lived in the cove below Ellen. She was a plain little woman, soft-spoken and as retiring and timid as Sarah was bold and outspoken. Ellen told Will, "Nellie puts me in mind of one of them little gray house wrens the way she flits around and works all the time. Folks say she's the best cook in this settlement. She's got them three little girls of hers cookin' too. I vow they'll make good wives when they're ready to marry."

Mary Plemmons was a large raw-boned woman whom her husband bragged could outwork any two men in the fields. She had reddish blonde hair that she kept braided in a coronet around her head. Her hands were rough and callused, but her stitches were as tiny and delicate as any of the others. The Plemmons had no children.

Sarah had told Ellen, "Pore Mary, she ain't got no young'uns to love, so she takes in every stray animal and bird that comes her way. I never seen so many different critters as she has hangin' around her barn. She's got everything from a raccoon to that one-winged owl she rescued. Jesse said he thought the critters had passed the word that Mary's a soft touch."

Julie Phillips was nearest to Ellen's age and was five months pregnant with her first child. She and her husband, Elisha, were the largest landholders in the cove. Julie was Elisha's second wife and was stepmother to his two sons and three daughters. His first wife had died in childbirth. He was considerably older than Julie.

"Sometimes I feel more like a sister to the children than their mother," Julie told Ellen. "I hope that when the baby comes I'll feel more grown up than I do now. Elisha would spoil me just like he does his children if I'd let him. The girls are real excited about the baby though, and I may not get to do much motherin'."

Julie was a delicate blonde with sparkling blue eyes. She looked as if she belonged in an elegant drawing room instead of the rough wilderness cabin that was her home.

Louisa McGinty was the other quilter. She, too, was expecting a child, her third. She had two sons and was longing for a daughter this time. A tall slender woman with black curly hair, she was the most accomplished seamstress in the group. She and Sarah Cole lived closer to Ellen than the others, and so Ellen felt she knew them better. Louisa had been especially kind to Ellen when she and Nola were both sick with the grippe. Twice that week she had climbed the mountain trail to bring fresh baked bread and hot soup to them.

The quilters were working on a Log Cabin quilt for Ellen. She had used a scrap of Nola's first apron as the center of the pattern. It was a rich mulberry red, and the dark strips fanning out on one side were supposed to represent the shadows in the cabin. The light strips on the other side represented the sunshine radiating from the center square, which represented the fire.

Ellen took short, neat stitches as she outlined the strips in the pattern. The talk rose and fell, each quilter absorbed in her work. Ellen had missed her turn with the quilters in February. The snow and ice had been too severe for even the hardiest travelers, so everyone was working hard to make up for the lost turn.

"Well, Ellen," said Sarah, "I think we'll finish your quilt today, and then you can get it bound off and ready before yore next young'un gets here. It'll come in handy next winter if we get as much snow and ice as we did this past one."

"I don't reckon I've ever been so happy to see the spring as I was this year," Nellie Mann spoke softly. "Seems like the violets and trillium has plumb outdone theirselves, and the Judas' trees has never been this red."

As the women talked around her, sharing the news they had accumulated since their quilting last month, Ellen pondered on the feelings the quilting bees roused in her. Words formed in her thoughts:

> *Oh, the joy one feels,*
> *When first the quilt reveals*
> *The patterns and stories of old*
> *They weave with stitches so bold*
>
> *'Tis soothing to me*
> *When with my friends I see*
> *The cloth and colors combine*
> *With love the pattern to define.*

She was brought out of her reverie as the baby she carried moved in protest at the cramped position of her body. She moved and, stretching her back, put her hand on her abdomen in a soothing motion. It had been a difficult pregnancy this time, as if to make up for the ease of the first one. She was still having bouts of morning sickness and her already in her eighth month.

"Why they call it morning sickness I'll never know," she told Will. "This baby has woke me many a' night from a sound sleep, and I've had to run for the slop jar. Even before I missed my first time, I'd already got mincy about my eatin'. Seems like I've had mornin', noon and night sickness."

With a start, Ellen realized the last bit of quilting was finished, and the women were taking the quilt off the frame. "Well, that finishes another one, Ellen," said Sarah. "You've got a fine, warm quilt. Next month don't forget, it's my turn. I hope you'll be able to get there. It's a hard walk over the ridge to our place. But I've got a Wedding Ring quilt put together against the day my Mollie gets married, and I want to get it quilted and in her chest."

"Oh yes, Sarah, the baby is due in about two weeks, and I'll be fine by then. Will said I could have the wagon and mule if I don't feel up to walkin'."

"When is Will comin' home?" asked Mary Plemmons. "If he wants to get his 'taters in the ground by Good Friday, he better be gettin' on home soon."

"I expect him home by tomorrow. He couldn't wait a day longer to pick up that new doctorin' book he ordered. We needed some supplies and he used that for an excuse to go," she laughed as she stretched her back, massaging it with her hand.

"Hmmm, seems to me you look like that baby's gonna come quicker'n any two weeks," Sarah Cole said. "Are you shore you're a' feelin' alright? Low as that baby's settin', it can't be much longer. I recollect my second one was a mite earlier than we thought it would be."

"Oh Ellen, if you're afeared at all that it's comin' early, I'll be proud to stay on the night with you. Miz Cole can send her boy over to tell my family where I am. I'd feel a lot better if you'd let me stay. What on earth would you do here by yoreself if it come early?" Nellie Mann asked her.

"Goodness no! I'll be fine. Why I'm not the least bit uneasy. You just go on and tend to yore family and don't fret about me," Ellen protested.

"Well now, if you're right shore," Nellie said reluctantly.

"I am. I'm sure I'm goin' to be perfectly fine," Ellen said emphatically.

One by one her friends began picking up their baskets, drawing their shawls around their shoulders and readying themselves for their treks home. Each gave her a reassuring pat or hug as they

left. As Ellen watched them out of sight, she felt somewhat uneasy, but she put her feelings down to sadness at ending the companionship the gatherings afforded her.

She put away her sewing supplies with a sigh and began preparations for a simple meal for Nola. The thought of food made her
feel suddenly nauseous, and she ate nothing. When the child had
eaten, Ellen took her hand, picked up the bucket by the door and
started for the spring. It was not far from the cabin, and Ellen was
suddenly grateful she did not have far to walk. She felt a more
pronounced feeling of heaviness in her abdomen and suddenly
longed for the safety of the cabin.

The first pain struck her as she lifted the brimming bucket of
water, and she gasped as much from surprise as pain. Trying not
to trip over the trailing hem of her dress, she urged Nola up the
path ahead of her. As she entered the door, she felt the warm gush
of liquid down her legs.

Oh no, she thought, *it can't be a' comin' now, it's too early. Besides, I
ain't even got the cradle down from the loft yet.*

Nola looked at her mother with big, brown questioning eyes
and spoke a tentative, "Mama?"

"Go on, honey baby, and fetch Papa's satchel to the bed," she
told the child.

Ellen knew the supplies she needed would be in Will's doctoring bag. She closed the cabin door and made her way to the bed,
shedding her damp under garments and dress as she went. She
slipped her long white cotton gown over her head, grateful for its
voluminous size.

Nola dragged the satchel to her mother, wondering at the sight
of Ellen going to bed before dark. "Nola, you must get yoreself to
bed now," Ellen told her. "Never mind about yore night dress.
Just pull yore shoes off and get under the quilt. Mama will take
care of everything directly. Just go along and be a good girl now."

When she was sure Nola was settled, Ellen began preparing for
the ordeal ahead of her. She took out clean sheets and searched
through the satchel until she found scissors and string. Only then
did she give in to the pains and lie down.

"Oh, Lord," she prayed, "the good book says you won't give us
any more'n we can bear. I hope you know what you're a' doin',
'cause I'm not shore I can bear what's a' comin'. When little Nola
come, I had my own ma and sisters to help me. Now it looks like
I'm just a' gonna have to help myself."

Time stood still as each new pain washed over her, and she was borne up to the crest of it until she could bear no more. Then it would blessedly ease off for a few minutes. The perspiration poured off her, and the rag she stuffed in her mouth to stifle her moans almost gagged her.

The cabin grew darker, and only the waning fire gave off a little light. Her eyes adjusted to the dark as time passed. One pain now merged with the next until her whole world was engulfed in a red blaze of agony. She knew it couldn't last much longer, and steeled herself for the final contractions. Bearing down with all of her strength, her body gave one final contraction, and the baby was born. Knowing she must find the strength to complete the job, she raised herself up and pulled the baby up onto her stomach. She felt the cord, took the scissors in trembling hands and cut and tied it off with the string she had made ready. The baby cried, and she pulled it up to her breast and wrapped a sheet around it, then fell back exhausted. As she drifted into unconsciousness, she murmured the words of her favorite Psalm: "I will lift up mine eyes unto the hills from whence cometh my help. My help cometh from the Lord." Her last thought was of the baby, and she pondered, "Little baby, are you a girl or a boy? Never mind. Whatever you are, you are a tough one, 'a pushin' yore way into this world all by yoreself."

Will woke her, laughing and crying at the same time. "Ellen, Ellen, what have you done now? You've gone and birthed the baby by yourself! Oh, my dear, brave, strong Ellen."

She opened her eyes and looked up into Will's tear-streaked face and cried out in relief, "Thank the Lord you're finally home. This has been the longest night of my life."

"Oh Ellen, I'm so sorry. How on earth did you manage by yourself?"

"Just stop talkin' for a minute, and hold me, Will," she said. "Just hold me and tell me yo're really here."

Will pulled her into his arms and she clung to him. They sat thus until a small, sleepy voice stirred them from their embrace.

"Mama, Papa's home," Nola said as she stumbled across the cabin floor to them, rubbing the sleep out of her eyes.

"Yes, and that ain't all that's home. Here's yore new baby. . . . Oh, my soul, Will, I still don't know if it's a boy or a girl! Look at it and tell me."

Will took the baby from her and chuckled as he examined it. "Why, for sure, she's a brave strong-willed girl just like her mother," he said. "Guess we'll just have to call her little Ellen."

"No such thing, Will Johnston," said Ellen. "She'll be her own person, and nobody's little anything. I've had it in mind to call her Matilda. I heard once that Matilda means 'powerful in battle,' and little Tildy shore battled her way into this world!"

She caressed the baby and murmured, "First thing tomorrow I'll have to get busy and start piecing you a quilt for your bed. Maybe I'll make a pretty little Dutch Girl quilt. Next time it's my turn for the quiltin', I aim to have it pieced and in the frame so's we can get started workin' on it. I don't aim to get caught short like this again.

"Now, Will, please get up in the loft and get this baby's cradle ready so she can have a proper bed. And get Nola a clean apron to put on. Pore child went to bed in her clothes last night without even gettin' her face washed. Go get the brush, honey, so Papa can brush yore hair for you. Be careful, Will, she's got such thick hair and it's tangled. Don't brush too hard, she's right tender-headed."

"Stop fussin' with my hair, girl," Nola scolded Cindy. "You're pulling it out by the roots. I can't stand for anybody but Mama to brush my hair. She knows how to get the tangles out without hurting me. Sam said he never did want me to get my hair cut, and I never have. He called it my crowning glory. Said the color reminds him of chestnuts when they're dead ripe. Martha's hair was never as pretty as mine, and she was always envious of me. Don't tell Mama what I said, she'll switch me. She says it's sinful to be vain."

"Yes, Grandma," laughed Cindy, "I'll try to be more careful."

Deftly she twisted the old lady's thin white locks into a bun on top of her head.

Nola grasped her arm suddenly and asked, "Is the cradle ready for the baby? Papa said he built it good and stout so it'd last through all the babies. Fix it pretty now, and put the special little quilt Mama made in it. Poor little Tildy, she didn't use it long. They put her in the cold, dark ground all by herself. Don't put me too deep where it's so dark. I was always afraid of the dark. Tildy looked so little and frail that day and so lonesome. Wonder if it's hard making the trip to the other side? Mama says Jesus is waiting for you. I hope he stays near by when I'm making my journey."

rue to her promise, Ellen began the new quilt for Tildy. She could only spend odd moments at night on the quilt, because her days were filled with work from the time she rose at dawn until the last glimmer of light at evening. In addition to the children and household tasks, she had to help Will with the crops. He had cleared another field where he planned to plant corn with seed saved carefully from last summer's crop. It was back-breaking work for both of them, and they took turns with the mule and plow. The black earth had a special scent of its own and was rich and loamy.

"I declare, Ellen," Will said as he paused to mop his brow, "this is the richest land I've ever seen. If corn don't grow here, it won't grow anywhere."

"Humph," replied Ellen, "I just hope the corn will grow half as thick as these roots have!"

Ellen had brought the children to the field with her and had placed them under a big oak at the edge of the newly cleared ground. As she toiled back and forth with the mule, she tried to keep them content. Although Nola was not much more than a baby herself, she sensed the importance of keeping watch over Tildy. The baby was still tiny and had not yet made up for her premature birth. She nursed hungrily when Ellen fed her, but she never seemed satisfied and did not fill out as Nola had.

One morning she was particularly restless and fretful, and Nola rocked the cradle with a little too much vigor. It upended, spilling Tildy out on the ground with all the bedclothes landing on top of her. Nola screamed for Ellen, but she was at the far end of the field

25

and did not hear her. She pulled the covers off Tildy and tried to lift the baby the way she had seen Ellen do it, but the wriggling, screaming child was too much for her and she tumbled off the little knoll into the damp earth beside Tildy.

When Ellen turned to work her way back across the field, all she could see was the upended cradle. No babies were anywhere in sight. She ran as fast as the sticky, plowed ground would let her, fearing the worst. She was almost fainting with fear by the time she reached them. When she did, she cried and laughed in relief. Both children were covered with black earth and were screaming in indignation. As she picked them up and brushed the dirt from their faces, she made crooning sounds, trying to comfort both children at once.

"This is one day I'm a' goin' to quit early, and this field can be hanged for all I care," she said. She picked Nola up, placed her on her hip and, with Tildy in her other arm, made her way back to the cabin. There she filled the wash basin with water and washed both children. She gave Nola a piece of ash cake to chew on and put Tildy to her breast.

When Will came to the cabin to see where they were, he was astounded to hear peals of laughter as Ellen trotted Nola on her foot while she recited an old nursery chant,

> "*Trot a little horsey,*
> *trot down town.*
> *Trot a little horsey,*
> *nearly fall down!*"

On the last line, she tossed Nola up in the air and caught her in her arms.

"Ellen," Will said in mock severity, "what on earth has got into you? The day is only half gone, and you're sitting around playing like a young'un! Have you taken leave of your senses?"

"Now, Will Johnston, you just calm yoreself. We've all been workin' day and night till we're near 'bout wore out. I just decided it's time me and these babies have a little fun for a change. After all, Will, I may be wife to you and mother to these two little ones, but that don't mean I'm too old to enjoy a few minutes of foolishment."

Will's eyes twinkled as he looked at the face of his wife, flushed and framed in dark curls escaping from the tight bun she had hastily put up that morning. He saw again the sixteen-year-old girl he had fallen in love with, and he marveled at his good fortune.

He gave a whoop of laughter and fell to his knees by the rocker. Encircling Ellen and Nola with his arms, he joined them in their childish game. Their laughter mingled with the sounds of the birds in the forest as they celebrated. It was a rare moment for the little family, one that Ellen would savor many times as she remembered the day.

As she lay in Will's strong arms that night, Ellen knew she was the luckiest woman in the world. After they finished their lovemaking, Ellen felt utterly content and complete.

FIVE

Т he crops had been bountiful, and Ellen was justly proud of her summer's store of food. She had spent many hot days over the fire canning and preserving food for the winter. Will had dug pits in the garden and had lined them with hay to store the cabbages, potatoes and winter squash.

"None of mine will go hungry this winter," Ellen thought smugly as she surveyed her shelves of jars and preserves. "When I get my apple butter and jelly made and fix us some dried apples for fried pies and the like, we'll be all set for anything. Then it can snow all it wants to. Me and mine will fare right well."

Calculating by the phases of the moon, Ellen made pickled beans and kraut when the signs were in the shoulders. First she had asked Will to carry out the crocks so that they could be washed and sunned. Then she prepared the vegetables as her mother had taught her, cooking and cooling the beans first. Then she packed the beans in the crock, sprinkled them with salt every few layers and covered them with cold water from the spring. Nola and she looked long and hard before they found the right rock to weigh down the beans. After the fermentation time was over, she rinsed off the salt water, covered it with clean water again and stored the crocks in the cool springhouse.

Ellen rose early in the morning and began her apple butter. She laid her fires and began peeling the apples. This was an all-day job, and the fruit had to cook slowly until it thickened.

This meant someone had to stir the mixture constantly to keep it from scorching. The spices, bought so dearly on Will's last trip to the settlement, were stirred in at the proper time and sent up tantalizing aromas all day. Nola scurried about, helping Ellen carry wood to keep the fire at the right heat and entertaining Tildy. Once Ellen had the fruit bubbling to her satisfaction, she began slicing apples and placing them in the sun for drying.

Will had gone into the woods to look for a new herb he had heard about. He hoped it would help Tildy's bouts of diarrhea. The child remained sickly and thin, never getting over one spell of illness before another struck her. Will was beginning to feel helpless and frustrated because he could not help Tildy. None of his books helped him with her problems. Although she still ate hungrily, the bouts of diarrhea kept her weak, and she gained very little weight. Ellen had finally stopped breast feeding her and was giving her cow's milk hoping that would help the problem. So far there was no improvement.

Ellen was pouring up the last of the apple butter when Will came rushing in, his eyes bright with excitement.

"Ellen, Jesse Cole came by awhile ago and said they'll be having services at the Shook house next week. Bishop Asbury himself is going to be there. What a treat we'll have hearing the word preached by Asbury! They say he's one of the finest preachers in the whole church. First thing tomorrow we must begin getting things together so we can go."

"Well, fancy that!" exclaimed Ellen. "It'll sure be good to listen to a fine preacher like Asbury, but it'll be real nice to have some womenfolks to talk to also. I've shore missed our quiltin's this summer. Gardenin' and cannin' sure don't leave no time for settin' and talkin'. We'll have to get up early tomorrow if we get everything ready."

"Now Ellen, don't make too much fuss. Just fix us something to eat and put in the clothes we need."

"What does a man know about woman's dress? You're lucky, all you have to worry about is keepin' the dust off yore black suit. It's been so long since I've been out of this cove, I don't know what womenfolks is a' wearin' these days. My dresses from my dowry is a' gettin' threadbare and faded. I 'lowed I'd be makin' me some new ones when the cannin' was out of the way, but there'll be no time for that now. Maybe I can sew some of that lace tattin' I made last winter on the collars to perk 'em up a little. I wish I had one more petticoat to make my skirts stand out. Sarah Cole says that's real stylish now. Oh well, I can always starch 'em extra stiff."

Will grabbed her and swung her around the room laughing, "Oh, you'll be the finest looking lady there. Just wear that blue

calico that matches your eyes, and I'll be the envy of every man
there."

"Just hush, Will Johnston," she laughed. "I guess when you get
all fixed up with your white shirt and vest and that black hat of
yores on, you'll cut a right fine figure yoreself. Maybe I'd better
keep my eye on you!"

They talked far into the night, making plans for the trip, and
rose eagerly the next morning to begin their preparations. Ellen
aired the clothes she thought would be needed in the warm au-
tumn sun and then began baking breads and pies to take with
them. She packed food enough to last the family for the week they
would be gone, while Will looked to the condition of the wagon
and mules. Her last chore was to sew the dried fruit in bags and
hang them in the pantry along with the strings of leather britches
and hot green and red peppers. As she surveyed her handiwork,
she vowed, "Now that's as purty a sight as a body ever seen!"

The next morning they piled into the wagon at dawn and began
the trip. Will wanted to get as much of the journey as possible
behind them the first day so they could arrive by noon on the
second day of their trip.

Once they left the cove, the trip became more difficult. The road
was little better than a cow's path, and the rocky terrain made
traveling rough and uncomfortable for all of them. They moved
slowly through a countryside, overpowered by huge balsams and
hemlocks. The pine needles were so thick in places that the wagon
almost became mired, causing Will to call them needles of mud.
They passed through silent forests of huge evergreens, marveling
at the centuries of isolation that had fostered them. Even Nola's
chatter was stilled for a time.

After they topped the ridge and began their descent into the
next valley, the scenery changed, and the blood red of dogwood
leaves blended with the golds and oranges of maples. Ellen told
Will, "If I live here a hundred years, I'll never get used to the way
these mountains change."

That night they camped in a grove of willows near the Pigeon
River, then finished their journey to Shook's place the next morning. This was Ellen's first visit to the campground, and she was
enthralled at the sight of all the people. The area had been set
aside by Jacob Shook for use in religious meetings, and wagons
and campsites covered the whole field. Ellen nervously smoothed
her dark calico and straightened her bonnet as she surveyed all of
the activities.

There were wagons and people everywhere, with families greeting each other after months of separation. Children were running in every direction, trying to escape their mothers, and mothers were frantically corraling their children before they could get out of their sight. The women were dressed in homespuns and calicos and bonnets of every description. Their long dresses swept the ground and flared out over their many petticoats.

The men were dressed in buckskins, black suits with vests and string ties and combinations of both. Their hats ranged from coonskins and broad-brimmed felts to high-crowned stovepipes.

"Land alive, Will, I'd forgot what it was like to see more'n four or five people in one place. I guess we're goin' to have to get off of our mountain more often before I forget how to act in civilized society."

"I reckon you'll get the hang of it back soon, Ellen," Will chuckled.

Will's prediction came true as old acquaintances were renewed and new friendships established during the camp meeting. They were pleased to see most of their neighbors. In the area where Will parked the wagon, the McGintys, the Coles and the Manns all made camps.

Will was just getting his own team unhitched when Jesse Cole summoned him. "Will Johnston," he called. "You're needed over here, friend. We've got a pore fellow that looks like he's broke his arm. I told him I'd fetch you to fix him up. I knowed you'd take care of him."

"Gladly," replied Will, "just let me hobble these mules first, and I'll be right along. Ellen, I'll be back soon's I can."

"Please hurry, Will," Ellen pleaded. "They's lots to do before we can fix a fire and cook."

Louisa McGinty strolled over with her baby, and while they fed their babies the two women began comparing notes about their summer's canning and preserving. Louisa's baby was born just one week after Tildy.

"I tell you, Ellen, I couldn't believe I finally had me a little girl," Louisa said. "She was like a precious jewel to me, and it just seemed fitten to call her Pearl. She's a real good baby, too. Growin' like a little weed."

"Good land, I reckon she is," Ellen exclaimed. "Why, she's twice as big as Tildy. I declare it's plumb worrisome the way Tildy eats so much and just don't seem to grow a'tall."

"Well, some young'uns is just like that," Louisa reassured her. "They just take longer to get started. She'll fatten up one of these days."

"Yes, I suppose," Ellen sighed. "Tell me, Louisa, couldn't we make one campfire and share it? Seems like it'd be less work and a lot more sociable. It looks like Nola's goin' to be trailin' your John and Sam all the time anyway, and it'd sure make it a lot easier to keep track of her."

"Why, that's a fine idea, Ellen," Louisa exclaimed. "I declare, I hunger after woman talk so! All I hear is man talk. What's growin' and what's not growin' and if the fish is a' bitin' or not bitin'. I'll be right proud when Pearl gets big enough to talk to me."

"Poor Will might be just as glad to have some men folks to talk to him," laughed Ellen. "He must be tired of bein' the only man in the family. This'll work out just fine."

The next day, after all the families were settled in their campsites, the people gathered to hear the great Asbury preach. He and his traveling companions, McGee, McKendree and Boehm, took turns preaching to the some seventy-five gathered at the campground. Jacob Shook himself gave a personal testimonial about his conversion.

"I tell you, friends, the spirit of the Lord plumb overwhelmed me while I was a' plowin' one day. I had been workin' up to this for some months, and I knowed the spirit had come on me that day. First I fell down on my knees right there in the middle of the field, and then I ran up and down the rows a'shoutin' the good news to everybody that would listen. My life has been changed since then and I know I have to tell it to all who'll listen."

They were disappointed that poor health prevented Asbury from preaching more than once. His message was powerful though, and Ellen knew she would never forget the haunted look on his face as he admonished them, "In all things, obey first the will of God and read your Bibles daily. If you do this, then surely the kingdom of God will be yours in the next life!"

Late Saturday afternoon, Asbury left with his entourage for his next meeting over in Buncombe County, but the people stayed on for several more days, hungry for companionship and reluctant to bring an end to the meeting.

More and more the families from their cove turned to Will for answers to questions they did not understand, and their campfire became the center of discussions after services at night. Ellen watched proudly as Will took on this new role of leadership as naturally as if he had been trained for it. She had never before realized how much more extensive Will's education had been than that of his neighbors.

The close proximity of the McGinty camp became a mixed blessing for Will and Ellen. They enjoyed the companionship of the other couple, but little Sam McGinty soon proved himself to be a problem.

"I declare, Ellen, that Sam is as wild as a young colt," Will complained. "He's up to some devilment every minute of the day. He's made himself known to everyone at the campsite. I don't understand how two brothers can be so different. John is just as obedient and dependable as a man could want, but that Sam . . . he's something else!"

"I know," Ellen sighed, "I felt so sorry for Jacob when that Trull fellow complained to him that Sam was the one that threw them buckeyes in his campfire. The explosion nearly scared his mules to death. It took him and Jacob the better part of the morning to get them rounded up and settled down."

"I think that was one time that Jacob took to heart what the Bible says about 'spare the rod and spoil the child.' I think everybody in the camp enjoyed that thrashing."

All of these things were put behind them the next morning when the people began to gather after breakfast for their first Sunday morning services. It began with the amen-corner singing, "Father's Gone To Glory." One after another voices took up the hymn, and people began assembling under the shelter Shook had erected. They sang without books, as most of the hymns had never been printed but were passed on from one generation to the next.

After the singing, Brother Hiram Ferguson took over where Asbury had left off. His method of preaching was impressively simple. His lack of education was overcome by his obvious sincerity, and he expounded the gospel fearlessly as he knew it.

Ferguson looked over the crowd of people, mainly farmers and their families, crowded into the shelter. As was the custom, the men sat in front and the women and young children took their places at the back of the congregation. He announced that his text would be on prayer. He recounted the prayers from the Bible— David's prayer, the prayer of the Pharisee and the publican, the prayer Jesus prayed in Gethsemane, and the prayer Jesus taught his disciples to pray.

"Prayer is our one sure way to reach God," he told the congregation, "but it also has to do with vows and responsibilities." He talked on for the better part of an hour, never referring to any notes but speaking easily and simply from his heart. His sermon ended with an appeal to the sinners to repent and come forward, to be prayed over that they might be saved. Some twenty people made their way to the front to give him their hands while the congregation sang.

Three more days of preaching and hymn singing followed and at the close, some forty souls had professed their belief in Jesus Christ. On Wednesday evening the new converts were baptized in the Pigeon River.

Ellen and Will left early Thursday morning and returned to their mountain home, renewed and ready to take up their lives again.

"I vow, Will, I never have felt such a fulfillment of my soul," Ellen said. "These has been the finest times I've spent in many a day. My heart is near bustin', it's so full."

Will quietly nodded his head in agreement as he urged the mules back over the mountain trail. Nola and Tildy slept contentedly on their pallets, rocked by the swaying of the wagon.

SIX

The Indian summer weather lingered through October, but by the second week of November winter's icy fingers began to slip down the valleys past the hoar-crusted mountain tops. As the sun lost its strength, little Tildy also began to lose hers. Never a contented child, she became even more fretful and Ellen spent most of her time trying to pacify her. She seldom spent an uninterrupted night, but walked the floor interminably with Tildy. Will read and re-read his medical books and herb diaries trying to find something to help her.

On the last day of November, he noticed that Tildy's eyes had a yellowish cast to them and that her skin had taken on a definite yellow tinge. For the first time he began to fear that she had something that would snuff out her tenuous hold on life.

"Ellen, I'm afraid Tildy has something wrong with her innards," he said. "Seems like her food just don't do her no good, and my books say that yellow janders means her liver isn't doing its work. I don't know what else to do for her. I've tried everything I know from butterfly-root to sassafras tea, and it don't seem like anything I do makes any difference." He bowed his head dejectedly, overwhelmed by the weight of his failure.

Ellen covered his hand with hers. "Hush now, Will, you've done all you could and more than most. We just got to try a little harder and have a little more faith. Just think of all the folks you've helped with your doctorin'. I know you'll find somethin' to help soon."

Will looked at Ellen gratefully for her words of encouragement, but he was afraid that her faith in him would be disappointed this time. Never before had he felt such despair. He began to spend more and more time in prayer. He believed that was their only hope now.

That night Tildy's fever shot up so high they could feel the heat radiating from her tiny body. Will forced more butterfly-root tea down her throat, trying to break the fever, but to no avail. Sometime after midnight, the child went into convulsions, and even Ellen was forced to admit how gravely ill she was. After the seizures passed, she lay quiet for the first time in days. Will told Ellen, "This isn't a natural sleep. God help us now, 'cause there's nothing else we can do to help her."

He fell to his knees by the bed and began to pray, "Dear Lord, help us to bear what is to come. Give us the strength to accept thy will."

"No!" cried Ellen. "Don't give up, Will. There must be something else you can try. Bring me some fresh water, I'm goin' to bathe her again. If we can just get her fever down, I know she'll be all right. God wouldn't take her from us. Help me, Will!"

Nola slept peacefully through the ordeal, unaware that her little sister was slipping away from them.

Near dawn Ellen and Will sensed a change in Tildy. Her breathing became more shallow, and finally she drew her last breath and was still.

Frantically, Ellen picked up the tiny body and tried to breathe life back into her. After several minutes, Will gently took the baby from her.

"Give her up now, Ellen. She isn't ours anymore. She's His again. He won't let her hurt anymore."

He laid her gently on the bed and covered her frail body with the sheet. Ellen and Will clung together, weeping bitter tears and seeking comfort from each other.

"Hold on to me, Will," Ellen sobbed. "If you don't, I'm shorely goin' to drown in this pit of darkness we've fell into. Oh, God, why did you take her? Why did you take my baby? Oh, Will, I want her back. Please get her back for me. I can't stand this. It's a' tearin' my heart out!"

"We can't help her anymore, Ellen. Now we'll just have to help each other as best we can and depend on God's love and strength to get us through this."

After a time, Will rose and helped Ellen to the rocking chair where she had spent so many hours holding Tildy.

"Will you be all right now, Ellen?" he asked gently. "I must go and get Sarah and Jesse to come and help us do what must be done. I will be as quick as I can."

Numbly she nodded her head and wrapped her arms around her bosom.

Will had not gone far when he met the Coles coming down the mountain trail.

"How did you know? I was just on my way to get Sarah to come and help Ellen."

"We knew how sick Tildy was, Will," Jesse said gently, "and when Sarah heard an owl callin' early this mornin', we knowed somethin' bad had happened. I brought my tools with me, and I'll make her a fine box for the buryin'."

Sarah and Ellen washed the tiny body and dressed her in the best she had. Will took two new pennies from his money box and laid them on her eyelids. Jesse fashioned a strong box from some chestnut wood Will had put aside, and the two women lined it with material from Ellen's quilt scraps.

Word spread quickly through the mountain community, and soon neighbors began coming with offerings of food and sympathy. Nola was confused by all that was happening. She was afraid of the sad, dark look on her mother's face, though, and asked no questions. She longed to pick Tildy up and play with her, but the solemnity of the faces around her constrained her. Never had she seen the baby so still. Even when she slept, she had tossed and turned restlessly.

Most of the neighbors sat up that night. Those who lived too far to go home made a pallet on the floor in the cabin or slept in their wagons.

They buried little Tildy on a knoll near the first cabin Will built for the family. Before they closed the coffin, Ellen took the Dutch Girl quilt she had been working on for the baby and wrapped it around her tiny body. She gazed stonily and silently as they lowered the box in the cold, dark earth.

Nola shivered in her bed. The people gathered around her sang, "Happy Birthday," peering down at the old lady and smiling when she closed her eyes tightly. Two tears coursed down her withered cheeks.

SEVEN

Ellen sat motionless in the rocker, her arms clasped around her bosom hugging a baby that was not there. She watched passively as Will made stabs at straightening up the mess in the kitchen.

Nola ran up to Ellen holding out her doll, its leg dangling by a thread where she had torn it. "Mama, will you please fix my baby for me?"

Ellen looked down at the child and shook her head disinterestedly.

"Please, Mama," Nola persisted. "Can't you get your needle and just sew her leg back on?"

Ellen frowned and pushed the doll away from her. "You tore it, now you can just do without. I've got no time for wastin' on a doll."

Nola's eyes clouded with tears, and she ran back to Will and flung herself in his arms. "Why is Mama being so mean, Papa? Why won't she fix my doll for me?"

"Hush, Nola, just put the doll aside and Papa will take you with him this morning to look for herbs. Don't cry now, and don't bother Mama, she doesn't feel good," he told her as he hugged her to him. "Hurry now, and find your coat and mittens. Don't forget to put your toboggan on too. It's damp out today."

"She never feels good anymore," Nola pouted as she went in search of her coat.

When Nola left the room, Will turned to Ellen and said, "Ellen, you must pull yourself together and try to put Tildy's death behind you. Can't you see what you're doing to Nola? She needs her

38

Mama. I need you, too. None of us can bear this grief alone. Please don't shut us out like this, let us help you. Let God help you, Ellen. Pray and ask for His help. He'll listen."

"Pray, you say? I've done all the prayin' I mean to. I prayed the night Tildy died, and what good did it do me? He took my baby away from me anyhow," she answered bitterly.

"Oh, Ellen, please don't talk like this. It's not like you to be so bitter. You must let me help you."

"Help me? How can you help me? You weren't there to help me the night she was born. You couldn't even help her with all your herbs and your books. How do you know what I'm feelin'? You don't know what it's like to carry a child in yore body for nine months. You don't know what it's like to lay for hours a' birthin' a baby when you feel like yore whole body is bein' wrung out. You don't know what it's like to feed it the milk from yore breasts and watch it starve before yore eyes. Don't talk to me about grief. Nobody knows how my heart aches and how empty I feel. Just leave me be!"

Nola had returned to the room and shrank back against her father, frightened by the anger in her mother's voice. She clutched Will around his leg and stared wide-eyed at this mother who had become a stranger.

"Please think about what I've said, Ellen," Will said sadly. "I'll take Nola with me, and perhaps you'll feel better when we come home. Why don't you work on that new quilt pattern Sarah brought you? You know how much you love your quilting. Louisa said to tell you she'd be over to help with the house when little Pearl gets over her croup."

Ellen shrugged indifferently and stared stonily out the window as the two left the house. Will had been taking Nola with him lately as Ellen slipped deeper into her depression. He wished he could share with Ellen the pleasure he took from Nola's quickness in learning the plants. He had only to show her an herb once or twice, and she could spot them almost as readily as he could. They shared an interest in the plants, and their need to comfort each other had developed a strong bond between the two. Nola now turned to Will for all her needs.

"Papa, when is Mama goin' to be well again?" asked Nola as they headed to the barn to feed the livestock.

"I don't know, Nola," he answered sadly. "I just know that we have to be very patient with her and ask God to help us all through this bad time. You must remember that no matter what

she says or does, your mama still loves you. It's just hard for her
to show it right now."

"I hope it won't be much longer, Papa," Nola sighed. "I want
things to be happy again like they were before Tildy went away.
Why did she have to go away? Is it because God is mean like
Mama said?"

"Oh, no, honey. We can't always understand why God does
things, but we do know there is a reason for it and we have to
trust in Him."

"Was it because I was a bad girl, Papa?" Nola asked softly.
"Maybe if I'd helped Mama more Tildy wouldn't have got sick."

"Oh, Nola, is this what we've done to you? No, no, you were
not in any way to blame for what happened to Tildy. She was very,
very sick and was hurting so bad that God took her to be with
Him, so that she wouldn't have to hurt anymore. You must believe that, Nola. Someday your mama will understand that too."

As Ellen looked out into the bleak gray day, she felt the very
drabness of the mountainside adding to her misery. The naked
gray of the tree trunks against the overcast wintry skies was like
the bleakness in her heart. Gray mists swirled about the ground,
and low-hanging clouds, so weighted down with moisture that
they could not rise, surrounded the mountain peaks. Ellen felt as
if she was encompassed in a world turned gray.

She rose from the chair and paced around the room. She picked
up the quilt pattern her neighbor had brought her, then flung it
aside. She began wringing her hands as she paced. Finally, she
held them out as she first implored and then demanded an answer from God.

"Oh, God! Oh, God! Why? Why? Why have you done this to
me? What did I do to make you punish me like this? Why did you
have to take my sweet baby? Oh, my pore Tildy. All alone and so
cold with no mama to hold her and love her. Oh God, how can I
bear this hurt any longer?"

Ellen went back to the window, looking out into the gray fog
swirling along the grounds and creeping closer and closer to her.

As she gazed into the mist, a woman appeared, followed by a
young man. She was tall, raw-boned and somber-looking, like the
day. Her silvery gray hair was pulled severely back from her sharp
face and was wound in a tight knot at the back of her head. She
was wearing a cotton dress covered by an apron, both as gray and

somber as her grim countenance. Her feet were bare and cal-
loused, as were those of the man with her.

Ellen watched unmoving as the pair approached the cabin and,
without waiting for an invitation, pushed open the door and entered.

"Ellen Johnston?" the woman asked sternly. When Ellen did
not reply, the woman stepped further into the cabin, followed by
her companion.

"I be Lizzie Conners. Ye lost a young'un awhile back, I heard.
Ye think the good Lord's got somethin' again ye 'cause He took
yore baby. Ye think yore burden is the worst they is. It ain't.
They's worse things than death, missus, and they's worse bur-
dens than yores!"

Numbly Ellen looked at the woman, then flushed in anger as
the words sank in. She opened her mouth, an angry retort on her
lips, when a grunting noise caused her to look into the face of the
man behind her. As she looked at him, she was overwhelmed by a
stench that had pervaded the whole room. Her eyes widened in
shock as she took in the figure before her.

He was a pathetic caricature of a man. He had a vacuous grin on
his face and though his eyes roved from side to side, it was obvious that he comprehended nothing. The saliva drooled down
his chin and left gray tracks through the dirt on his face. When he
opened his mouth, it revealed the black, rotted stumps of his
teeth. The sounds he made were unintelligible. He pulled
aimlessly at his lips with his fingers, and shuffled his feet constantly, as if he wanted to move about but had no place to go. He
was filthy from his scarred bare feet to his greasy black hair, which
hung in his eyes and straggled on his shoulders. The front of his
overalls was wet with urine. Ellen felt a sudden need to vomit.

After Ellen had looked at him in shocked silence for several
minutes, Lizzie took him by the hand and led him to the door.
She turned to Ellen and said in a harsh, bitter voice, "I prayed to
God too, and asked him to spare my baby. He was a' burnin' up
with the fevers and a' havin' one fit after t'other. I begged God to
let him live. He answered my prayers. He's alive, and I'm the one
that's to blame fer that!"

She took another step toward the door and then turned back
and fixed Ellen with a haunted stare. "Git up off yore backside,
woman, and bend yore knees to the floor and thank God He took
yore baby to a better place. The burden I've got to live with is the

worry about who's goin' to look after him when I'm gone. Hit won't be his pappy, 'cause he left me a long time ago."

As abruptly as she had appeared out of the fog, Lizzie Conners disappeared with her "baby." Ellen sat back in the rocker and stared out at the fog. She sat motionless for what seemed like hours until she suddenly become aware that a weak winter sun had come out and burned the fog away.

Dazed, she sat up and looked around her at the disarray of her home. She rose and began touching the things in the room. She fingered the dusty furniture and picked up the dirty dishes from the table, then wandered into the bedroom and stared in dismay at the unmade bed and the scattered clothes.

Turning, she ran back into the great room and sank to the floor in front of the rocking chair. She began to cry. This time they were not bitter, hopeless tears, but sad ones of relief and healing.

Finally she rose from the floor and methodically began to clean the house. She swept, scoured and washed everything in sight. Then she set about preparing a meal for her family.

Some time later, Ellen watched Will approach the cabin with Nola trailing behind him. She cried out in remorse as she saw how his shoulders were stooped in dejection. She rushed out to meet him and flung her arms around him.

Will took her by the shoulders and looked deep into her eyes. What he saw there caused him to clasp her to him. She held tightly to her husband, reveling in the comfort and warmth of this nearness.

Nola tugged tentatively at her skirt. "Mama?" she asked. Ellen bent down and picked up the child, covering her face with kisses as the three of them entered the door to their home.

Nola pushed the covers back fretfully. "My hip's hurting," she said peevishly. "Can't you get me a little poppy? Papa says that's the best thing for the pain. Just mix it up and give me a little spoonful. Just enough to ease me a little. Then make me a hot poultice with some of that snakeroot and sassafras in my medicine box."

"Would you listen to her," laughed her great-nephew. "Still doctorin' herself. Don't she beat all! Pa said she never saw a real doctor till she broke her hip."

"Well," replied Alma drily, "as Doc Rogers said when I told him she doctored herself, 'Don't knock it. How many other people do you know who're one hundred years old?'"

EIGHT

Their first son was born the next June, as healthy and robust as Tildy had been sickly and frail. They named him William Blaine Johnston, Jr., but Willie seemed to fit him best. That is how he was called all his life. Ellen reveled in his energy and good health, and Will experienced all the pride men feel in their first son.

Nola was her mother's devoted helper. Tending Willie was like having a living doll. When he began to walk, he seemed bent on escaping her attentions and it was common for Ellen to hear Nola call, "Willie, Willie, where are you? You'd better come here right this minute, or else!"

Sixteen months later another daughter was born to them. They named her Martha, after Will's mother. She too was a healthy baby, and at last Ellen felt she had put the pain and grief of Tildy's death behind her.

Nola was seven years old when Will told Ellen, "It's time for some real schooling for Nola. I can teach her at home, but she needs classroom experience. And she's not the only one in the cove."

"What can we do about it? With no schoolhouse, there's not much hope for a school."

"Well, someone has to take the responsibility to get a school started and it looks like it has fallen on me. I will leave first thing in the morning and see if there is enough interest among the other families to start a school."

At daybreak Will saddled up one of the mules and began his journey through the cove. First he traveled over the ridge to the Cole's and from there to the next cove where the Manns lived. By dark he had covered the entire community, finding seventeen children of school age. He and Ellen talked until late in the night, trying to work out a plan for the school.

"Everyone agrees on the need for one," he said, "but no one wants the job of starting one or doing the teaching. I've been thinking about our first little cabin, and I think we could use that for awhile, at least until we can build a real schoolhouse. Of course, the main need will be for a teacher and some way to pay him."

Every time they talked about the problem, they were faced with the fact that Will was the only person in the community with enough education to teach the children.

"I couldn't even consider doing anything until all of my crops are in," Will mused, "and by then we could only get in a few weeks of schooling before bad weather. Maybe we could get in a few weeks in the summer before harvest time. I guess that would be better than what they're getting now."

Most of the families shared Ellen and Will's concern for their children's schooling. When he called a meeting of all who were interested, seven families came to the gathering.

"We all seem to be of a mind that we need this school for our young'uns," Elisha Phillips said. "I propose that we just make this a workin' meetin' and get on with what needs to be done."

There was enthusiastic agreement with the proposal, and so their first meeting turned out to be a working one. While the women swept and scrubbed the cabin, the men constructed rough benches for the children and a table for the teacher's desk.

The parents promised to furnish slates for their children and what books they could find. Will dug out his books, too. His main book would be the Bible. In addition, he had copies of *Treasure Island*, *Pilgrim's Progress*, a Latin textbook, three precious books of poetry, one arithmetic book and his various medical books. When he realized what he was undertaking and how little he had to work with, he began to wonder aloud about what he would be able to teach the children.

"Don't worry, Papa," Nola told him, "you'll be the best teacher that ever was. Why, just look how much you've already taught me. I can read 'most as good as Mama, and I'm learnin' to cipher too."

Will laughed. "I only hope I can find some more students who are as easy to teach as you are."

On the first day of school Nola was up before anyone else. She was ready to start the new venture almost an hour before Will was through with his chores and ready to go.

Nola fairly danced up the mountain trail toward the little cabin that was to be their schoolroom. "Look, Papa," she exclaimed, "did you ever see the sky so blue or the leaves so pretty? It's just a perfect day to start a new school."

Will opened the cabin door and watched the eager, but apprehensive, children straggle in a little later. Most of them clutched tin pails containing their lunches. Except for Nola and one other little girl, they were barefooted and would remain so until the first snow fell.

As the other children entered the room, Nola found herself suddenly shy. She looked at her Papa standing at the front of the room, and he looked suddenly unfamiliar in this new role. She became as subdued as the rest of the children, looking in big-eyed wonder at all the strange faces around her. She knew the McGinty boys, John and Sam, who were about the same age as she. Zac Mann was at least ten years old, and the Cole's oldest boy looked like he must be about seventeen. He was the biggest child there, and he obviously was not very happy about being there.

As they seated themselves, the girls sat on one side of the room and the boys on the other. Any other arrangement would have been looked on with disfavor as a "courtin'" school. The strict mountain parents would not have allowed it.

"Nola, will you please help me get a roll started of all the pupils?" Will asked her. "Then we will try to find out who has had some schooling and who has not."

Nola's heart swelled with pride at being selected to help the teacher. As the other girls looked at her with envy, she could not help feeling important.

When the roll was completed, Will found that only two of the children had been exposed to any kind of schooling. "I see by the way things are that we will have to start with very basic reading and ciphering," he told the class.

"Now, children," he began, "we will begin each day with a reading from the Bible, and I expect you to pay strict attention to God's word. Today I will read from the book of Psalms, number 24.

'The earth is the Lord's and the fulness thereof; the world, and they that dwell therein. For He hath founded it upon the seas, and established it upon the floods. Who shall ascend into the hill of the Lord? Or who shall stand in His holy place?'

As Will read the beautiful words of the Psalm, Nola's face glowed and she sat up a little straighter on her bench. Surely no one had a papa as smart or as wonderful as hers.

Will got through the first day of school with no calamities. He felt very good about his first attempts as a schoolmaster.

As they made their way home that afternoon, Nola ran ahead of him and burst into the house shouting, "Mama, Mama, you should have seen Papa today. He was the most wonderful teacher that has ever been. Willie, I bet you wish you was big enough to go to school, but you ain't. Come on and I'll teach you what I learned today."

Ellen laughed at Nola's exuberance and told Will, "Well, if you done half as good as Nola says, you must be real pleased with yoreself."

Will grinned and admitted that the day had indeed been a success. He was to look back on this first day later as one of the few uneventful ones. As the children overcame their initial shyness, their love of fun and mischief overcame their awe, and Will found his patience taxed to its limits.

One of the chief pranksters was Zachary Mann. "Mischief comes as naturally to Zac as breathing," Will complained to Ellen. "I tell you, he sorely tries my patience with his pranks. He does everything from hiding toads in the girl's lunch pails to setting that pet coon of his loose in the schoolhouse. Then he acts as innocent as a babe."

"I don't see how he could be anything but mischievous," Ellen laughed. "That tow-head and freckled nose of his couldn't mean anything else. To say nothin' of that cowlick on his forehead, and them blue eyes that just sparks meanness when he looks at you."

"If he wasn't one of the brightest children in the class, I'd set down on him harder. But just about the time I'm at the end of my patience and ready to tan his britches, he'll come up with an answer that has just escaped the rest of the class. One of these days he'll go too far, though, and then Mr. Zac Mann better look out!"

Not many days passed before Zac ran out of luck. It was a cold morning, and Will built a fire in the fireplace to take some of the chill out of the room. He was late getting there, and after he lit the fire, he busied himself getting things ready for the students. He failed to notice that the chimney was not drawing properly.

He stepped to the door to summon the children in, and as they began to enter, Samantha Phillips shouted, "Law me, teacher, the school's a' fire!"

Will turned to see smoke boiling down the chimney and filling the room with thick clouds of smoke. He hastily shooed the children back out the door and went to investigate the cause of the trouble. He climbed on the roof and found brush and mud stuffed in the top of the chimney.

When he had cleared out the mess, Will summoned the class around him and eyed each in turn. Sixteen pairs of clear, innocent eyes returned his gaze. Zac Mann was studying the circle his toe was digging in the dirt with a great deal of interest.

"I think I will dismiss school for the day," Will told the children. "This smoke won't clear out anytime soon, and it's too cold to hold class outside."

As the children started eagerly home, Will grasped Zac firmly by the collar of his shirt. "I think you will have to stay awhile, Zac," he said sternly. "You and I have some cleaning up to do before we can go home. First you can clean that mess off the roof, and then we'll see how much work needs to be done inside."

After Zac had scrubbed all the benches and the teacher's table, Will told him, "Now, Zac, I think you could learn a lesson from this, and I can think of no better source than God's own words. Before you return tomorrow, you will learn by heart and recite to me and the class Psalm 51. This is a prayer that David made to God for forgiveness when he had done something that was very displeasing to Him. It begins, 'Have mercy upon me, O God according to thy loving kindness: according unto the multitude of thy tender mercies blot out my transgressions.' Do you know what the word transgressions means, Zac?"

"Well," Zac answered sheepishly, "I reckon it means don't stuff the chimbley full of mud again."

"I reckon it does for sure," Will agreed. "Furthermore, after you have recited this passage to my satisfaction, you may also clean the schoolroom for the rest of the month. If I think you are sufficiently impressed with the gravity of what you have done, I will think about forgiving you!"

When Will recounted Zac's punishment to Ellen, she laughed and said, "I think there was a difference in Zac's 'transgression' and David's. Ain't that the prayer David prayed after he'd been with Bathsheba?"

"Yes, but I don't think Zac is going to do that much research into the passage. Anyhow, the prayer seemed right fitting to me at the moment."

This did not stop Zac's pranks, but after that he was careful to avoid playing any more that directly affected Will.

NINE

While the cabin was a poor substitute for a real classroom, it worked out quite well. As Will thought about how he was using the cabin, he wondered if it could not also be used to fill another important need in the community. He decided to discuss his idea with Ellen.

"If we can make use of the cabin for a schoolroom during the week, Ellen, why can't we use it for a meeting place on the sabbath? It's a long trip to the Shook's meeting ground and with our family growing, it's getting harder and harder to make the trip."

"Why, that's a fine idea, Will. The women folk were talking on the idea of startin' up a church at our last quiltin' bee. For some it's just near on to impossible to get to the camp meetin's. If we had some place that was close by, it would be a blessin' to us all. Let's do it, Will."

So Will set out a second time on a tour of the mountain coves. He met with even more enthusiasm for the church than he had for the school. Most of the people he talked to expressed almost identical longings to his and Ellen's.

Everyone expressed a desire to have at least one service before the cold weather set in, and so it was decided that they would hold their first meeting on the following Sunday.

The pupils cheerfully cleaned up the schoolroom on their last day at school that week. They were proud that their schoolroom had been chosen as the first meetinghouse for the community. Even Zac put aside his foolishness and worked as hard as the others. He could not resist one last prank, though, and while everyone was getting ready to go home, he tossed two buckeyes into the fire.

The coals were hot, having burned all day long, and it did not take the nuts long to reach the explosive stage. He had timed his prank perfectly and as they started out the door, the nuts exploded with a loud bang, scattering coals and ashes all over the freshly swept floor. Zac looked so startled at the success of his prank that the other children, after a good laugh at his discomfiture, fell in and cleaned up the mess in a few minutes. Will shook his head in helplessness and sent the children home. Zac left feeling very fortunate that Will was in such a good mood.

Sunday morning dawned crisp and clear, one of those rare, beautiful November mornings. The sky was an October blue, and the mountain peaks stood out in proud grandeur against the skyline. Most of the trees had shed their leaves, but there were still some burnt golds and deep reds showing up the mountainsides. They contrasted sharply with the greens of the balsams and pines. The weather had a bit of the warmth of Indian summer and a promise of winter's cold breath. Everyone agreed that the weather could not have been more to their liking.

Jacob McGinty, a man recognized by his neighbors as a God-fearing man with a gift of expressing himself well, had consented to bring the first message to the group. The room was filled to overflowing, with several of the men standing outside the doorway.

Occupying the front bench with Will were Thomas Mann, Jesse Cole and John Conners. They had worked the hardest getting the new church organized.

Across from them on the women's side sat Jacob's wife, Louisa, surrounded by her five children, John, Sam, Pearl, Mary, and Thomas. Ellen and her children occupied the next bench, with the baby Martha in her mother's arms and Nola and Willie sitting decorously next to her. Will had worried that the children might misbehave due to their familiarity with the surroundings, but either the large number of people or the solemnity of the occasion served to keep them quiet.

After a period of hymn singing, Jacob rose and stationed himself behind the table that served as teacher's desk during the week. Stroking his long, gray beard, he began to read from his Bible. When he had finished his reading, he asked that everyone kneel with him in prayer.

"Oh Lord, who has made Heaven and earth and all the poor critters living here, we ask that you look down on us today and bless what we are about to undertake. We come together to this place where we can give thanks and praise to thee for all thy bountiful blessings. We come seekin' guidance when we don't know which-a-way to turn, and we come out of gratitude for what you've already done for us poor sinners. But most of all, we come seekin' forgiveness for all our wrongdoings and assurance that there'll be a place for each one of us when we leave this place on earth. And now, Lord, we ask that you bless every man, woman, and child here today and be with each one of us durin' the days ahead. All this we ask in the name of our Savior, Jesus Christ! Amen!"

This prayer was followed by a chorus of amens from the men seated on the first two benches. Jacob laid aside his Bible and began a simple sermon based on his text, the twenty-third Psalm. He spoke with deep conviction and sincerity, searching out each face in the congregation as he spoke.

Jacob was careful to steer clear of speaking for any specific doctrine, for surely there were almost as many doctrinal beliefs as there were families present. He spoke for the better part of an hour and closed with a long prayer exhorting God to follow the paths of His children and the children to follow the path God intended for them to follow.

After the singing of three more hymns, the first meeting in the little cabin disbanded. A few who were able pressed a few dimes and pennies into Jacob's hand as they left. Will promised to meet with some of the men to plan for a time when they could come together again.

With Martha nestled in Ellen's arms, Nola tagging at her mother's skirts and Willie riding majestically on his father's shoulders, the little family set out down the mountain trail to their home.

"Well, Ellen, my dear, did you ever think that our little cabin we built so long ago would someday be honored in such a way? I guess that might just be one of the poorest excuses for a church building the Lord ever looked down on, but I bet there's never been a more sincere bunch of Christian people gathered in one place."

Ellen was lost in her own thoughts and did not reply, but Will had spoken as much to himself as to her and so did not notice her silence. She was thinking of the words Jacob had read from the Bible and they seemed to burn themselves into her very soul: "Yea, though I walk through the valley of the shadow of death, I will fear no evil for Thou art with me." She thought back over the days and weeks following Tildy's death and the deep depression she had fallen into. She realized that God's hand had steered Lizzie Conners to her. She was so overcome with awe that it was all she could do to keep from falling on her knees and thanking Him right there. Clutching Martha to her breast, she raised her eyes to the blue sky, and silently uttered her prayer of thanksgiving.

TEN

Winter set in with a vengeance that year. The beautiful November Sunday of the church meeting marked the end of Fall, and the mountain community found itself wrapped in ice and snow for months.

Following two weeks of rain came the sleet and snow. In the peaceful cove the cabin was almost covered with snow drifts and Will had to dig tunnels to the barn so he could feed and care for the livestock.

As winter tightened its grip, Ellen was hard put to entertain the children. In desperation she began teaching Nola to sew so that she would stay occupied while the younger children napped. Ellen taught Nola to sew quilt squares together, just as her mother had taught her. Nola was a quick student and soon was occupied with making quilts for her doll. Before long she knew all the patterns Ellen had taught her: Log Cabin, Churn Dash, Dutch Girl, Jacob's Ladder, Bear's Paw, Shoofly, Honeycomb, Joseph's Coat, and the pattern all girls learn on, the Four Patch.

As they sat by the fireside one afternoon while Will was in the barn repairing his equipment, Ellen decided Nola was ready for a more serious project. "Nola, it's time for you to make a quilt for yourself."

Nola wanted to start at once. "What should I make?"

"We'd better start with somethin' simple like the Four Patch. It makes such a pretty bride's quilt. You could put it in your dowry."

"What's a dowry, Mama?"

Ellen laughed and tried to explain. "Well, it's the things you take with you when you get married, Nola. When me and your papa married, I had sixteen quilts in my chest."

"Really? What did you do with all of them?"

"Well, most of them are on yore beds keepin' you warm," Ellen said. "And besides my quilts your papa had one of the prettiest Freedom Quilts you ever did see. His ma made it for him."

"Oh, can I see it, Mama?"

Ellen laughed, "See it, honey? You see it all the time. It's the beautiful red, white and blue one we put on the bed when company comes. Come on, we'll get it out and look at it again."

As she lifted Will's quilt out of the chest, Ellen lovingly fingered the bold colors. "Yore papa's ma said she made it from scraps brought all the way from Cornwall, England. It's traveled a far piece when you think about it. Crossed a big ocean and then all the way up to these mountains . . ." her voice trailed off, and her mind traveled back to the days when Will and she made their own trip to the mountains.

Nola's tugging at her arm brought Ellen back to the present.

"Why do they call it a Freedom Quilt, Mama?"

"Well, it's because when a boy comes of age he's considered free to do as he wants."

"I don't understand."

"Well, when a boy reaches twenty-one, he's free to make his own way in life. If he's a bound boy, he's set free from his master. If he's livin' with his folks, they can't take his wages or make him work at home for nothin' anymore. When this happens, his master or his folks usually gives him a new suit of clothes. A Freedom Suit, it's called. Likewise he's sometimes given a Freedom Quilt."

"Who makes it for him, Mama?"

"Well, that depends. Sometimes it's his mother, or his sisters, or his friends. If he's not about to get married, his quilt is put away till he decides to wed."

"Why don't they call it a wedding quilt then?"

"Sometimes they do call it a Bridegroom's Quilt, but I like to call it a Freedom Quilt. I like that name better."

"Mama, can I put my quilt on your frame and let the ladies quilt it for me the next time they come?"

"Well, maybe someday you can. Not right away though. It'll have to grow an awful lot before it's big enough to fit on these frames."

"How old were you when you made your first quilt, Mama?"

"Hmm, well, I reckon I wasn't much older than you are when I pieced my first quilt top. Still got it too."

"You have? Where is it?"

"That's the one on mine and Papa's bed. I was shore proud the day Mama said she was about to take it out."

"What do you mean, 'take it out?'"

"That's what they say when your quilt is finished and ready to be bound off."

"Did you quilt it yourself?"

"Law no, child! I didn't do any of the quiltin' in it 'cause I wasn't good enough with the needles then. It takes a heap of practice before you can take yore place with the quilters."

"What did you do to get good enough to quilt? How did you learn?"

"Why, by practicin' on scraps and watchin' the others quilt. I ran many an errand and fixed many a meal 'fore I got good enough to take my place around the frame. I recollect how proud I was the first time I set in on a quiltin'."

"I'll be glad when I'm old enough to quilt. Can I help fix the food the next time the quilters come?"

"Well, we'll see. You work on yore Four Patch, and we'll see how well you do."

"Do you remember the rhyme you made up with the quilt's names, Mama? Say it for me, please. I like it."

"Let's see if I can remember it. Some day I'm goin' to set these poems down on paper when I don't have nothin' better to do." Ellen replied.

She thought for a few minutes and then recited:

> Churn Dash, Churn Dash,
> Honeycomb, too,
> Log Cabin, Joseph's Coat,
> Drunkard's Path blue.
> Crazy quilt, Four Patch,
> Bear's Paw true,
> Jacob's Ladder, Freedom Quilt,
> Shoo Fly Shoo!

Nola laughed delightedly, "Mama, it sounds just like a song! Tell me some more stories about your quilts."

"Well, let me see now, this one here is called the Log Cabin, and I guess it's just about my favorite one."

"Why, Mama?"

"Well, I guess it's 'cause it's about homes. The yellow in the center is supposed to be the fire or the chimney in the cabin. The light pieces shows where the firelight falls and the dark pieces is supposed to be the shadows.

"What's this one here? It's funny looking."

"That's the Bear's Paw pattern. It was supposed to remind folks of the dangers they faced when they first settled the frontiers."

"What's this one that twists and turns so?"

"Oh, that's called the Churn Dash. I guess it was named that way 'cause the pieces is shaped like the dasher in a churn. I guess some woman dreamed that one up while she was a' settin' and a' churnin' one day," Ellen laughed.

"Oh yes, I see the shapes now! What's this? It looks like a puzzle or a maze of some kind."

"Now that one's called Drunkard's Path 'cause it just wanders all over the place like it was drunk. Now this last one is interestin'. It's called a Crazy Quilt. You don't have no pattern for that one. It's made up of all the little old scraps you've got left when you finish up yore quilts. You just fit 'em all together ever which-a-way. Then you do some fancy stitches in between each one."

"Have you got every quilt pattern in the whole world, Mama?"

"No, Ma'am! One quilt my Mama would never have in her house was Wanderin' Foot."

"Why not? What's wrong with it?"

"'Cause, it was supposed to bring bad luck. Any child that slept under it was supposed to grow up discontented and a' wantin' to wander all its life."

"Where did all the other quilts' names come from, Mama?"

"Lots of quilts like Jacob's Ladder, Joseph's Coat and Robbin' Peter to Pay Paul was named from Bible stories. I think two of the funniest names I ever heard of for quilts was Crazy Ann and Old Maid's Dream. Maybe one of these days you'll make up a new pattern and we'll call it Nola's Nonsense! How would you like that, child?"

"Oh, I'd like that a lot, Mama," Nola laughed. "Did you have lots of quiltin's at Grandma Henderson's when you were a girl? Were they like the ones you have here when Mrs. Mann and Mrs. Cole and the other women come?"

"Well, sometimes they were and sometimes when we was ready to take a quilt out, we'd have a party and all the men and boys would come, too."

"Was that a lot of fun?"

"Oh yes, I recollect that it was when we was takin' my sister Katie's Double Wedding Ring quilt out that it turned out to be a real important night for me."

"What happened?"

"Yore Papa was there. He'd come with Grandma and Grandpa Johnston for the party, and when we went walkin' together after supper, he asked me to marry him."

"He did? Did you know he was going to ask you then?"

"Well, I had a suspicion he was. Anyhow, he asked my Papa's consent right then and there and Papa said yes. I can still see Katie's face when we made our announcement. She was that mad!"

"Why was she mad? Didn't she like Papa?"

"Oh yes. All my family liked yore papa. She said we'd stole her thunder 'cause it was her Bride's Quilt they was a' takin' out. She soon got over it, though, and was happy for us. That very night they basted my quilt on the frame so they could get started on the quiltin'. Now, Missy, that's enough quiltin' talk for now. Run along and let me get some cookin' done before your brother and sister gets up. I promised yore papa I'd fix him a mess of leather britches for tomorrow and I got to get them in to soak."

Nola skipped away and Ellen chuckled as she heard her chanting, "Churn Dash, Churn Dash, Honeycomb too—."

"Grandma," Cindy said, "are you going to show me how to put that quilt pattern together like you promised? Remember, you said every girl worth her salt had to have at least a dozen quilts when she married."

Nola looked at her great-granddaughter and replied with a twinkle in her eyes, "I expect I'm good for at least one more quilt. "What pattern are you thinking about starting with?"

"Why, I thought you said it had to be a Four Patch," Cindy laughed. "Of course, I had something a little fancier in mind. Maybe like Flying Geese!"

"All right," Nola answered, "but none of that lazy machine sewing. It's got to be done properly by hand, Missy, just like my Mama taught me. Churn Dash, Churn Dash—" she murmured, drifting off to sleep again.

ELEVEN

The cold weather continued through December and January, and Ellen told Will, "I vow, I think the whole world has turned into one great big icicle!"

The mountains were waist deep in snow, and in some places the coves had drifts as high as the houses. Melting snow for the animals to drink kept them busy.

One day Will struggled for nearly two hours to lead the cow through the drifts to a stream, and when he finally got there, she refused to drink from the running water. Since then, Will and Ellen had melted the snow and had carried it to the tub in the barnyard.

"I'm getting worried about the hay and corn, Ellen," Will said one afternoon as they were feeding the livestock. "I had counted on the animals being able to graze the pastures some this winter. If the weather don't moderate soon, we'll have to cut back on their feed, and that'll mean less milk."

Later that afternoon they were startled by a loud banging on the door and opened it to find Sam McGinty, Jacob's eldest son, half frozen on their stoop. "Please, Mr. Johnston," he cried, "You've got to come help my pa!"

His teeth were chattering so hard he couldn't talk any more. After they got him inside and warmed, he continued his story. "Ma sent me to see if you'd come and tend my pa. He fell out of the barnloft this mornin' when he was throwin' hay down to the livestock. His leg's busted up bad. Me and John carried him in to the house, but he's in a bad way and we need your help. It ain't just broke, the bone's a' stickin' out of his leg. We couldn't do nothin' for him. Ma said you'd come and fix it if I could get here."

"Of course I will, son. Just let me get my things together and I'll go at once. Ellen, get me some poppy seeds to help him with the pain, and put me in some of that black plantain and snakeroot and sassafras in case the wound mortifies. Quick, Nola, run and get my bag while I get my things on."

Everyone scurried about carrying out Will's orders. Ellen and Nola got his medical supplies while Willie helped him with his boots and coat.

When Sam began to put on his coat, Will stopped him. "You stay here for the night, Sam," he said. "You're worn out and will only hinder me. Rest tonight, and then strike out for home first thing tomorrow."

Sam breathed a sigh of relief. "I confess, Mr. Johnston, that I wasn't lookin' forward to makin' that trip back today. Tell Ma I'll be there quick as I can in the mornin'."

"Will, take care now," Ellen told him. "I hope you won't have to stay long. It's just not fair of people to expect you to go off and leave yore own family for days at a time. We need you too, you know."

As soon as the words were out of her mouth, Ellen wished she could take them back. The displeased look Will shot her stopped her from saying anything more in front of Sam.

"Ellen, you know I'll be back as soon as I can," he told her shortly. "You surely would not have me refuse help to a neighbor. The path is clear to the barn and Nola is big enough to help you with the animals if need be. Everyone appears to be in good health to me."

"Oh Will, you know I don't mind takin' care of the stock. And of course I want you to help the McGintys. I don't know what got in me. I'm sorry if I've displeasured you."

"You could never 'displeasure' me, Ellen," Will reassured her. "Now take care and I'll be home the minute I see Jacob's all right."

Will hugged Ellen for a long moment. Then he took up his supplies and started off to the McGinty's.

Ellen watched until he was out of sight and then turned to the needs of the children and Sam. "The first thing we need to do is get you in some dry clothes, Sam McGinty. I think some of Will's things will suffice until we can dry your things. While you're a' changin', I'll fix you a cup of sassafras tea. My mother used to say it was the best thing in the world to ward off a chill."

When Sam slipped back into the room in Will's oversized clothes, she gave him the tea. Then she began preparing their evening meal.

The children looked warily at Sam and he fidgeted, sensing their disapproval of him. His reputation as a troublemaker had not lessened since the camp meeting, and they were recalling the times they had heard their papa discuss his behavior with Ellen.

Sensing the tension in the cabin, Ellen decided to fix a special treat for supper. "How would you young'uns like some of my special fried pies for supper?" she asked. "Sam, does your ma ever fix them?"

"Oh yes, ma'am, she shore does. I reckon I like 'em about as well as anything."

"Oh boy, fried pies," Willie whooped. "Can I have two? I don't never get enough fried pies!"

"Well, we'll see," Ellen laughed. "Nola, come on and you can help me."

Ellen took a bag of her dried apples down and put a generous helping of the fruit to stew. When the spicy apples were thick and to her liking, she rolled out her pastries and filled them with the sweet mixture. Nola crimped the edges, and they dropped them in deep fat to fry until they were golden brown. Supper was put away in short order as the children rushed through their meal in anticipation of the delicious treat.

Ellen gave them their fill for once, and laid aside the rest to send home by Sam the next day. She had already put a loaf of bread for the McGintys in the oven. She knew Louisa's mind would not be on food for the next few days.

When she had told Willie for the third time to ready himself for bed, she gave him a smart slap on the rear of his britches. Thoughts of Will out on the cold mountainside made her short-tempered, and she told him sharply, "Willie, you step lively now and mind what I tell you! Just because Papa's gone, don't think you can forget how to mind me."

Finally they were all ready for bed and a pallet had been prepared for Sam in Willie's room. Nola pushed up close to Ellen and said, "Mama, please tell us a story before we have to go to bed. Papa was going to tell us one tonight, but he's gone now. I just don't think I could go to sleep yet anyhow."

"Well, all right," Ellen replied, "I guess we're all a little uneasy. Which story do you want tonight? David and Goliath, Moses and the Bulrushes, or . . . ?"

"Oh please, Mama, tell us the story about Grandma Cunnigan and the outlaws," Nola and Willie chorused.

"I never heard of that story," Sam said.

"Course you didn't," Nola laughed. "It's about our own grand-mother and how she crossed the plains."

"Hush, Nola, let Mama tell it," Willie squealed.

"Now, now, Willie, just calm down. I'm gonna tell it. Well, it happened like this: your Grandma Mary and Grandpa Josiah Cunnigan, my Pa and Ma, was hard workin' folks who built their homeplace in the mountains of Tennessee. They worked together a' buildin' their cabin and grubbin' up stumps to clear their fields. 'Cept when she's havin' babies, Mary worked just as hard as Josiah. First they was Lucinda, the oldest girl, then Jessie, and Sue Anne, and finally baby John. Josiah was always partial to Lucinda 'cause she was their first-born. He called her his mountain girl."

"Tell about her hair, Mama," Nola interrupted.

"She had hair that was as brown as chestnuts and it hung clear down to her waist when she loosed it at night. Her eyes was what her pa called chinquapin eyes, they's so black. Well, when Lucinda was fifteen, Josiah took sick with what they thought was the grippe. He never could seem to throw it off, though. They put horseradish poultices on him to draw the poison out of his lungs and dosed him with boneset tea and butterfly root for the fevers, but nothin' helped him. Finally one mornin' he drawed his last breath and give up the ghost."

"That means he died, Sam," Nola whispered.

"Well, the Cunnigans was right well thought of, and neighbors come from all over the mountainside to help lay Josiah out. Grandma washed him and dressed him in his good black suit, and then they buried him near the willer tree he loved so much."

"How did they live after their pa died, Mama," Nola prodded.

"The neighbors was good to Mary and helped her with her crops and such for a time. 'Neighbors is kind,' Mary told Lucinda, 'but how long can you expect menfolks to leave their own crops to tend another's? I don't see how we can make it alone. If the boys was older, we could do it, but me and you can't make enough crops to keep food in our bellies. I won't be beholden to others for my livelihood. Josiah would never have wanted it that way. It 'pears to me all we can do is pack up our household plunder and go back to Missouri where we've got some kin to help us out.'"

"Did Lucinda want to go to Missouri?" asked Sam.

"No sir! Lucinda 'most grieved herself to death at the thought of leavin' those mountains. She had the same love for that wild land as Josiah had, and she couldn't stand the thought that she might never see it again. 'I knowed somethin' bad was a' gonna happen when I fergot and looked at the new moon through the trees the first night it rose,' she lamented. 'And everbody knows the blue jays is evil birds that brought us bad luck a' hangin' around so close to the cabin all summer.'"

"That's true enough," Sam exclaimed. "I've heard my pa say that many a' time!"

"Well, anyhow Mary told them to start gettin' their belongin's together so's they could get on the trail before bad weather set in. The old folks said it was goin' to be a hard winter on account of all the signs. There'd been more spiders around than usual, and the hickorys and oaks was loaded with nuts and acorns, and the bears and other wild critter's coats was thicker than common."

"Papa says you can tell by the stripes on woolly worms how bad the weather'll be," Nola volunteered.

"They piled all their belongin's in the wagon and hitched the mules up early one mornin' and set out. As Mary looked back at that lonely grave under the willers, she promised herself that some day she'd come back."

"Where did they go then, Mama?" prompted Nola.

"They joined up with a caravan in Knoxville, turned north toward the Cumberland Gap and started a trip that was nothin' but hard daily toil. They struggled over mountain passes so rough it took men and critters pushin' together to get through, and they forded rivers like they'd never seen before. Mary had been lucky to find a man named Lon Woody in Knoxville who was lookin' for a way to go west, and they made a trade. In return for food and a place to bed down, he promised to help her drive her wagon. They traveled most of the daylight hours, and at night they's almost too tired to eat anything before they'd fall on their pallets. The next day, they'd be up at the crack of dawn and off again.

"When they crossed the Missouri border, they left the rest of the wagon train and turned up north toward Jefferson City. The first night by themselves, they made camp early and had their first fresh meat since they left home. It was two rabbits that Lon managed to snare. Just as they sat down to eat, two men rode up to the camp and hailed them, askin' for leave to come into the camp.

"Was they scared?" asked Willie.

"Oh no, it wasn't nothin' unusual to meet folks on the trail. They made them welcome and invited them to share their food with them.

"Now these men's horses was all lathered in sweat, and the men was covered in dust from the trail. They rubbed their horses down and washed up and set down to eat.

"'Ma'm, this is mighty tasty stew, and we're much obliged to you,' the dark-haired man said. 'My name is Joseph Truitt, and this here is my brother Bob. We're on our way to Kentucky to buy some horses for our spread back in Kansas. We been ridin' hard for two days, and this is the first decent food we've had since we left.'

"'Why don't you fellers just bed down with us for the night?' Lon asked them."

"Did they stay?' asked Sam.

"No," Ellen said, "the men said, 'That's mighty neighborly of you, but we'd best git on the trail. My brother here is anxious to git back to his old woman. Thank you again for the fine vittles, ma'm.' Then they saddled up the spare horses they'd been leadin' and left at a hard gallop."

"What happened next, Mama?' Nola asked.

"Mary had just got all the children settled and was gettin' ready to climb into the wagon to her pallet when six men come ridin' into the camp. 'Howdy ma'm,' the leader said, 'we're lookin' for two men who may have come this way. They was ridin' hard and had two spares trailin' 'em.'

"'Who might you be, mister?' Mary asked him, 'and why are you lookin' for these gentlemen?'

"'Gentlemen, haw! That's a joke,' said the leader. 'Them "gentlemen" is outlaws. I'm Sheriff Jim Morgan and these men are my deputies. We've been trailin' them rascals for three days now. They burned out and robbed three families in St. Louis and shot up two of my men aways back.'"

"I bet that scared Grandma Cunnigan," Nola said.

"It shore did," Ellen said. "She told Lon, 'If I'd a' knowed that's who they was I'd shore never let 'em near my camp, much less feed 'em my stew!'

"Lon showed the posse which way the outlaws had gone, and the posse rode off after them. When they was gone, Lon got out his shotgun, laid his bedroll between the campfire and the wagon and got ready to spend the night on guard. He dozed and woke up the whole night long, a' jumpin' at every little noise.

"Tell Sam what Lon did, Mama," Nola urged.

"Well, around four in the mornin' somethin' woke him up a' creepin' through the brush. He raised up ever so careful and stared into the shadows. He made out a dim shape comin' his way by the light of the dyin' campfire."

"He thought it was the outlaws come back to get him for sure," Nola said.

"He raised his gun, steadied his shakin' hands, took careful aim and squeezed the trigger. The awfullest sound they'd ever heard woke Mary and the young'uns up. They jumped out of that wagon sure that their end was near, just in time to see one of their mules a' runnin' through the brush."

"He'd shot their mule," Nola laughed.

"Mary hollered, 'Look what you've gone and done, Lon Woody, you've done shot that pore critter's ears plumb off!'"

"Boy, I bet that was one surprised old mule," Sam laughed. "What did they do then?"

"Well, after Mary and the young'uns rounded the mule up and doctored its wounds, they packed up their plunder and turned around and headed back to Tennessee. Mary 'lowed as how she wasn't goin' to live in no heathen country where outlaws ate up folks' rabbit stew and people shot the ears off of mules!"

"Was Lucinda glad they was goin' home, Mama?" asked Nola.

"Yes. They all whooped and hollered for joy, and when Mary seen Josiah's lonely grave under the willers, she knowed she'd done the right thing."

"Did she ever go back to Missouri again, Mrs. Johnston?" asked Sam.

"No, she stayed there and raised her family. She had lots of trials and tribulations, but she never had no hankerin' to go back to Missouri again.

"Now, it's way past bedtime and this fire is a' burnin' low, so you young'uns get to bed. Sam's got to get up early tomorrow and get hisself home to help his ma."

"Thank you Mrs. Johnston. That was a fine tale. Boy, I bet that was fun travelin' across the plains," Sam said dreamily. "Someday I'm goin' to travel all over this country and see everything."

"Wouldn't you be scared to leave your ma and pa!" Nola asked, eyes shining in admiration.

"Shucks no. Don't reckon I'm scared of nothin'! 'Sides, I'll be a growed man by then," he swaggered.

"Well, that's enough talkin' now," Ellen said. "I hope you'll all say a special prayer for your papas tonight. Pray that yours got to the McGintys safe, Nola, and Sam you pray that yours is a' gonna be all right."

Nola gave her mother a quick hug before she climbed up to the loft. "Someday I can tell my own children about Grandma Cunnigan and the outlaws, just like you told us. It's my very favorite story. I think I'm like Lucinda. I don't ever want to live anywhere but right here in the mountains with you and Papa."

TWELVE

Will alternated between walking and riding the mule over the mountain ridge and to the cove where the McGintys lived. He made good time, considering the weather. As he traveled, he thought about Ellen's reluctance for him to leave her and felt guilty because he had been short with her. He knew she was remembering being left alone when Tildy was born. He had agonized many times that somehow Tildy's illness might have been prevented if Ellen had been tended properly.

There had not been many calls for his doctoring skills since Tildy's death, other than the delivery of his own children, but he had continued to keep his supplies in good order and he reviewed in his head what treatment might be needed for an injury like Sam had described. His failure to help Tildy weighed heavily on him and made him less sure of himself. He prayed that he would be able to do what must be done to help Jacob.

The cold began to chill him, and he suddenly felt older than his thirty years. The mule must have noticed the difference, too, and it balked at having to struggle through the snowdrifts. About dusk he got his first glimpse of the smoke from the McGinty cabin, and it gave him heart to forge ahead. Louisa was watching for him and rushed out to meet him as he came in sight.

"Thank the Lord, Will. You are the answer to my prayers. I don't know what we'd of done if you hadn't got here," she said as she helped him into the cabin.

"How is he?" Will asked.

"He's bad. He fell from the barn loft this mornin' and his leg is busted bad. He ain't one to let on, but he's sufferin' somethin' terrible. Didn't Sam come back with you?"

"No, Louisa. The boy was so tuckered out I made him stay. Ellen will fill his belly and see that he gets a good night's rest and send him on first thing tomorrow. Now, let's see what we can do for Jacob."

The three younger children were huddled in the corner, big-eyed and scared. They looked at Will with relief when he came in with his medicine bag.

John was by his father's bedside, applying cool cloths to his forehead and holding him down as he thrashed about the bed, moaning in pain.

Will's heart sank as he drew back the sheet and looked at Jacob's leg. It was swollen almost twice normal size and was blue and purple from the injury. The shin bone was protruding from the outside of his leg. The lower part of his leg lay at an unnatural angle. Jacob was obviously in a great deal of pain. His speech was garbled, and he did not recognize Will.

"He's been like this since half past noon," Louisa told Will. "He don't know who I am half the time, and he keeps tryin' to get up and go feed the stock."

"Can you help him, Mr. Johnston?" John pleaded. "It's a fierce wound."

"Yes it is, John, and we've got a hard job ahead of us. It's going to take all three of us to do this job. I'm going to need help from both of you."

"I stand ready to do what ever you tell me, Mr. Johnston," John said looking him squarely in the eyes. "Just tell me what you want me to do."

"The first thing we must do," Will said briskly, "is ease his pain. Louisa, bring me some water so I can mix him something strong enough to help him through this. Then, John, I want you to fill all the kettles you have with water and put them on the fire. What I'm going to have to do will be hard on him and you, too, I suspect. We've got to get this leg set and the bone back where it's supposed to be. I just hope mortification hasn't set in. You've helped by keeping the wound covered with clean rags."

"Will he lose the leg, Will?" Louisa asked fearfully.

"I don't know, Louisa, and that's the truth. Like John said, it's a fierce wound. I promise I'll do the very best I can, and with the Lord's help we'll pull him through this. Now, Louisa, you get me all the clean rags you can find, and a bedsheet if you can spare one."

Will rolled up his sleeves and went to work. First he laid out the ground up poppy seeds he'd brought and mixed them in a little water. Then he took the snakeroot and sassafras and made a poultice for the wound on Jacob's leg. He fed Jacob the poppy mixture a spoonful at a time and waited for it to take effect.

"I'm going to need you and John both to hold him when I try to set this leg. Even with the poppy, it's going to hurt him, but you must hold him as still as you can."

When the drug had taken effect, Will tied Jacob's arms and sound leg to the bed with strips of cloth and said, "John, you stand on this side of the bed and Louisa, you stand on the other side. You must hold him as still as you can." When both were in place, he grasped the broken leg and pulled down on it, at the same time twisting it back to its normal position.

Jacob screamed in pain, and it was all Louisa and John could do to hold him down. The bone slipped back into place, and Will gave a great sigh of relief. Jacob had mercifully fainted.

The perspiration was pouring off Will's face, and his hands trembled as he thought about his next steps. He looked at John and Louisa. "Are you all right?" he asked.

Louisa whispered, "Yes." John nodded. Both were pale and, like Will, perspiring heavily. Will was aware of the soft weeping of the girls in the corner.

"The worst is over now," he said. "I'm sorry I had to hurt your pa, but there was just no other way. Let's look to this wound now. John, you go and find me two good boards, and Louisa, start bringing me some of that hot water."

He began applying hot poultices where the bone had penetrated the skin, changing them as quickly as they cooled. He continued the treatment for a long time, hoping to draw out all the poisons. Next he covered the wound with a salve made of wild geraniums and ginger that an Indian medicine man had shown him how to make. Louisa tore up a sheet, and Will bound the strips tightly around the wound. John helped him secure the two boards he had found on either side of the leg, and they tied them firmly with more strips of cloth.

After Louisa fed the younger children some milk and bread, she put them to bed. Then she and Will began a long vigil. John sat with them, refusing to go to bed until he knew his pa was all right.

When the sedative wore off, Jacob became irrational, and they had to tie him down to keep him from hurting himself further.

Will continued to give him small doses of the poppy mixture, but the pain was so severe it didn't seem to have much effect.

Sam returned home early the next morning, and he and John went about taking care of the livestock and doing the other chores around the barn.

The next two days were a continuation of the night's ordeal, and Will and Louisa were able to sleep only in snatches. John and Sam helped as they could, but much of the time it took all four of them to subdue Jacob. Will continued applying the hot poultices and salve to the wound, but on the third day when Will took the bandage off the wound, he knew something drastic would have to be done if Jacob's leg were to be saved. It was swollen and had turned an ugly purple color with bright red streaks creeping toward his trunk.

"Louisa, I'm going to have to lance the wound and let the putrefaction out. If I don't, there's danger that he might lose his life as well as the leg. Take this knife and boil it, and then I'm going to need all three of you to hold him."

When they were all in place, Will cut into the wound with one swift motion. A stream of pus and putrid liquid spewed out of the gash. The odor was overpowering and Sam made a wild dive for the door. Will heard the sound of the boy's gagging. He looked up just in time to see Louisa sink to the floor in a faint.

"John, are you still with me?" he asked.

A weak, but steady voice answered, "I'm here, Mr. Johnston."

"Good, now hold on a few more minutes until I get this poison drained out, then bring me more hot water."

When he felt the wound had drained as much as it would, he began applying hot poultices again. Sam had returned and helped his mother into a chair.

"Put a cool cloth on her head, Sam. You might try one for yourself too."

"I'm so ashamed of myself, Will," Louisa said. "I've never done such a foolish female thing like that before in all my life."

"Don't you feel bad, Louisa. It takes a mighty strong stomach to take something like that. Sit and rest awhile. Boys, keep that hot water coming. We've got to get all the poison out this time, or we won't get another chance at it, I'm afraid."

Once the poison was drained, Jacob's recovery was almost miraculous. In two more days, he was so much improved that Will felt he could go home. He left instructions about changing the bandages, promised to be back in a day or two to check on Jacob and then set out with his mule for home.

When he got home, Ellen said, "Will, you look tuckered out. I want you to go to bed and rest. We'll look after things. You just rest yoreself up."

"Ellen, my dear, I've never felt better in my life. I didn't realize how much my failure to help Tildy had affected me until I saw Jacob recovering and knew I'd saved his leg."

"Oh, Will, I never faulted you for Tildy's death!" Ellen exclaimed.

"I know, but I faulted myself. Now I know there was nothing I could have done that would have changed things. God knows best after all."

Jacob McGinty walked with a limp the rest of his life, but he kept his leg. When he tried to thank Will for what he had done, Will told him, "It is I that should thank you. If you want to thank somebody, thank the Lord. He guided my hand when I lanced that wound."

Jacob credited Will with the deed, though, and as soon as the weather moderated, he had Sam and John load a sled with corn and hay and take it to Will for his animals.

THIRTEEN

Spring came early in the mountains that year. As often happens after unusually cold temperatures, the flowering trees and shrubs were unusually beautiful.

"The whole mountainside looks like one big ball of color," Ellen told Will. "I think the wild cherry and redbud trees are the prettiest I ever seen, and then the dogwood and crabapple trees comes along and outdoes 'em."

"Have you seen the Sarvis trees down around the creek?" Will asked. "Their blooms are the closest things to lace I've ever seen."

"Yes, and the blood root and spring beauty no more'n got through until along come all them violets a showin' their stuff."

"That Nola is going to wear her legs to a nubbin' running to me with her flowers. She can't stand it when she finds a new blossom until she can name it," Will bragged. "She's brought me everything from Dutchman's Breeches to May Apples to identify. Said she was going to make her a flower book like my herb book."

"Yes, I know. What you can't name, I've had to. She'll go wild when the wild honeysuckle and ivy starts a' bloomin'."

Ellen was again big with child, and her movements were slow and deliberate. She was impatient with herself and her body.

"I declare Will, I just can't figure why I'm so big this time. Do you reckon we misfigured? I'm already bigger'n I was with Martha and by my way of figurin' I'm just a' startin' my seventh month."

"Maybe we lost our notching stick this time," Will laughed.

Springtime became a period of quiet contentment for the family. Will prepared his fields for planting, and Ellen scrubbed the

71

cabin from floors to rafters, trying to get rid of the winter's smoke and dirt before the new baby arrived. She kept Willie and Nola busy carrying water from the spring.

"Mama ain't let that pore old washpot rest a minute," complained Willie. "She's washed every quilt and piece of clothes on the place."

"Quit complaining, Willie," Nola scolded him. "Just hurry up and bring that water so you can help me carry out the bedticks. Mama wants everything aired."

"I'd rather be in the field helpin' Papa."

"Don't worry, there'll be plenty of that to do too," Nola told him. "Then you'll be fussin about that."

"Nola," Ellen called, "when you finish there, start foldin' up them winter clothes we've finished with and put 'em in the chest. They're all clean now, and all we'll have to do next winter is air 'em out, and they'll be ready to wear."

"Mama, why are you washin' everything?" asked Willie. "Are we goin' somewhere?"

"No, but when I dropped that dishrag last week, I knowed it meant somebody dirtier'n me was a' comin' to visit, and I decided I'd make shore they wasn't cleaner'n me," she teased him.

"I tell you what! It seems to me like we've all done a fair to middlin' good job on this old house, and I think we deserve a day of rest. Tomorrow we're goin' to fix us a basket and go up to that purty rock we found last summer and have us a picnic. How would you like that?"

Squeals of delight answered her question, and after that there were no more complaints from Willie about the work. When the children finally settled down for sleep that night, she got herself ready for bed, feeling unusually tired.

"Guess it's the new little one a' wearin' me down so," she told Will. "Seems like I can't turn out no work a' tall anymore."

"Seems to me you've done well to get everything cleaned so quick. I'm glad you're taking some time tomorrow to rest. I wish I could go too, but I've got to get that upper field turned so we can get the corn in. If our animals keep multiplying, we'll need even more grain to get us through next winter.

The next morning everyone was up early, anxious to start on the picnic. Ellen sliced slabs of ham she had cooked the day before, boiled eggs, baked sweet potatoes, dished up a bowl of leather britches from the pot simmering over the fire, packed some biscuits and then added fried apple pies to the ample basket.

With the three excited children, Ellen set off across the meadow for their rock, some two miles up the ridge. It was a gradual climb with only one really steep section to maneuver. Nola and Willie took turns helping Martha, half pulling and half carrying her over the steep places. Ellen managed the basket, pausing frequently to catch her breath and to "spell" the children.

"Mama, look at the wild honeysuckle," exclaimed Nola. "That bush has got every color on it. They's red and yellow and orange and pink colored ones on it. I didn't know they was so many different colors."

"Looks like that bush has caught 'em all. Don't this sun feel good? It won't be long till summertime now."

Ellen's long skirt kept catching the brambles, so finally she pulled it up and tucked it in her waistband, feeling more freedom in the narrow slip she wore underneath.

At last they reached their destination and were all content to lie back in the grass and catch their breath for a few minutes. The place, simply known as "the rock," was in the middle of a large meadow carpeted with phlox, violets, primroses and buttercups. The large outcropping rock dominated the area. It was twenty feet in diameter and the top was partially covered with green moss, as soft and springy as carpet. The edge of the rock formed a natural roof where it protruded from the earth and formed a shelter where at least six grown men could be protected from the rain.

Ellen looked up at the mountain ranges surrounding them. The colors in the mountains ranged from the yellow greens of the new leaves to darker greens of the balsams and pines. As the peaks overlapped each other in the distance, they changed to different shades of blue. The mountain slopes were spotted with splotches of whites where the apple trees and dogwoods were blooming. The smoky blue of the sky made a perfect backdrop for the majestic peaks.

As Ellen drank in all the colors around them, she heard Nola say softly, "Oh Mama, look at the baby rabbits. There's at least six of them, and they look like they're playing leap-frog!"

The rabbits did appear to have a complicated game of leap-frog going as they bounded back and forth over each other, sometimes jumping forward and sometimes springing just as easily backward over each other. They sat entranced watching the show before them.

Suddenly a huge bird dropped out of nowhere, and before their horrified eyes, grabbed one of the rabbits in its talons. With the same graceful motion, it soared back up into the sky clutching the wriggling rabbit and disappeared into the nearby forest. The other rabbits vanished, diving into their burrows.

"Oh Mama, the poor little thing," Nola cried. "Why did the mean old bird take him away from his family? Why did God make birds that hurt little rabbits?"

"Hush, Nola," Ellen said, "that's a red-tailed hawk, and it's probably got a nest with hungry babies in it. It's just doin' what comes natural for it. They's a purpose for everything God puts on this earth and a reason behind everything that happens."

"What do you mean, Mama?" Nola asked.

"Well, just like when Tildy died. I thought for a time that God was just a' punishin' me by takin' my baby away from me. That wasn't it at all. He took her 'cause she was a' sufferin' and couldn't have ever been well again."

"Why did He let her get sick, Mama? Why does God let people get sick and die like Tildy and Grandma Henderson?"

"I asked that question myself, Nola," Ellen answered sadly. "Then somethin' happened one day that let me know that God don't make us sick. They's just things on this earth that makes us sick, like diseases and accidents and gettin' old. God just helps us get through the pain and takes us out of our misery to a better place."

"What happened, Mama? Who told you that? Did Papa tell you?"

"No, honey, it wasn't Papa. He probably already knew it. It was a pore old woman and her 'baby' that showed me how merciful God had been to Tildy and to us. Some day when you're old enough to understand, I'll tell you all about it. Right now you must know that Tildy could have never been well, and Grandma Henderson, well, she was old and she was hurtin' too. That's why God took 'em. To help them, not to punish us."

"But I don't understand, Mama. What's that got to do with the baby rabbit?"

"Well, not a whole lot I reckon." Ellen smiled. "But I guess what I wanted you to see was everything that happens is a part of God's plan. When He made this world, he made all kinds of critters. He had to have some kind of plan to take care of them critters, so maybe he put rabbits here to feed them big birds, and maybe he put them big birds here to keep the earth from bein' overrun with rabbits. Just remember, everything is part of God's plan to replenish the earth. Some day even me and you will go back to the earth to make new life grow."

"Mama, I'm gettin' hungry! When are we gonna eat?" came Willie's plaintive cry from across the meadow.

"Right now," Ellen said, starting to spread the cloth on the rock. "Come on now, you young'uns, and let's eat!"

"Please say one of the blessings you made up, Mama," Nola said. "I like them better than the regular 'God blesses.'"

As they bowed their heads Ellen said:

> "God of earth and God of sky,
> Hear our prayer and stay close by.
> Guard our hearts and guide our hands,
> That we might always tend Thy lands.
> Accept our thanks for this good life,
> And keep us safe from harm and strife."

"Amen. Now let's eat!" said Willie.

"Here, eat a bite of your birthday cake," Cindy told her great-grandmother

Nola pushed it away impatiently. "Not until it's been blessed." she said firmly. "You've been raised to know better."

"Yes ma'm," Cindy said contritely. "Do you want us to say the one you taught us, or can I say one I made up, please?"

The room quietened as Nola nodded her consent and closed her eyes. Cindy prayed:

> "God of our Universe and all mankind,
> Give us wisdom to someday find
> Peace for our world and help us be
> A loving and kind close knit family.
> For this dear life this special day,
> We thank thee humbly and truly pray,
> For her good health 'til the day when she
> Finds peace and joy in Heaven with Thee.
> Amen!"

FOURTEEN

Ellen and the children returned home that afternoon rested and happy after their picnic at the rock.

Will told Ellen, "I'll be finished with my spring plowing and planting by the end of the week. I think it would be good to have a few weeks of school before the children are needed for help with the crops."

Word was passed from neighbor to neighbor, and on the day he had set, almost all of the students showed up for lessons. Making up a roll and placing students was not necessary this time, and Will dove right into the assignments.

"Now, boys and girls," he told them, "we can get more accomplished if you children who are further along will help the younger ones in the morning and in the afternoon while they do reading and writing assignments, I can give instructions in algebra and Latin to you."

Although Nola was younger than most of the children, she fell in the latter category. She thrived on the challenge of learning the complicated subjects, and soon was ahead of most of the other students. Zac Mann was the only one who seemed able to stay ahead of her.

Will told Ellen, "I've decided the secret of keeping Zac out of mischief is to keep him so busy he doesn't have time to think up pranks. He and Nola are very competitive. He's the only one in the group that can really keep up with her. She absolutely thrives on algebra and Latin."

"Another thing I've decided to do is have a spelling bee every Friday. I think the children will enjoy the change. Quite a few of them are really good spellers, and maybe this will make some of the others want to do better."

Will divided the class into two groups. The leader among the younger children alternated from week to week, but Nola and Zac dominated the other. Nola won the first week, Zac the second and third and Nola the fourth. The fifth and final week was to determine the champion.

Will's plan for keeping Zac out of mischief had worked well, but on this last day Zac could not resist trying one last prank. He had a special relationship with animals and kept a variety of creatures. His mother had tolerated them fairly well until one day when a mischievous raccoon pillaged her pantry and either ate or overturned everything in sight. Since then he had been ordered to keep them away from the house. Will had been hard pressed to keep the animals out of the school room.

On the day of the final spelling bee, Zac brought his pet skunk, Rosie, to school with him. He concealed her in his shirt, but Will was suspicious of his studied look of innocence and the obvious bulge around the middle.

Fixing Zac with an icy stare, he said, "I suggest, Zac, that you make sure there are none of your friends hiding in your shirt. Maybe you'd better step outside and find a place to leave it until school is dismissed. Unless of course, you want to concede the spelling bee this afternoon."

Zac sheepishly left the room and returned shortly, looking much slimmer around his middle. When the snickering had stopped, Will announced that they would begin the final spelling bee.

Pearl McGinty won the contest among the younger children by spelling the word *sleeve*. The older group began their competition, and eventually the field was narrowed down to Nola, Zac and Sam McGinty. They successfully spelled fifteen words, then Will gave Sam the word *propinquity*.

Sam shifted from one foot to the other, thought for a long moment, then took a deep breath and said, "Propinquity, p-r-o-p-i-n-c-i-t-y."

"Wrong!" whooped Zac. "It's p-r-o-p-i-n-q-u-i-t-y."

Glowering, Sam sat down. Nola and Zac spelled *acquirement, enticement, incitement, suscitate, transmigrate, indurate* and *misanthropy*. Finally both missed the word syllogistic. Zac successfully spelled *parenthetic*, but Nola missed her next word, *hyperbole*.

"Hyperbole," she said, "h-i-p-e-r-b-o-l-e."

"That's wrong," said Zac gleefully. "Hyperbole, h-y-p-e-r-b-o-l-e. I won! I'm the champion speller of this here school. I beat you, Nola Johnston!"

Nola sat down, blinking back tears.

Will shook Zac's hand. "That was a fine job, Zac. I'm real proud of you. You will be a fine student if you'll put about half as much thought to studying as you do on them pranks of yours."

He turned to Nola and was distressed to see tears welling up in her eyes. "Now, Nola," he said, "here can be a good example to all of you younger students. Zac is three years older than Nola, but she stayed right with him and beat everybody else. Many students much older than she is. I'm very proud of you, Nola!"

"Yeah," Sam spoke up, "she shore beat me good!"

"Thank you, Papa, thank you, Sam," Nola said quietly.

"Nobody else better not say nothin' about Nola gettin' beat," Sam muttered, glowering at Zac.

"I want to give each one of the winners a book of *Aesop's Fables*," Will said. "There is a story in one of them that talks about friendship. This seems to be a good subject for us to end our spring session on. We get through life by helping each other and encouraging each other."

He then proceeded to read the story:

The Bear and the Two Friends

Two friends setting out together upon a journey which led through a dangerous forest, mutually promised to assist each other, if they should happen to be assaulted. They had not proceeded far, before they perceived a bear making toward them with great rage.

There were no hopes in flight; but one of them, being very active, sprang up into a tree; upon which the other, throwing himself flat on the ground, held his breath and pretended to be dead; remembering to have heard it asserted that this creature will not prey upon a dead carcass. The bear came up and after smelling of him some time, left him and went on. When he was fairly out of sight and hearing, the hero from the tree called out, "Well, my friend, what said the bear? He seemed to whisper you very closely." "He did so," replied the other, "and gave me this good advice, never to associate with a wretch, who, in the hour of danger will desert his friend."

"What lesson do you think this teaches us, children?" asked Will.

"Well, it teaches you how to fool a bear," Zac snickered.

"Yes," Will said dryly, "it does that, although I wouldn't advise trying it. It teaches something else though."

"Mr. Johnston," John McGinty said, "I think it means if you make a promise to somebody, you're supposed to keep yore word. It said 'they mutually promised to assist each other,' but when it come down to it, he run off and left his friend to shift for his self."

"Very good, John. That's exactly what it meant. Here's something else I read once. 'A man is only as good as his word.'"

While the children were still digesting the story, a dog began barking frantically outside the school. The barking was followed by a series of pitiful yelps. Before Will could investigate, Zac rose up from his seat and, to Will's astonishment, ran out the door.

"Phew," Sam yelled. "It's a skunk!"

All of the children began running from the room, holding their noses and gagging. It did not take Will long to follow.

The dog, a brown spotted hound belonging to the Mann children, was still yelping and running for home with his tail tucked between his legs.

Looking chagrined and dismayed, Zac was frantically pulling off his jacket and shirt. The children cut a wide path around him.

"Mr. Johnston," said John McGinty, "I reckon school's out for a spell, ain't it?"

"Yes, I reckon it is," replied Will. "You children can go on home now, unless you've got some words of farewell you want to say to Zac."

Will held a handkerchief over his nose and stood well up-wind of Zac while he told him, "Well, Zac, I don't expect you'll be bothered with a lot of friends seeking your company for awhile. I think you had best get yourself home—or as close to it as your mother will allow. We'll take this matter up when school convenes again."

Thus ended the spring session of the little school on the mountainside.

FIFTEEN

T

hree weeks after the dramatic closing of the spring school session, Will and Ellen were eating breakfast when they were startled by a knock on their door. When Will opened the door, he found three men on his doorstep.

"Will, do you remember me?" asked a tall, darkly handsome man. "We met at the camp meeting over at Shook's."

"Well, I declare!" exclaimed Will. "It's Alfred Silver. What on earth brings you to these mountains? Are you looking for some of those herbs I told you about? Come in, man, and welcome."

"Well, I shore wish it was good that brought me. Truth is, I'm needin' the help of some good men who know this area, and I recollected how you told me you had tramped these mountains here abouts."

"What's the trouble? You know I stand ready to help any way I can."

"My brother, Charles, is a' missin'," Silver replied soberly, "and we've had reason to believe he come over in this area huntin' bear. Anyways, that's what his wife said. He's been missin' fer over a month now, and we can't find hide nor hair of him anywheres."

"What makes you think he came over here?" asked Will.

"Well, he had a friend that lived jest over the county line that he liked to hunt with and his wife Frances heard him mention his friend's name. When we asked him about hit though, he says he never seen him. Said he never made no plans to go huntin' with him. We 'lowed we'd come and look anyhow and see could we find anybody that'd seen anything of him."

"Let me get my things on and we'll see if we can't round up some help. Thomas Mann and Jesse Cole know the area better than I do, and I'm sure they'll help if they can."

"I'll shorely be much obliged to you, Will," Silver told him gratefully. "My pa is jest about out of his mind with worry. He's looked everywhere he can think of. He's done got so desperate he's gone off over to Tennessee to see a' old Guinea Negro that claims he can find lost people with a conjurin' ball."

The party set off and recruited Mann and Cole to go with them. They combed the area for the better part of three days, contacting every family in the area and picking up help as they went along. They found no trace of the man nor anyone who had seen him. After three days, Silver and his companions gave up and started for home.

Before they left, Will told Silver, "I'd be obliged if you'd let me know what you learn about your brother's disappearance. I regret we couldn't find him for you."

"I'll shore do that, Will," Silver said, "and I'm mighty obliged fer yore help. I'll git word to you one way or t'other."

Almost a month passed and one day Will received a crudely printed note saying, "Bruther Charles is dead. Done in by his wif. Truil is set fer Monday next in ashvil. your frind, A. Silver."

"I think that I'm just going to have to go and sit in on that trial," Will told Ellen. "I've puzzled over what might have happened to Charles Silver, and I don't think I can rest until I hear the whole story."

When Will told Jesse and Thomas about the message, they decided they would go to the trial with him. The three men set off early the following Sunday morning and rode into Asheville in time for the trial Monday.

The jurors had been sworn in by the time they arrived. The Attorney General of the State of North Carolina was the prosecutor. The judge's name was Donnell.

"Who is defending the woman?" asked Will.

"She ain't got no counsel," one of the spectators told them. "She ain't said nothin' nor answered no questions. Jest sets there a' lookin' straight ahead."

Charles Silver's father was the first witness called by the prosecution. "Now, Mr. Silver," the prosecutor said, "I want you to tell us a little something about your son. What kind of man was he, and was he a good son to you?"

"Well sir," Silver replied, "Charles was a strong, healthy, good-lookin' man and so far as I know always agreeable. He had lots of friends and everybody seemed to like him. He was always a favorite at all the parties 'cause he could make merry by talkin' and laughin' and playin' music on his fiddle and his guitar."

"Why do you think the defendant would want to kill him?" asked the prosecutor.

"I reckon she took hit in her head that she had cause to be jealous of him. 'Twarn't so, though. He was true to her and he loved their little baby daughter. As fer what kind of a son he was, why I couldn't a' asked fer a better one. He just lived right acrost the ridge from us and was good to come and help when we needed him."

"Now Mr. Silver, I want you to tell the jury how you first come to find out your son was missing," the attorney said.

"Well, hit happened this way," Silver replied. "Frances, his wife, come by the house and told us that Charles had gone up the river a' ways to visit with his friend, George Young, and she was worried 'cause she thought he should've been home by now."

"Weren't your worried about him too, Mr. Silver?" asked the attorney.

"No. We never thought too much about hit 'cause we knowed how much he loved to hunt with his friend," replied Silver.

"What happened that made you begin to worry?"

"Well, jest a few days later Frances come back again and she was that mad at him fer staying away so long. Told my woman that she didn't care if'n he never come back. Said she's goin' to pack her things and the baby's things and move back to her pa's place."

"What did you do then?"

"Why I went straight away and got some of the neighbors to help us, and we commenced to look fer him."

"And what did you find?"

Silver shook his head sadly and replied, "We couldn't find no track nor trace of him nowhere. We went up to George Young's and asked had he been up there to see him."

"What did Mr. Young tell you?"

"He said he hadn't been there, and furthermore he'd never expected him to come. I tell you I was gittin' plumb desperate by then. One of the neighbors told me they was a old Guinea Negro over in Tennessee that could find lost people with a conjurin' ball, and so I jest took off to look fer him."

"And did you find him, and if so what did he tell you?"

"I couldn't find him, but the man he worked fer said he could read the ball as good as the Guinea. So we hung the ball up like a pendulum and marked off the points of the compass. Then I drawed him a map of the section where Charles lived, but that there ball wouldn't point away from the house a'tall."

"What did you surmise that meant, Mr. Silver?"

"Well that feller said he thought hit meant hit was possible that Charles had been done away with at home. Well, we set there and jawed awhile, and then he tried the ball again. This time he said hit showed him the body had been found."

"What did you do then?"

"Why, I lit out fer home as fast as I could go, and when I got there, I found out that what he said was true."

"Thank you, Mr. Silver," said the attorney. "You may step down."

"Just a minute," Judge Donnell interrupted. "Mrs. Silver, do you wish to question the witness?"

Frances Silver never looked up from her hands in her lap where she had been staring the whole time during the testimony. Silently she shook her head.

"Very well," sighed the Judge, "call your next witness."

"I call Jack Collis to the stand," said the attorney.

When Collis had been sworn, the attorney said, "Mr. Collis, I want you to tell this jury what you found when you searched Charles Silver's property."

"Yes sir, I shore will. When I went in his cabin, I stirred the ashes in the far place with my walkin' stick and seen some pieces of bone. I also seen that the ashes looked awful greasy."

"Did you observe anything else?"

"Yeah, we poked around in the yard some and turned up some ashes that had been dumped in a hole near the spring. We found some more pieces of bone and gridiron such as Charles wore on his huntin' moccasins. Then we took a closer look at the cabin and under the floor, we found a circle of blood as big as a hog's liver."

"What did that lead you to believe, Mr. Collis?"

"It 'pears to me that anybody with any gumption can see that Charles Silver was murdered and his body was hacked up and burned right thar in his own farplace."

Will had been sitting tensely on the edge of his seat, and when Collis made his dramatic accusation, he gasped and sank weakly back against the backrest. The thoughts of such a heinous act made him feel physically ill, and it was all he could do to control himself.

Judge Donnell pounded his gavel until the spectators quieted down and then motioned the prosecutor to proceed.

"Thank you, Mr. Collis," the attorney said, "you have been most helpful. I would now like to call Sheriff Bob Noland to the stand."

Again, the Judge gave Frances Silver the opportunity to question the witness, and again she shook her head silently.

"Sheriff Noland, will you please tell us of your involvement in this case?" requested the prosecutor.

"The first I knowed about it, Mr. Alfred Silver over there come to see me and said his brother Charles was missin' and they'd found some evidence around his cabin that showed he'd been murdered. I went up there and looked around the barn and found Charles's axe where it had been hid under some hay in the loft. It had blood on the blade and the handle. I seen all the other things Jack Collis told about, and then I went up to the Stewart's place where Frances Silver had gone to and asked her what she knowed about all of that blood and them bones and ashes."

"And what did she tell you, Sheriff Noland?"

"Well sir, she never said a word. Jest set there and shook her head kind of numb like. Then her Ma and her two brothers lit in a' cussin' Charles Silver and said he got what he deserved for the way he'd treated Frances."

"What did you do then?"

"I jest arrested the whole crowd and took 'em in to the county seat to the jail. We never could prove the Stewarts had anything to do with it, so I had to let 'em go. It seems to me though, that she had to have some help from somebody to have hacked that body up like she did."

"Thank you, sir, you may step down now, I don't have any more testimony to present, Your Honor. The State rests its case," said the attorney.

"Frances Silver," said Judge Donnell, "since you refused to have an attorney, do you wish to speak for yourself? Is there anything you wish to ask any of these people who have testified against you?"

Frances Silver sat staring stonily at the floor, her face expressionless.

"Very well then," Judge Donnell said, "let the record show that the defendant refused to testify in her own behalf."

The prosecuting attorney summarized all of the evidence for the jury, and then Judge Donnell turned the case over to them.

Will watched the faces of the jury as they filed out to begin their deliberations. He told Ellen later, "I've never seen such a sober looking bunch of people. I was surely grateful I did not have to sit in judgment on that woman."

The jury deliberated all night and the next day recalled the witnesses, Collis and Noland. After questioning them again, they announced they had reached a verdict.

Will watched the jury file solemnly back into the courtroom. They all stared straight ahead, and none of them looked at Frances Silver where she sat alone at her table. Her hands were clasped tightly in her lap, and she stared stonily at the table in front of her.

"Have you reached a verdict?" Judge Donnell asked.

"We have, Your Honor," said the spokesman for the jury.

Will found himself holding his breath as the foreman opened up the paper he held and read, "We find Frances Silver guilty of the crime of murderin' her husband, Charles Silver."

Will heard Frances's mother burst into tears, but as he turned his eyes to Frances, he saw that she neither flinched nor changed expression as the words were read.

Judge Donnell said, "You have been found guilty of murdering your husband, Frances Silver, and for that you will be hanged by the neck until you are dead. You will be taken to Morganton to await the date of your sentence."

He banged his gavel and announced wearily, "This session is over."

Will and his two neighbors began their journey home that very day, sickened by all they had learned and anxious to be back in their mountain community. None of them slept very well on the trail that night, and they rose early to complete their journey.

"I have never been so shaken by anything," Will told Ellen that evening. "Frances Silver is a right comely woman with fair skin and bright eyes. She would not say why she did such a terrible thing, and she expressed not one word of remorse for her act. Surely her family helped her commit the murder, but there was no proof of it, and she would say nothing. It will be many a day before I forget the terrible things I heard."

"I reckon the best thing you can do is try to put it out of yore mind," Ellen replied sadly.

"I'm afraid that's easier said than done. I don't think I'll ever forget the cold look on that woman's face."

Some weeks later, a drummer was in the area and brought them news of the conclusion of the trial of Frances Silver.

"I was travelin' near the town of Morganton," he told them, "when this man and a young boy rode up in a wagon and asked could they travel along with me. It gets pretty lonely a' travelin' around by myself, so I told them, 'Why shore, come right on.' Well, sir, we hadn't gone along very far when this sheriff and two deputies come ridin' after us hard as they could. The sheriff rode up close to the boy and said, 'Frances?' He turned around and said, 'I thank you sir, my name is Tommy.' The man he was with, who turned out to be his or her uncle said, 'Yes, her name is Tommy.' Well sir, that sheriff snatched the hat off'n the boy's head, and bless my soul, but it was a woman dressed up like a man. It seems this woman, name of Frances Silver, was in jail a' waitin' to be hung for murderin' her husband, and she got some boy's clothes somehow and tried to escape. That sheriff took us all back to Morganton, and I like to never have convinced him that I didn't have nothin' to do with it."

"What happened to her afterwards?" asked Will.

"Well, she's gone on to her reward, or punishment, I guess," the drummer replied. "They hanged her the very next day. Let's see, that would have been July 12th. You never seen so many people who had come a' hopin' she'd confess before she died."

"And did she confess?"

"No sir. I thought for a minute she was goin' to tell what happened when she was a' standin' up there on the scaffold waitin' for 'em to hang her, but her pa yelled out at her, 'Die with your secret, Frances,' and that's just what she did."

"Then no one will ever know what really happened or what made her do it," Will said sadly.

"They was a' passin' out slips of paper with this here ballad printed on it at the execution. Some claim Frances Silver wrote it as her confession, but I don't know. All I know is she give me the cold shivers the way she stood up there with that cold look on her face and spoke nary a word when they hanged her."

Will took the paper gingerly and read:

> *This dreadful, dark and dismal day*
> *Has swept my glories all away,*

My sun has set, my joys are past,
  And I must leave this world at last.

Oh God! What shall become of Me?
  I am condemned the world can see.
To endless doom my soul must fly,
  All in the twinkling of an eye.

Judge Donnell has my sentence passed,
  To that All-wise Judge I go at last;
No hope to lift my drooping head,
  And none when numbered with the dead.

Alas, that dreaded Judge I fear!
  Shall I that awful sentence hear
"Depart ye cursed, murderess, fell,
  Into a quenchless, burning hell?"

I feel that I shall tended be
  By frightful ghosts of misery
Eating my flesh by endless plan
  For the innocent blood of a helpless man.

And shall I meet that manly face,
  Whose blood I spilled upon his place,
With flaming eye he'll accusing plead;
  "Why did you do th' unholy deed?"

In that last calm sleep I see him now,
  The beautiful peace on his handsome brow;
Our winsome babe on his heaving breast
  The crimson blade and the dreamless rest.

Now that I can no longer live
  Oh, pitying Lord, my crime forgive.
When I hear the call of the judgment roll
  May I appear with a bloodwashed soul!

SIXTEEN

Ellen's time was near, and she had been hard put to tend the stock while Will was away at the trial. The children had helped her as much as they could, but by the time Will got home she could hardly maneuver the path from the cabin to the barn. She was much bigger with this baby that she had been with any of the others, and it had become an effort for her to stand. Will was quite concerned about her and, as a precaution, he alerted Aunt Addie Carver, a granny woman who had delivered nearly a hundred babies in her lifetime, that he might need some help when the time came. He arranged for the oldest Cole boy to go for her when Ellen's birthing day came.

On the morning of July 23rd, Ellen said, "Will, I know my time is not far off. You'd better send Willie over to the Cole's and have them fetch Aunt Addie."

Will stirred up the fire and, with Nola's help, set pots of water on to boil. He helped his daughter prepare a sparse breakfast for Willie and Martha and then sent his son on his way.

Will told Nola, "You take Martha outside and take care of her, but don't go far. If Aunt Addie doesn't get here in time, I may need you to help me."

Nola did as she was bid, praying that Aunt Addie would soon get there. She did not relish the possibility of having to assist her father in the birth.

Will had prepared as much ahead of time as he could. He had clean sheets and cloths ready and had only to lay them out. He boiled the scissors he would use to cut the umbilical cord and set a basin of cool water on the bed with a cloth to wipe Ellen's face.

Ellen's pains had started out sharp and strong and she already was perspiring heavily. Last he tied a sheet to the bedpost at the foot of the bed for Ellen to pull on when the time came.

Nola's prayer was answered. It was not long before the wizened little old lady came hurrying along the trail to the cabin.

"I had a presentiment last night that Ellen's time was here. The moon was full, and I knowed it couldn't be much longer. I got my things together this mornin' and left out early. I was 'most half way here when the Cole boy come fer me."

She got busy immediately, first putting on her white apron and tying a clean cloth around her head. She washed her hands thoroughly, made sure everything was fixed for the cradle, and stood by awaiting Will's instructions.

"From the looks of her, it'll be a big baby," she said. "I've fixed some catnip tea for the child. It's good to break the hives out and to clear up the liver. Oh my, I nearly fergot the knife."

She got a butcher knife and stuck it in the floor under the bed, explaining to Will, "Hit's to cut the pain."

Ellen's labor intensified until the pains were coming so close together that she could not tell when one left off and another began.

Will examined her and saw the baby's head ready to deliver. He told her, "Now bear down, Ellen, and push. This baby is ready and it will all be over in a thrice."

Ellen pushed with all her might, pulling on the sheet and straining as hard as she could. She felt the baby emerge and fell back on the bed in relief and exhaustion.

Will took his son, cut the umbilical cord, and tied it off. Aunt Addie had put a square of cloth on a shovel and scorched it brown over the fire. She cut a hole in it and slipped it over the cord, fitting it snugly against the child's belly. She then cleaned the baby with oil and, after diapering it, wrapped him in a warm blanket and laid him in the cradle.

"Well, this little man sure fooled me," Will told Ellen. "I thought he would surely weight at least ten pounds, but I swear I don't think he's much more than six."

"Will," Ellen said, "I feel queer, I feel like I'm still havin' this baby."

"It's probably just the afterbirth, Ellen. I assure you, you've had a fine healthy boy with a head as pretty and round as you ever did see. And the blackest hair! You'll feel better when you get rid of the afterbirth."

He turned back to her just in time to see another head emerging. "Oh my, Ellen, it seems like your work isn't over yet. There's another baby coming, sure enough. Bear down once more, my dear. Surely this will be all!"

Ellen did as she was told, anxious for the whole ordeal to be over. A second baby, another little boy, was born minutes later. The flustered Aunt Addie treated him in the same manner as the first and laid him in the cradle by his brother. She tied a string around the first-born so they could record which was the oldest child.

When the afterbirth was delivered and had been taken out and buried by Aunt Addie, Will called the children.

"Nola, Willie, Martha, come and see what has happened! Not only do you have one new baby brother, but there are two of them! God has surely blessed us this day."

The children crowded around the cradle, wide-eyed and awestruck at the sight of the identical babies lying side by side. "Papa, what will we call them, and how can we ever tell them apart?" Nola asked.

"We'll have to think about names for awhile," said Will. "I had not settled on one name, much less thought about needing two. They will have to be very special names, that's for sure."

Nola was fascinated with the twins, and her eagerness to tend to them caused Aunt Addie to laughingly say, "You didn't need me, Mrs. Johnston. You've already got a granny woman here! I never seen a child so taken up with babies as this one. It's a good thing too, 'cause with all the hippens you're goin' to have to wash, you'll need all the help you can get."

This proved to be true. They no more than got one baby dry and settled until the other one needed attention. Ellen's back was paining her, and so for the first time after having a baby, she stayed in the bed for a few days. But she could not abide being idle for long, and was soon up and about, helping to wait on the new babies and caring for her family.

They chose the names James Cunnigan and John Calhoun for the twins, and their lives settled down into a routine of tending babies and trying to keep ahead of the mountain of washing that accumulated every day. The big, black wash-pot in the yard was fired up almost every day now and it kept Willie busy bringing wood to keep the fire going. It was not his favorite chore and he told his papa one night, "If these babies don't soon let up a' wet-tin' and messin' up clothes, we're goin' to have these whole woods burnt up!"

Aunt Addie extended her stay past her normal two weeks, "Seein' as you got twice the need for me," she told Ellen. She was a great story-teller, and at night the children urged her to tell them more tales. She did not require much begging and told them one hair-raising tale after another.

One night Nola begged her to tell them about the hardest birthing she had ever attended.

"Well, without doubt hit was one of the first ones I did when I was just a young'un myself. I was just about sixteen or seventeen, I disremember which, when a hollow-eyed boy about ten years of age appeared on our doorstep late one evenin'. He asked fer my maw, but she was off over to Thickety Creek a' tendin' to another birth. I hadn't done none by myself, but that pore young'un was so scared I told him I'd go and do the best I could. He 'lowed that the whole family 'cept'n him was down with the summer fevers and if I didn't come, he didn't know what they'd do. When I got there, I could see why the pore young'un was so desperate. The whole kit and kaboodle of 'em was down with typhoid, 'cept him. They was nine young'uns besides him and the one acomin' and the old man and his maw.

"I knowed right away hit was the typhoid. If'n you've ever smelt it, you don't never fergit hit. They was sick people a' layin' all over the room, and that pore woman in the middle of hit about to give birth. I sent the boy to the spring for water to boil and then tried to do what I could to help his maw. She was in the last stages, though, about all I had to do was to catch that little girl baby when she come out. The woman had no more than birthed that baby, when she lit in to bleedin' from her lungs, and they wasn't nothin' in the world I could do fer her. Seems like she had just held on till she could get that baby borned.

"Well sir, before that night was over six of them people had died, includin' the old man. I done what I'd heard my maw say she done for folks that had the typhoid. I sponged 'em down as much as I could to get the fever down and washed their mouths out to keep the yellow fur from coatin' their tongue, but in spite of everything I done, they dropped off one right after t'other, till they wasn't but just five of 'em left. That pore little baby never had a chance and right after the first cock crowed the next morning, hit died too.

"I sent the boy back to the house to git me some help, but I lost two more 'fore he come back with my maw and a neighbor woman. Well sir, they said they'd never seen such a sight of dead folks all laid out as they seen that morning, and I was so tired, I was about to fall down myself. Maw flew in and we got things cleaned up and fixed the other three young'uns up best we could. When I'd rested fer a little spell, I took me off fer home and got my Paw and two oldest brothers to come and bury them pore folks.

"Hit took 'em two days to build the boxes and dig the graves fer all of 'em. We put the little baby girl in her mother's arms and buried 'em together. The other three young'uns lived, but one of 'em never had good sense after that. The fever plumb burned his brains out. I reckon none of my other birthin's ever come up to that one!"

Will looked over at Ellen as Aunt Addie concluded her tale and saw the look of pain in her eyes. He knew she was remembering the difficulty she had endured alone when Tildy was born and then the pain of the loss when she died.

Ellen looked up into Will's face, and they quietly clasped hands, feeling a bond of remembered sorrow, but overwhelming love, at the shared grief.

Will spoke huskily, "This seems like a mighty appropriate time to bow our heads and thank God for these two strong healthy babies He's seen fit to bless us with."

Silently they bowed their heads together as Will spoke his simple words of thanks.

"Heavenly Father, thank you for James and John. We know they'll make a place in our family for themselves just like Nola and Willie and Martha has. We know, Lord, that with your help we'll be able to care for them and help them grow up into fine men. We're thinking about our little Tildy too, and we know you're caring for her and that comforts our hearts. Amen."

Nola looked solemnly at her mother and father and saw the look of love and understanding that passed between them. She determined to help with the new babies as much as she could.

When Aunt Addie got ready to return to her cabin, she cautioned Ellen to remember certain rules about raising babies, declaring that these things had all been passed on to her from her mother.

"Always remember, if'n you want a child to rise in life, be shore to carry him upstairs when he's newborn before you carry him downstairs. And if you want him to have curly hair, why, what you've got to do is be shore and wet his hair and curl hit on the ninth day after hit's born.

"Another thing is to be shore you never cut a young'uns nails a'fore its first birthday, you bite 'em off instead, cause if you cut 'em, you'll never raise him. Now my Maw always said the way to make shore a young'un will cut his teeth without no trouble is to give him a bit of earthworm. Hit works every time.

"Well, I got to git on back home now and look after my own plunder. Hit's about time for the McQueen baby to be borned, and I promised Miz McQueen I'd be there for shore. You'uns come when ye can!"

SEVENTEEN

Will and Ellen endured another winter in the cabin. By spring they had decided they must build a larger house.

"I wouldn't have thought two little boys could make so much difference in a house," Ellen told Will. "Sometimes I feel like we're stepping on each other."

"I think I'm going to build us a frame house this time instead of a log cabin," Will told Ellen. "The Phillips's new house looks so fine, and I think we'd be better off to build that way, too. When I went to the trial in Asheville, all of the new dwellings were frame houses. I inquired about the cost at that sawmill over in Buncombe, and I think we can manage it."

"First thing you need to do is see if Elisha will sell you that piece of land next to ours. I declare I've plumb got my heart set on buildin' there." Ellen said. "That spring I seen bubblin' out from under that big walnut would be the finest place in the world for a springhouse. If we get it, I want you to promise me you'll build the springhouse soon as you get the house up."

"Ellen, I think you're more excited about a new springhouse than you are a new house," Will laughed. "I promise you that you'll have your springhouse right where you want it, but I do think we'll have to build the house first."

The site they had settled on was a lovely little cove with ridges of evergreens rising on either side of it. A stream ran through the property, and Ellen was as taken with it as she was the spring. Will could already envision where he would place the house and the barn. The stream would wander down between the barn and the house and cross back in front of the dwelling. The large area to the right of the house would be ideal for Ellen's vegetable garden. He planned to face the house to the east so they would be assured of the morning sun.

Will approached Elisha about the land the next time he saw him.

"Elisha, I've had something on my mind for some time, and I would like to see if we could strike a bargain."

"Well now, it wouldn't be that piece of land that joins our places, would it?" asked Elisha.

"How did you know?" Will asked, startled.

"I didn't figger you was lookin' at it because you admired the view that much. I guess it's no secret that yore family has about outgrown yore cabin. I'd say it's jest a matter of time till you'll be thinkin' about more space."

Will laughed heartily. "No, that's no secret. Those two little fellows have sure filled up all the corners in the cabin. Ellen and I feel the need for some more room. What I'd like to do is build me a nice, two-story frame house on that piece of land where the creek curves around the level area. If you and Julie would be willing to part with it, I figure it'd take just about three acres or a little more to do what I want to. Since it joins my land, it would sure work out fine for us."

"I see no reason why we can't strike a bargain, Will," Elisha replied.

After further discussion, they settled on the following terms:

> For value received, I, William B. Johnston promise to pay to Elisha Philipps, fifty dollars. The said amount is to be paid in corn, at fifty cents, and wheat at one dollar, and bacon at the selling price.

Will hauled the lumber for the new house in his wagon. It took him several days to bring all that he estimated he would need. He then began approaching his neighbors for help with the house.

He traded off work with Seth Mann for the laying of the foundation of the house and for building the huge fireplace that dominated the great room. He did most of the work himself, but he enlisted the aid of his neighbors on what he could not do alone.

The house rose slowly that summer. When Will had to work in the fields with the crops, he had no time to spare on the building. The house was a rambling two-story structure with a wide porch encircling three sides. The first floor consisted of the great room, to be used for sitting and as a central heating room, and a smaller dining room and a bedroom for Will and Ellen. The kitchen and pantry was connected to the house by a dog trot. The upstairs was divided into two large bedrooms, one for the girls and one for the boys. The house was set in a stand of beech trees with the mountains as a backdrop.

As he had promised, Will built Ellen's springhouse as soon as the house was finished. He built it so the cold water from the spring flowed through and made an ideal cooling place for Ellen's milk and butter. She and the children spent many hours finding rocks for lining the stream. When she finished, it was as snug as the house itself.

They had begun the house in the spring. They moved into it in late October of the following year. The twins were two years old.

Ellen told Will, "I think everyone will be grateful for some privacy, except for James and John. I declare if they're not right in the middle of everything! What they don't think to get into just ain't worth thinkin' about. If it wasn't for Nola, I don't see how I'd manage. Willie helps too, when I can find him. Sometimes it takes more work a' locatin' him than it does to look after them myself."

"I know what you mean. Willie is good help in the garden when he's there. The trick is to keep him there. Don't know when we've had such good luck with our garden as we have this year. I expect you'll be able to fill that fine springhouse of yours up this year."

"Yes," Ellen said dreamily, "I know right where I'll store the pumpkins and candyroasters. And there'll be plenty of room for the turnips and my crocks of pickled beans and corn and kraut."

"I hope you'll leave a little room for the milk and butter," Will said dryly.

"Come next spring, I'm goin' to plant the banks with violets and forget-me-nots where the water comes out of the house. There won't be a finer or prettier springhouse anywhere!"

"Maybe you can give a little thought to what you want me to plant around the house when you get your springhouse fixed up," Will laughed. "I thought I'd bring some rhododendron and azaleas for the front and put some mountain laurel around the sides."

"My sister Katie has promised to send me some seeds from her flowers and root me some slips from her bushes this fall. Some of the plants she has was brought over from Ireland with Mama and Papa, and I would treasure havin' a startin' of them."

Will looked around him at their home and heaved a sigh of pleasure. "You know, Ellen, both our other homes have given me pleasure, but I've never felt quite like this about the other ones. I feel like this will be our home for good now."

When they were finally settled in the house, Will turned his energies to a new project that he had been thinking about for some time.

"Since Zac's skunk paid us that visit, we've never been able to get the odor out of the schoolroom completely," Will told Ellen. "I've decided it would be easier to build a new school than to try to make that one habitable again. I think I'll feel out Elisha Phillips about the location and see if he's interested in helping me with the project."

Elisha and Julie Phillips were the largest landowners in the valley. Knowing their generous nature, Will felt comfortable approaching Elisha about the new school.

"I know you are as interested in the education of our children as I am," Will said to Elisha. "You are also aware that since Zac's skunk 'baptized' our cabin, it has not been very pleasant. It's kind of hard to teach Latin while you hold your nose."

"Yes, I can see where it'd be a problem," Elisha laughed. "What have you got in mind, Will? Knowin' you, I'd bet you've already got things planned out."

"Well, I might as well tell you that I've got a spot picked out to build a new school on," Will admitted. "It's that spot with the nice little grove of poplars on it. About halfway between your place and mine. It would be more central for everybody and not as hard to get to in bad weather as the cabin is. Then too, we wouldn't have to haul logs in. We could just fell the poplars right there. There'd be plenty to build with."

"By golly, I'll do it!" exclaimed Elisha. "We got no dearer dream than to see our young'uns get better book learnin' than we did. We both got enough to get by, but we shore do covet more for our children. I know the spot you're talkin' about, and I can't think of a better spot. There's a fine spring on that piece too, and I don't never recollect it goin' dry. You get everybody together Will, and we'll build us a school to be proud of. Of course, maybe we better make it skunk proof."

"Ha," Will laughed, "I'd be a sight happier if we could make it Zac proof."

He turned to go and then added, "There's something else, Elisha. I'm thinking that this building can also serve as a meeting house on Sunday, just like the other one did. I think we should keep this in mind when we plan our building and allow for space to hold all the families on the sabbath."

"I agree. It did my heart good to see how eager everybody was for some preachin'."

Will busied himself on the project and came up with a plan for a type of building his father had told him about in Tennessee. It was variously known as a "double-pen," "dog-trot house," "possum-trot house," or as a "two-pens-and-a-passage." Its basic form was two single rooms separated by an open passage, with both sections covered by a common roof. This would give them a separate room for their sabbath meetings, and if the school grew, they could always use the other room as a classroom. For the present, they would build the one log cabin and, as time allowed, add the other one to it.

They set the first Friday in November to begin. The morning dawned crisp and clear, and the workers began their work with much laughter and good humor.

The neighbors were accustomed to helping each other with their buildings, and so tasks were assigned with a minimum of confusion. They divided into four work parties, each choosing the job at which he was most capable.

One group would fell the huge poplars and cut them into their maximum length, which was about thirty feet. Will and Elisha were in this party. They would hew the logs with their broadaxes so that they would be flat on two sides. This would allow the logs to fit more snugly and require less clay to chink the cracks.

Jacob McGinty and his boys, John and Sam, were recognized as the best shingle makers in the cove. They set to work splitting blocks of oak for the roof.

Another crew, called the "corner men," would notch the logs and fit the timbers together. When the logs were ready, it would take the combined strength of all the workers to raise them in place. If the corner men had done their job correctly, the logs would fit snugly on the corners, and the sheer weight of the timbers would hold them in place.

Jesse Cole and Lon Severs were accomplished stonemasons and would supervise the laying of the hearth and the chimney stones. They had also laid the foundation for the building.

By the second weekend the walls were ready to be raised, and when they had been set in place, everyone not involved in putting up the roofing timbers and readying the roof for the shingles helped haul in the stones for the fireplace. The doors and windows were cut in the logs after the sides were raised.

After the walls were up, the women and girls filled the cracks and crevices with mud. This task was known as chinking. After all the walls had been chinked, the roof beams set in place and the shingles nailed down securely, they brought in the benches and tables from the old schoolroom.

Will looked at all they had accomplished and said, "It seems to me we should have a party to properly dedicate this new school building. I think we've done a fine job."

"Well, I'm shore all fer that!" exclaimed Jesse Cole. "Jacob, if you and yore boy Sam will furnish the music, we'll have us a dance nobody'll fergit."

"We'll be happy to bring our fiddles, and I think I can find some banjos to help us out," declared Jacob.

"I'll take care of gettin' the food here," volunteered Ellen. "I reckon we've got enough good cooks among us to fill up everybody."

"Seems to me that Saturday night would be a mighty good time to have this shin-dig," Elisha said.

The date agreed upon, they all went their separate ways to make their party plans. Ellen's prediction was true, and the tables groaned from all the food the womenfolk brought. Benches and tables were pushed back, the music began, and the dancers formed their circle.

Jacob McGinty called out, "Now circle up with your pretty little lady and all go left, then dance with your girl with a do-si-do, and circle right. Promenade now with ladies in front and gents behind, then circle up four and open and shut them garden gates."

He continued with the familiar, but intricate, patterns of the square dance while the music grew fast and furious. He concluded the set with, "Promenade now and take your pretty little lady home."

Skirts swirled and feet flew as the dancers shuffled and clogged to the beat of the music. Everyone danced, with the adults in one big circle and the children making their own little circle in the corner.

When it was over and the families had dispersed for their homes, Will told Ellen, "This was surely a good beginning for our new school. Everyone worked hard getting the building up, and I did not hear one word of dissent the whole time. If I never do another thing for our children, this was time well spent."

Ellen looked up at Will with love and admiration. She knew that this would certainly not be the last thing Will did for their children and the other children in the community.

"Will," she said, "I ain't got all the fine words that you have to tell you how I feel, but I want you to know that I must be the proudest woman alive right at this minute because of what you've done. My heart is jest plumb bustin' with love for you tonight."

EIGHTEEN

Th he week following the party, Jesse Cole and Lon Severs finished laying the rock for the school's chimney. They made sure the draft was correct by holding a feather under the flue and observing that it rose to the proper height and at the accepted rate of speed. When they were satisfied that the chimney was working properly, they helped Will replace the benches.

Mild weather enabled Will to get in about five weeks of lessons before the weather became too bad for the students to get to school. Will was pleased with the progress the children had made, but he felt they needed a trained schoolmaster.

"I have done my best for these children," he told Ellen, "but since we have a proper school building, I think it's time we found a schoolmaster for them. I'm going to write to my brother Zeb in Tennessee and see if he can find us one."

"How would we pay a teacher? Do you think the community can afford one?"

"Surely everybody could spare half a dollar a month. I've been figuring and if everyone's willing, we could pay him about ten dollars a month. We could raise him up a cabin near the schoolhouse and give him enough land to make a garden so he could feed himself. Seems to me a man would be quite comfortable on an income like that. I think it's worth a try anyhow."

Zeb Johnston responded to Will's request and began to search for a schoolmaster. After much effort, he found a young man named Joshua Perkins who promised to be there in time for the spring session.

Nola was almost thirteen years old now and had become as adept at supervising the household as Ellen. Willie was old

101

enough to help Will in the fields, and Nola and Martha helped their mother with household chores and tended to the twins.

With all the work to be done, Ellen had little time to herself. She formed the habit of taking an early morning walk before the others rose. She used this time to plan her days and to reflect on her and Will's life.

One morning she chose to walk along the stream that flowed through her springhouse. It was a beautiful morning and the rising ground mists promised the day would be clear and warm.

This weather between fall and winter is kind of like me right now, she thought. *Here I am with a growin' family and more'n half my life already spent. I reckon my children's kind of like that new quilt pattern I'm makin'—Grandmother's Flower Garden. I reckon my family's sort of my flower garden. They're shore fine blossoms though. Reckon me and Will is lucky to have five healthy young'uns.*

She sighed heavily. *I still miss little Tildy though. Can't help wonderin' what she'd be like had she lived. Well, no use grievin' over somethin' I can't change, Lord, I'm just happy for my blessin's. A fine new home, good children, a good man by my side.*

She looked up and smiled at the sight of her snug springhouse. *And the purtiest little springhouse in this whole mountainside!*

As she looked more closely she frowned and exclaimed, "What in tarnation! I know I closed that door good when I left yesterday evenin'. I bet some pesky varmint has pushed it open. No tellin' what kind of mess I'll find."

She approached the door cautiously and eased it back, half expecting a marauding raccoon to burst out. It took her eyes a few seconds to adjust to the dim light of the springhouse, and at first she saw nothing amiss. But a slight movement in the corner where she stored her sacks caught her eye, and as she went closer she saw that someone was curled up under the sacks.

Her first impulse was to get Will, but just then the person rolled over and the tousled head of a young girl appeared. Ellen leaned down closer and saw that she was a child no older than fourteen or fifteen, very thin and with dirty red hair. Her face was streaked with dirt, and the arm Ellen could see was painfully thin.

"Wake up, girl!" Ellen said in a loud, firm voice. "What in the world are you a' doin' sleepin' in my springhouse?"

The girl raised her head and looked at Ellen with large startled eyes. She jumped up and would have run past Ellen, but just as she started out the door, she half stumbled and fell. When Ellen reached her, she realized the child had fainted.

"Humph," exclaimed Ellen, "I guess you're about starved to death from the looks of you. Well, let's get you up to the house and see what I've found. I shore never expected to find the likes of you when I opened that door."

Ellen half carried and half dragged the girl up the path to the house, pausing frequently to catch her breath. When she finally managed to get her to the porch steps, she called to Will, who was just getting up, to come and help her.

Will looked in astonishment at his wife and her burden as he opened the door. "What on earth, Ellen? Where did you find that child?"

"Quit askin' questions, and come help me," Ellen told him shortly. "This pore child looks like she's half starved. I never seen such a pore, bony creature. I bet she won't weigh over eighty pounds soakin wet."

Will helped Ellen carry her into the house and put her on their bed. After a cursory examination he said, "She's half starved all right. I can't tell what else is wrong with her till we get some of this dirt off her. Where did she come from?"

"Found her in the springhouse. Land alive, I don't think I ever seen such a bedraggled lookin' thing in all my life. Her clothes ain't nothin' but rags, and she ain't got a sign of a shoe on her. Look at her pore feet, they're bruised all over."

"Yes, she looks like somebody threw her in a briar patch and then rolled her in a mud hole."

"Can't tell what color her hair is, but it looks sort of red," said Ellen. "I recollect her eyes looked green, what I could see of 'em."

Will brought a basin of water from the bucket on the porch and Ellen took a soft cloth and began to wipe some of the dirt from the girl's face and arms. As Ellen gently rubbed the cool cloth over her face and neck, she began to moan and regain consciousness. Finally she opened her eyes and looked around her.

"Whar am I?" she asked huskily. "and who mought ye be? I never meant ye no harm. I 'us jist a' lookin' fer a place to git out of the cold fer a few hours. Please, ma'am, ifn' ye'll just leave me go, I promise I won't bother ye no more."

She tried to rise, but weakly fell back and closed her eyes again, resigned to whatever fate awaited her. When she got up the courage to open her eyes again, she stared up into the bluest and kindest eyes she had ever seen.

"Why bless you, child," Ellen said, "we don't mean you no harm either. We'd just like to help you if you'll let us. I have never turned a hungry man or critter away from my door, and I don't intend to start now, and you're just about the hungriest looking soul I've ever seen. Let me get into my kitchen and stir you up somethin' to eat, and then we'll talk some more. Do you think you might be able to force down some eggs and ham and a biscuit or two?"

"I reckon I shore could try, ma'am," the girl replied weakly. "I disremember when I last did eat, but I think it was two or three days past, and that was jist a old raw 'tater I dug in a garden I come acrost."

Ellen wasted no more time on talk, but went quickly to the kitchen and began to prepare some food for the girl. She fried up slabs of cured ham, scrambled up a dozen eggs and hastily patted out biscuits. When all was ready, she poured a glass of cold sweet milk, and Will helped the girl to the table. By this time the children were all gathered around the table looking big-eyed at their strange guest.

Ignoring the silverware Ellen had laid by her plate, the girl picked the food up in her hands and stuffed it in her mouth as fast as she could chew and swallow it. The children were horrified at her bad manners and cast surreptitious glances at their parents.

Ellen and Will looked at each other in surprise, but neither rebuked the girl. Will only told her mildly, "You'd better slow down a mite. If you haven't eaten lately, it will make you sick if you eat too fast."

When her hunger was appeased somewhat, the girl looked around at the other people at the table. Nola and Martha had dressed the twins and had combed their hair neatly. Both were dressed in clean calico dresses with an apron, and their hair was neatly braided. Willie was also dressed in clean overalls and shirt and had done his best to slick down his unruly cowlick. Realizing how totally different she looked from the rest of the people at the table, the girl dropped her head in embarrassment.

"Now that you have eaten a little, my dear, perhaps you would care to tell us your name," Will said gently.

The girl ducked her head still lower and in an almost inaudible voice said, "My name is Cassie, sir."

"Cassie! Well, that's a right pretty name. Since you've properly introduced yourself to us, I think we should do the same for you. My name is Will Johnston, and you have already made the acquaintance of my wife, Ellen Johnston. These are our children, Nola, Martha, Willie, James and John. And now children, if you have finished your meal, you may be excused from the table and go about your chores. I think our guest needs to rest for a little while."

The children rose reluctantly and left Cassie alone at the table with Will and Ellen. She cast an imploring look at Ellen and said, "I'm much obliged to ye fer the good vittles, ma'am, but if'n ye don't mind, I'd best git on my way now."

"Why, where would you be goin', child, all alone and at your young age?" asked Ellen. "We wouldn't dream of lettin' you go off by yourself until you've at least had a chance to rest a spell. I know you couldn't have got much sleep last night. That pile of sacks was a mighty uncomfortable lookin' bed to me. Wouldn't you like to rest for just a spell here with us? Seems to me there's nothin' so pressin' that you couldn't stay for just awhile."

Cassie stared at her hands, which she was twisting nervously in her lap. "Well, ma'am, I reckon that I could set fer a short spell. I am a mite tared. I couldn't lay myself on your clean bed kivers though, dirty as I am, so ifn' ye could jest give me a old quilt er somethin', I reckon I could jist curl up on the floor in one of the young'uns rooms fer a bit."

The child was obviously so tired that it was an effort for her to sit up straight. The combination of a full belly and a warm room was fast putting her to sleep.

Will bent down, scooped her up in his arms and carried her up the stairs to Nola and Martha's bed. Ellen laid an old quilt over the covers and after Will laid her down, covered her with another. She was asleep almost instantly.

Ellen shook her head in disbelief. "I wonder what on earth could bring a child to such a sorry state," she pondered. "She has to have been wanderin' through these woods for days to be in the state she's in. I don't think she's had anything to eat in a week at least. She's nothin' but skin and bones, and did you see the bruises on her arms and legs? They don't look like briar scratches to me. I declare, I think somebody has beaten this poor child."

Will stood beside Ellen gazing at Cassie. "My dear, I think you should know something else about Cassie I discovered. It may explain the bruises on her arms and legs."

"What are you talkin' about, Will?"

"Ellen, this poor child looks to be at least five or six months pregnant!"

Nola opened her eyes and stared at Alma who was washing her hands with a warm washcloth. "It isn't me that needs it, it's her," she said impatiently. "Can't you see how dirty she is?"

"Why, what do you mean, Grandma?" asked Alma. "I'm just washing your hands so you can eat your birthday cake. Lord knows we all realize how particular you are. I sure remember some of the baths you gave me when I was little. You'd nearly rub the skin off of us."

"Needed it too," Nola muttered, "never saw such a nasty young'un. But she learned. She soon learned."

NINETEEN

Cassie slept for a full twelve hours before she stirred. When she wakened, she looked around in confusion, forgetting for the moment where she was. The sound of the Johnston family at their supper table drifted up the steps, and the smell of food drew her to the top of the stairs. Timidly, she slipped down the steps and stood quietly at the door of the dining room. It was a scene completely foreign to her, just as the house and the furnishings were part of a world she had never imagined. A slight noise caused Ellen to look up, and when she saw the girl standing there, she rose hastily and urged her to come in and eat.

"Come on in, Cassie. We tried to let you sleep as long as you could. Now it's time to get some more victuals in your stomach. If you don't mind eatin' our poor rations, you're welcome to whatever you can eat."

"Pore rations? I don't think I've ever seen sich fine vittles in all my born days!" exclaimed Cassie.

"Mama, can we stay and watch the girl eat with her hands again?" asked Willie.

"Willie, you may be excused from this table at once," said Will.

Willie ducked his head and scooted out of the room as quickly as he dared. He knew he had said the wrong thing, and he wanted to get out of his father's sight before he felt the weight of Will's hand on the seat of his pants.

"Now don't you pay him no mind, Cassie," said Ellen. "He meant no harm, just a boy's natural mischief. We know how hungry you were, and that can excuse a temporary lapse of manners."

Cassie timidly slipped into the vacant chair at the table and watched big-eyed as Will heaped her plate full of beans, potatoes, fried side-meat and a large slab of cornbread. She looked at Nola and Martha, who were eating quietly, each with one hand in her lap and the other grasping a fork. She tried her best to do like-wise, but it was obvious to Ellen and Will that she was unfamiliar with flatware. They said nothing, but went on quietly eating their own meals.

When Cassie had again eaten her fill, Ellen allowed her to help Nola and Martha clear the table. After all was cleared away and the dishes washed and placed in the cupboard, she took Cassie into the great room and asked her to sit with her.

"Cassie, I'm goin' to talk plain with you. It's obvious to Mr. Johnston and me that you're runnin' away from someone or somethin'. It's not fittin' or safe for a young girl like you to be out in these woods alone. If you want, you're welcome to stay with us a few days until you can settle in your mind where it is you're a goin'. There's a trundle bed under the girl's bed, and you can sleep there. We can't make you stay, of course, but we want you to know you're welcome if you want to. When you get to know us a little better, maybe you'll tell us what it is that you're runnin' away from, but you don't have to tell us a thing if you don't want to."

"Oh ma'am, you're the goodest folks I've ever heared of," cried Cassie. "I tell you I jist don't know what to do no more. If I could jist stay a day or two till I can git rested up, I'd be ever so much obliged. I'll work fer my keep. I'm stronger than I look. Why I can tend young'uns gooder'n anybody. My Ma's got twelve young'uns, and I hep her all the time."

The mention of her mother's name caused Cassie's eyes to brim with tears. Ellen's heart ached at the look of utter misery on the girl's face.

"Well, that's enough talk about work," Ellen said brusquely. "The first thing we need to do is get you a good hot bath and see if we can't find you somethin' clean to put on. You look older than Nola, but you ain't no bigger, and I'm sure we can find somethin' of hers that'll fit you. If you don't mind my askin', Cassie, just how old are you?"

"Why I don't rightly know, ma'am. But my ma said as near as she could recollect I must be nigh on to fifteen years."

Will carried the tub into the kitchen, and Ellen began filling it with the water she had heated. When all was ready, she took an old gown of Nola's that looked as if it would fit Cassie, and asked her to take off her dress and step into the tub. When Ellen saw how Cassie's shoulder blades stuck out and how thin her arms were, she could hardly contain her shock. As she washed Cassie's back and saw her wince involuntarily, she could no longer contain her indignation.

"Child, who in the world has beaten you like this? Your poor back is a mass of bruises and welts. What manner of beast could do this?"

"It warn't no beast, ma'am. Hit was my pa that beat me," sobbed Cassie. "Don't think too bad of him, 'cause when you hear what I done, you'll likely say I deserved hit. I—I—I'm a'goin' to have a baby, you see, and my Pa says I've shamed him, and he put me out. He said I warn't no better than his old bitch dog, and he warn't goin' to put up with me bringin' in another young'un fer him to feed."

Cassie lowered her face into her hands and wept hot bitter tears, her thin shoulders shaking with emotions held in check too long.

Ellen could only pat her on the back and murmur, "There, there, don't cry so, child, don't cry."

When Cassie looked at Ellen from her red, swollen eyes, she said, "I don't blame ye none, ma'am, if'n ye want me to leave now."

"Nonsense," exclaimed Ellen. "This don't change nothin'. Hush now, let's have no more talk and no more tears tonight. Let's just finish this bath and get you to bed. We'll talk tomorrow."

The child sat submissively while Ellen washed her from her head to her feet, too tired to help. Ellen wrapped her in a soft quilt while she rubbed and brushed her matted, tangled hair dry. When she had finished, Ellen laughed with delight at the sight of the deep auburn ringlets that framed her face.

"I reckon when we get a little flesh on your bones, you're goin' to be a right pretty girl."

Cassie was so exhausted from her emotional outburst and the exertion of the bath that she fell asleep as soon as she was in bed. Ellen stood looking down at her and knew Will would agree with her that they would have to help this poor child.

Nola looked at Cassie sleeping as Martha and she were getting ready for bed. She felt a twinge of jealousy as she stared at the mass of red curls framing Cassie's face.

"Do you think red hair's prettier than black hair?" she asked Martha.

"I like brown best," Martha retorted, tossing her long brown pigtail over her shoulder.

Nola laughed and jumped in bed, pulling the quilt up to her chin.

The next day Ellen told the children what she and Will had decided. "The Lord has blessed our family with good health and a good home. Cassie has neither, and your papa and me think that we ought to share what we've got when we see somebody in need. We've decided that Cassie should stay with us for awhile till she's back on her feet. We hope you will make her feel welcome. We want her to feel she's a part of our family for as long as she stays with us."

At this point Ellen sent Willie and the twins out to play and told Nola and Martha that she had something to say especially to them.

"I might as well come right out and tell you girls now that Cassie is a' goin' to have a baby. Now I don't know nothin' about the circumstances that put her in this fix, and right now she ain't ready to tell us about it. But until she is ready to tell us, there are to be no questions asked her about it. Do I make myself clear?"

"Yes, Mama," they replied.

"Can I ask you one question, Mama?" said Nola. "I thought you had to get married before you had a baby. Is Cassie married? And if she is, how come she's runnin' away from her husband?"

"Nola, I guess you and Martha won't learn no younger, and it's time you know a few things that can happen in life. The fact is, sometimes girls does have babies without gettin' married first. It ain't right, but it does happen sometimes. As I said, I don't know what happened to Cassie, but I'm goin' to try and not judge her till I do. I hope nothin' like this ever happens to you girls, but I'd like to think that if it did, there'd be somebody that would help you if I couldn't. I guess it's because I love my daughters so much that I feel like I have to help somebody else's daughter."

"But Mama, what will we tell folks when they ask about Cassie? How can we explain why she's livin' with us and why she's havin' a baby?"

"You don't have to explain anything, Nola," Ellen replied. "Just say the truth, that she's a friend who needs us, and we're goin' to help her out. Now go on about your chores. Oh, and somethin' else, Cassie will pull her weight same as the rest of you. She'll need some help, Nola, 'cause I don't think she knows much about keepin' house. I know you'll teach her though. Just look what a fine job you've done with Martha."

Nola flushed with pleasure at the rare compliment from Ellen. "Well, I guess I'll teach her what I can. She sure acts funny though."

Nola's concern was well founded, and it took everyone's efforts to teach Cassie the basics of good hygiene. The everyday family life of the Johnstons was entirely foreign to Cassie, so poor had been her lot in life.

She confided to Ellen, "We had some spoons, but they's jist the wood kind that Pa whittled out fer us. I ain't never seed what you'uns call a fork before, and the onliest knives we had was the kind Ma cut with. Mostly us young'ns jist eat with our hands."

"Well, Cassie, you have a lot to learn I guess, but some of the things that has to do with stayin' clean and usin' good manners, you must learn. Some day you'll be glad you know these things."

Cassie was most impressed by the number of beds in the house. She told Nola, "Never in all my borned days did I think I'd have a whole bed all to myself. Why, at home they's jist two beds in the whole cabin. Ma and Pa slep' in one with the newest baby, and the rest of us slep' in the other'n ur else on a pallet."

Nola's role of teacher helped ease the jealousy she had felt that first night. Cassie was so open and grateful for every little thing that Nola did for her that she soon became Cassie's staunchest supporter. She was still very curious about Cassie's pregnancy, but Ellen's admonitions kept her from asking questions.

Cassie was very good with the twins and cheerfully took over much of their care. They, in turn, were fascinated with this strange girl who had become part of their family. As she grew more comfortable with the family, Cassie began sharing some of her many superstitions. She had a saying for any situation that arose and predictions of dire consequences if this or that superstition was not respected.

Nola's hair was long, and each night she would give it a thorough brushing before braiding it for bed. Cassie was appalled at the risk she was taking.

"Nola, don't ye dast let any of yore hair fall whar a bird mought pick hit up! If'n hit does and a bird weaves even one strand into hit's nest, ye'll have terrible headaches till the nest falls apart."

Then she would carefully gather up any fallen strands and burn them in the fireplace.

To Willie she confided, "If ye don't cuss, ye'll never raise gourds, and if ye ain't bad-tempered, ye can't git pepper to bear.

Also, if ye're hairy about the arms and chest, ye'll have good luck a' raisin' hogs."

Willie found this hilarious. He began to devise antics to upset Cassie and to tease her. On one occasion he put a bearskin over his clothes as he went out to feed the pigs. Will finally had to caution him about his shenanigans.

To Martha and Nola she imparted such bits of wisdom: "If yore bread's burnt, the cook's mad. And if yore fire won't kindle, you'll marry a lazy man. Likewise, if ye slop water on yore clothes, ye'll marry a drunkard."

John developed a sore throat, and Cassie earnestly begged Ellen to seek a man who had never seen his father so he could breathe on John and cure him. "If you won't do that, at least let John drink from an old shoe," she begged.

Will answered that he would rely on a brew he had made from the bitter golden-seal root. Much to everyone's relief, it cured John.

The children spent many nights shivering deliciously over her "hant" tales. One in particular they never tired of hearing was the tale about the mountain Boojum. This was a tale that Nola and Martha would tell to their own children in later years. The beast in the tale was a mixture of part bear, part man, and part panther.

"Hit started like this," she told the wide-eyed children.

"Old man Jim Winchester had started fer home one night, jist about this time of day. He knowed better than to be a' travelin' them woods atter dark, but he'd been held up helpin' a neighbor round up his cow. Well, he's a' goin' along jist as fast as his two laigs 'ud carry him when he got the feelin' that somethin' was a follerin' him, but try as he would, he couldn't make out hide nor hair of anything. Well, he got to walkin' faster and faster and whatever hit was a' follerin' him 'ud jist walk faster an faster too, till him and the beasty or whatever hit was, was both a' runnin' full speed.

"Finally old Jim jist couldn't run no more. He jist fell over on his back and told that beasty, 'Jist come on and git me, I can't run no more. Whatever hit is ye want of me, ye'll jist have to take, I can't go no further.'

"Well, with that he said this big black hairy beast cast a shadder over him like you wouldn't believe. He said hit must of been ten—twelve feet tall. Hit was so big, hit jist plumb darked out the moon. He said hit leant down and picked him up in hits big old paws and slung him acrost hits shoulder and then took off a'

runnin' on all fours jist like one of them big old mountain paint-
ers.

"Hit run on and on. First over one mountain, and then over
t'other till hit come to a big dark cave in the side of a mountain.
Then hit took him right on in to hits den. He said he knowed his
time had come and figgered this beasty was a' goin' to have him
fer his supper fer shore. But instead he said when hit got him in,
hit jist set him down and said plain as ever anybody could,
'Dig.' He looked around him and there set a pickaxe and he
picked hit up and commenced a' diggin'. He said there was
chunks of gold and rubies and ever kind of precious stone a
body could thank of in that cave.

"He dug all night long and finally when hit was nearly
daylight, he jist plumb swooned he was so tared. Well, the next
thang he knowed he woke up a' layin' in the woods right near
his cabin. He said his clothes was covered with dirt and dust and
his hands had big old blisters all over 'em. He said hit took him
nigh on to a week to rest up from all that diggin', and you can
shore bet he never got caught out atter dark in the woods again.

Now this warn't the only time the Boojum caught somebody
and made 'em do his diggin' fer him. They's many a man disappeared fer sometimes two or three nights runnin' and when
they come home, they's always covered in that same quare
lookin' dust and their hands 'us bloody and raw from diggin'.

"Now I'm a' warnin' you young'uns, ye'd better git yoreselfs
into yore cabin 'afore dark, if'n ye don't want the Mountain Boojum to catch ye!"

TWENTY

Cassie blossomed under the healthy influence of the Johnston household. The dark circles under her eyes disappeared, and her body filled out. She still would not tell Ellen the identity of her baby's father. For the most part, she ignored her pregnancy. Ellen tried to interest her in making clothes for the baby, but she was disinterested. When Ellen tried to talk about the future and what she would do once the baby arrived, Cassie looked at her vaguely and changed the subject.

"I don't know what else I can do," Ellen told Will. "I've tried everything I know to make her see she has to make some plans. She acts like if she ignores the baby, she can make the whole problem go away."

She sighed heavily, "Poor child, she'll have a hard enough row to hoe as it is. People are not quick to accept a child born out of wedlock. The poor thing will be shunned all its life, I'm afraid."

"My dear Ellen," Will told her gently, "you can't take Cassie's troubles on your shoulders. We'll do what we can for her, and beyond that we can't help her. There'll come a time when she'll have some hard decisions to make, but no one can make them for her. Not even you, I'm afraid."

"I know what you're sayin' is true, Will, but it don't make it any easier to accept."

"I've been meaning to caution you, Ellen. From the looks of Cassie, it won't be long until that baby comes. It looks to me as if it has dropped already, which means her time is near. You should keep her close to home now. Talk to Nola, and get her to help you. She and Cassie seem to have become close friends. Maybe she'll listen to her."

"I've been of the same mind myself, Will. I just hope it don't come while you're gone to help that new family of Caldwells with their cabin raisin'."

"Well, if it does, you'll know what to do, as many times as you've had to help me out. I want you to know, though, that I'm concerned about the baby. Cassie is just not big enough, it seems to me. I've watched her and if the baby shows much movement, she certainly don't let on. I wish you'd try again to talk to her about it and ask her how often she feels it move."

"I'll try, Will," sighed Ellen, "but I'm a'feared I won't make much headway."

Ellen's doubts were confirmed when she tried to pin Cassie down about the condition of the baby. "Oh, hit moves when hit's a' mind to, I suppose," was her disinterested reply. "Sides, I don't know how much hit's supposed to move."

Will left for the cabin raising, promising to return the next day if at all possible. It was February, and it was essential that they get a roof over the heads of this family as quickly as possible. They were fortunate it had been a mild winter, because ordinarily they could not have survived the two nights they had camped in their wagons. Even so, Will feared the cabin would not be much more than the most rudimentary shelter because of the time of the year.

All went well that day, and Ellen began to think that her fears were unfounded. However, when she called the children to supper, Cassie said she was not hungry and did not come to the table. When Ellen went to see about her, she found her curled up on the trundle bed, white-faced with pain.

"How long have you been havin' pains, child?" Ellen asked.

"Nigh on to two hours, I reckon. Hit jist comes and goes though. Like as not hit's jist somethin' I et fer dinner. If'n I could jist lay here quiet awhile, I reckon I'll be alright directly."

"Cassie," said Ellen firmly, "you will not be all right directly. You are in labor and a' fixin to have your baby. You've denied this as long as you can, and there's no way you can deny it any longer. Now you must let me help, and you must do exactly as I say. Is that clear?"

"Yes'm," Cassie replied meekly, "I'd be much obliged to ye if ye could jist make this hurtin' go away soon."

Ellen called to Nola and told her to put on plenty of hot water and to have Martha make sure the boys stayed downstairs and out of the way. Then she turned to examine Cassie. What she saw alarmed her. The girl had been bleeding heavily for some time, and something obviously was badly wrong.

Trying not to let Cassie know how concerned she was, she said as cheerfully as she could. "Well, now, Missy, let's get about the business of gettin' this child borned. I don't suppose you have any idea what you might like to name it, have you?"

"No'm, I don't reckon I've ever give it no thought. I guess hit don't really matter what I name hit. Folks has a name fer young'uns without no pappy already. I guess that's what they'll call hit no matter what name I set down fer hit."

Ellen ducked her head to keep Cassie from seeing her tears. For a while, they were too busy to carry on a conversation. Ellen wished desperately that Will were there. She did everything as much like he did as she could remember. Cassie's pains increased in intensity until they were coming about every five minutes. Nola was helping her mother, and Ellen felt sorry for the girl, who was suffering for Cassie with every pain.

"I'm sorry you have to see you first birthin' like this, Nola," she said. "Life is truly a wondrous gift, one of the most precious gifts from God to a man and wife. I wish I could tell you how happy your Papa and me was the day you was born. Your Papa called you his 'little bud of love,' and I reckon that truly described the way we felt about you. That's the way God meant for people to feel about their children. When things turn out wrong, it's our doin', not His."

"Mama, does that mean you think Cassie is bad? I don't think what happened to Cassie was her fault. I've got to know her as well as I know Martha and Willie, and I don't think Cassie is bad."

"Oh, no, child," Ellen said hastily, "that's not what I meant to say. You know as well as I do that sometimes bad things happen to us through no fault of our own. I've said all along that I won't judge Cassie, and I won't! Some day she'll tell us what happened to her. I believe Cassie is a good girl too. Well, whatever happens, we must help her the best we can. Look sharp now, I don't think this baby will be much longer gettin' here. Be sure you have the blankets warm and ready for it."

Cassie's labor went on for another three hours before the baby was finally born. It was a little boy and was stillborn. Ellen surmised that it had been dead for some time before its birth.

She did not spend much time speculating on the cause, as Cassie demanded all of her attention. Cassie bled profusely after the birth, and for a while Ellen feared she would lose her as well.

When she was sure Cassie was rid of all the afterbirth, she packed her as she had seen Will do on another occasion, and before long the bleeding was staunched.

Ellen and Nola sat up with Cassie all night, fearful that the bleeding would start up again. Ellen dosed her with as much sweetgum and blackgum bark tea as she dared, and finally Cassie fell into a natural, peaceful sleep. Ellen and Nola were exhausted, both physically and emotionally, after the ordeal. All of Ellen's old feelings about Tildy's death flooded in on her when she looked at the still form of Cassie's baby. She braced herself and took the little body up and bathed it. Then she dressed it in a clean white dress that had belonged to one of her babies. After wrapping it in a blanket, she laid it in the cradle at the foot of her bed. Only then did she and Nola lay down for a few hours rest.

Will came home late that afternoon and, after checking to be sure that Cassie was all right, began making a box to bury the baby. He used some chestnut that he had left from the construction of the house. When he had finished it, Ellen lined it with a soft blanket and placed the baby in it.

Cassie slept all that day, and Ellen finally decided she must rouse her and see that she took some food. When she had persuaded her to eat as much as she could, she gently told her about the baby.

"Cassie, your little boy was stillborn. He's with our Heavenly Father and will never have to suffer any pain or endure any troubles. I know your heart will ache for him but, believe me, he is where he will always be surrounded by love and will know only joy and peace. It will be hard for you to give him up before you ever held him in your arms, but he will know only kindness and love in the arms of God."

Cassie looked at her blankly and said, "I don't rightly see how I could grieve fer somebody that never even seemed real to me. I'm sorry that I ain't got no tears to shed fer him, Mrs. Johnston, but I shed all my tears when I knowed I's a' goin' to have him. I knowed they wasn't never anything in this here world fer him but shame and hurt, so I guess it's hard fer me to grieve 'cause he's been spared all of that."

"Cassie," said Ellen sadly, "it grieves me that you've suffered so much in your short life. Would you like to look at your baby before we bury him?"

"No'm, I don't reckon so. I'm afeared of the face I'd see on him. I don't want to hate him, and I would if he looks like—like him."

The next day Will and Ellen buried Cassie's baby beside their little Tildy. Now there were two graves on the knoll near the first little log cabin.

TWENTY-ONE

Cassie was slow regaining her strength, and Ellen fussed over her constantly, urging her to eat more. Finally, when the weather began to warm and spring approached, she seemed to take heart. She never mentioned her baby and, so far as Ellen knew, had never visited the knoll where he was buried.

It was time for the new schoolmaster to arrive, and everyone in the community was speculating on what he would be like and if he would be a hard taskmaster. Elisha Phillips had volunteered to board him at his home until the cabin could be raised and readied for him. Nola was beside herself in anticipation of his coming. She had pored over every book Will had, determined to impress the new teacher with her knowledge.

"I do declare, I never seen anybody as excited over a'body as that Nola is over this here teacher," Cassie declared. "You'd think hit were the president or a king or sich the way she's a' takin' on. I don't know why she's so all fired anxious to set in a old dark school. I shore never done nothin' that foolish. 'Pears to me like she's got all the larnin' she needs already!"

"You can attend school too, Cassie, if you'd like," Will told her. "We can make arrangements, and you can go along with Nola and the other children."

"No, sir," replied Cassie stubbornly, "meanin' no disrespect, Mr. Johnston, but I don't reckon so. I ain't about to set myself down with no bunch of babies. I reckon I know all I need to. 'Sides, my pa allus said that womenfolk don't need no book larnin' jist to raise young'uns and scrub floors."

Later, Ellen cautioned Will, "Don't push it, Will. Like as not there'll come a time when Cassie will want to learn, and that will be soon enough."

The first Sunday in April the whole community attended preaching at the school building, where they also met and appraised the new teacher. He was a tall, gangly young man whom Ellen described as "Right 'peart lookin', but a mite on the skinny side. What he needs is a good woman to fatten him up!" This was probably in the back of most of the young unmarried girls' minds as they looked him over and cast admiring looks at him. All but Cassie, that is. She gave him a frank appraisal and then seemed to dismiss him from her mind.

Joshua Perkins did not dismiss Cassie quite so casually, and asked Elisha Phillips, "Who is that striking looking red-head with the green eyes?"

"Why, she's a girl stayin' temporarily with the Johnstons," Elisha replied.

When Ellen invited him to their house, Joshua regretted that he had already accepted a dinner invitation from the Mann family. "I do hope you will ask me another time," he said, gazing longingly in Cassie's direction.

"Why, of course we will," Ellen replied. "Why don't you just come on home with Nola and the other young'uns from school Wednesday evening, and we'll see if we can't put a little meat on them bones of yours!"

"Thank you," Joshua accepted eagerly. "I'll be there on Wednesday."

When classes began the next day, he watched expectantly for Cassie. He was disappointed when the Johnston children appeared without her.

"Where is your older sister?" he asked Nola during the lunch break. "Isn't she going to come to school?"

"Why, no, sir. She says she already knows all she needs to know, and she isn't interested in coming to school. Mr. Perkins, I want you to know I have completed the second book of Latin that my papa got for me. I don't think I know everything there is to know. I just love to go to school and learn new things."

"That's just fine, Nola," replied Joshua. "I'm sure you are a fine student, and I shall depend on you to help me out with the younger children. There is surely a big age range in the classroom, and if I don't get some help from some of the better students, it will be hard for me to get around to everyone."

Nola beamed under the teacher's praise and vowed to herself that she would work just as hard as he did to help him teach the younger children. She went home that day bubbling over with plans on how she could help him and rattled on until Cassie said crossly, "I shore am a' gettin' tared of hearin' you go on and on about this here new teacher. Can't ye talk about anythin' else? My goodness, ye'd thank they wasn't nobody else but him no more. Come on, Nola, let's fergit about that old school and go see if'n we can find some bloodroot a' bloomin' up under the rock."

"Why don't you take Martha with you, Cassie," Nola replied. "I want to read this book Mr. Perkins loaned me. He said as quick as I read it he'd let me have another. I'm going to read every single book he has."

"Come on, Martha, let's go," Cassie said disgustedly. "I can't stand no more of this talk about readin' and sich. Hit's jist like my Pa allus said—book larnin' jist messes womenfolk's heads up!"

But if Nola heard Cassie's remarks, she did not acknowledge them. She was already lost in the pages of her book. She pored over it all afternoon until Ellen called her to help get supper on the table. As soon as the table was cleared and the dishes put away, she went back to her reading again.

Cassie pouted all evening and was heard to remark to Martha, "Some folks jist don't know how bad all that book larnin' kin be fer them. Why I knowed a gal oncet that had terrible headaches from readin' in books too much. I tell ye Martha, it jist ain't healthy to keep yore nose stuck in a old book all the time!"

Will chuckled when he heard what Cassie had said. "Well, it seems to me that someone's nose is out of joint. I don't envy Mr. Joshua Perkins when he comes to supper Wednesday. Cassie may set education back fifty years!"

When Joshua came home with the children on Wednesday evening, Cassie was nowhere to be seen. In a fit of industry, she had told Ellen that she believed she would clean out the springhouse and scrub down the trough where the milk was kept. It was not until Ellen had sent after her twice that she reluctantly came to the supper table, slipping in quietly while Will was offering thanks. She peered from under lowered eyelids at the teacher sitting diagonally across the table from her.

The conversation during the meal was carried on mainly between Will and Joshua and was concerned mostly with the status of the different pupils in the school.

Joshua told Will, "I am delighted and pleasantly surprised to find that the students are as far along in their studies as they are. I thought I would get a group of children with little or no schooling. It is obvious that you have done a good job with them. They are fortunate that they had someone like you to get them started."

"Well, I don't know how fortunate they were. I did the best I could for them, but it did not take me long to find out that I am not a teacher. At least not a long term one. I enjoyed trying it for a short time, but I don't think I have any regrets about giving it up."

"It's true that some people do find teaching dull," said Joshua, "but I personally find it very exciting to watch a child's mind open to grasp a new idea or become acquainted with a fascinating character in a book."

"I didn't mean to imply that I found it dull," Will said hastily. "Goodness knows, nothing that involves our friend Zac Mann will ever be dull. I suppose the children told you about Zac and the skunk, didn't they?"

"Oh, yes, sir, that was one of the first stories I heard," laughed Joshua. "You may be sure that I shall be on my guard with that young man. Of course, his saving grace is that he is so bright. It did not take me long to find out that he and your Nola are the two brightest students in the school."

Nola blushed and dropped her head. Cassie glared at Joshua, then turned to Ellen and asked abruptly, "Ma'am, kin I leave the table, please. I'm a' feelin' a mite sickish."

"Why of course, Cassie. Is there anything I can do for you?"

"No'm, I reckon not. I jist need a little fresh air, thank ye," Cassie said as she hastened out the door.

Joshua did not linger long after supper, feeling the need to get to the Phillips's before dark since he was unfamiliar with the path.

Cassie returned shortly after he left and silently took her place helping with the kitchen duties. She had little to say for the rest of the evening and went to bed early.

When Nola returned from school the next day, she found Cassie waiting for her about halfway from home. Cassie poked along until the other children were out of earshot and then said to Nola, "How hard is hit to learn how to cipher them words you read in them books."

"Why do you want to know? I thought you said you didn't want to go to school."

"Hit ain't that, Nola," Cassie replied with downcast eyes. "Hit's jist that I'd be ashamed to have to set with the little young'uns in school. Why, I'd have to be in the same class with little Martha. Now how would you feel if'n you's me?"

"Oh, Cassie! I'm sorry. I never thought of it like that. I guess I'd feel the same way. Can't you read at all?" Cassie shook her head in embarrassment. "If you can't read, Cassie, I guess you can't write your name either, can you?"

"No, I shore can't, Nola, and hits somethin' I've longed to do. I think hit must be the grandest thing in the world to be able to write out the letters that spells yore own name. Do you think you could show me? Or maybe ye think I'm jist too dumb to larn."

"Of course you're not too dumb, silly. Why, just look here! I bet I could teach you to write your name in nothing flat."

She knelt down in the path, took a stick, and in the dirt printed out the letters in Cassie's name.

"Air that my name, Nola?" asked Cassie in wonder. "Do them funny lookin' lines say Cassie fer shore?"

Cassie knelt down and, taking the stick, traced over the letters. "Well, I never!" she declared, "I never in all my borned days thought I'd be a writin' my very own name. Air ye shore them's the right words, Nola?"

"Of course I'm sure, and if you'll tell me what your other name is, I'll show you how to write it too."

Cassie looked at her hard for a moment and reluctantly said, "Hit's Martin, Nola. My other name's Martin."

Nola spelled out Martin in the dirt beside Cassie, and both girls stood looking at the words. Then slowly Cassie knelt down and with her finger traced around the letters in her name. She looked up at Nola with tears in her eyes and said, "That's the first time I ever seen my whole name wrote down. Do ye think I could ever larn to write hit by myself?"

Nola put her arms around Cassie. "I'll teach you to write your name, Cassie, and I'll teach you to read too if you want me to. I've helped the little young'uns, and I know I can teach you."

"First ye got to promise me somethin' though," said Cassie. "First ye got to promise me ye'll not tell nary a soul what ye're a' doin'. I couldn't stand fer everybody to know I ain't never learnt to write my name. And especially don't ye tell that smart alecky Willie. He'd blab hit all over the holler, and like as not he'd tell that skinny old teacher too. Ye got to cross yer heart and hope to die ye won't tell a soul. Promise now!"

Solemnly Nola crossed her heart and raised her hand. "I cross my heart and hope to die if I ever tell a soul, Cassie. It will be our secret. Then someday when you've learned to read really well, we'll surprise everyone. Papa will be real pleased. He sets a great store by book-learning."

"Yeah, I can tell he does. I shore don't want him to have to be ashamed of me. Nor yore ma neither. I guess it would please me if'n I thought you'd be proud of me too, Nola," she admitted shyly. "I shore do admar how smart ye are and how nice ye can keep house! Most as good your Ma can!"

"Oh Cassie, I am proud of you already—just for having the courage to tell me you want to learn. I'll teach you everything I know," Nola exclaimed. "When you've learned to read, I'll teach you to cipher too. It's not hard. You've just got to set your mind to it."

"Thank ye, Nola," Cassie said humbly. "I guess yore the goodest friend anybody could ever have!"

Nola and Cassie hugged each other again and then set out for home, excited about the adventure before them.

TWENTY-TWO

Nola was true to her word and told no one about the secret lessons she was giving Cassie. They spent the time between Nola's return from school and the evening meal each day on the lessons. There usually was about an hour in the evening before bedtime as well. Cassie proved to be an apt student, and before long Nola was able to tell her, "Cassie, you're as good as any of the children in Willie's class. It won't be no time at all till you're up with me and John and Sam. I wish you'd come on and go to the regular school with the rest of us. I just know Mr. Perkins could help you better than I can."

"Now Nola, don't ye fergit that ye crossed yore heart and swore ye'd not tell a soul what we's a' doin'," Cassie warned her. "Ye'd better not fergit yore promise ur else somethin' bad'll happen to ye fer breakin' yore solemn word."

"Don't worry," sighed Nola, "I won't tell anybody, but Mr. Perkins keeps asking me why you won't come to school with the rest of us. He sure does worry over you a lot. He's always askin' me questions about you."

"Do ye think folks knows about the baby, Nola?" asked Cassie fearfully.

"Well, I know Mrs. Cole does. I heard her asking Mama about it."

"What did yore ma tell her?"

"Mama told her it was an unfortunate incident that we should allow you to put behind you, and that was all she intended to say, except that she didn't hold you to blame for what happened to you."

"There ain't a gooder woman on this earth than yore ma," Cassie said fervently. "I vow ye don't know how lucky ye be, Nola, to have her and yore pa fer family. I—I guess if my ma'd looked after me like yore'n does, I wouldn't a' got in the fix I did."

Nola waited breathlessly, thinking that perhaps Cassie was at last ready to reveal what had happened to her. But in one of her mercurial changes of mood, Cassie started discussing Ellen's new pregnancy.

"Did ye know yore ma is a' hopin' fer another girl baby this time so hit'll even up thangs around here? That way there'd be three girls and three boys in yore family."

"I think things are already even, Cassie. You're our third girl. I couldn't feel any closer to you if you were my own blood sister than I do right now. I know Martha loves you just the same, too."

"Hush yore mouth," Cassie replied, blushing in obvious pleasure. "We'uns better git busy with these here chores or else we'll both be in trouble."

The three girls had taken over the bulk of the household chores for Ellen. This pregnancy had been easy compared to the one she had experienced with the twins. "I feel like some pampered high-falutin lady," she told Will. "Them girls won't hardly let me turn my hands."

"You'd better enjoy it while you can. When school's out, I'll be needing them in the fields some. I hate to work the girls, too, but until the twins get old enough to help, it's more than me and Willie can handle by ourselves."

Nola had planned the household tasks and had a set routine for getting everything done. On Monday and Tuesday the washing and ironing were done, weather allowing. Wednesday and Thursday were the days they did the sewing and mending. Ellen still did most of this. On Friday they changed and aired the bedclothes and did the weekend housecleaning. Saturdays were occupied with baking, as well as scrubbing and washing everybody for Sunday.

"You know, it seems we feel a need to clean ourselves inside and out for preaching on Sunday," Will laughed. "I'm sure God would accept us just as readily with the honest dirt on our hands, but somehow, it always makes me feel better if I'm looking my best when I go to services on Sunday."

The summer passed for the Johnston family with Cassie becoming an important part of the household. Only once did Ellen mention her returning to her own family.

"I know your mother must be worried about you and wonder what's become of you. Don't you want to get in touch with her and let her know you're all right? I'm sure now that he's had some time to get over his anger, your father'll forgive you, too. We could take you to see them some Sunday if you're a' mind to."

"No'm, Mrs. Johnston, I don't reckon so," Cassie answered. "I guess they's as glad to be rid of me as I was to go. And so far as my pa fergivin' me, I guess that works two ways. Maybe I ain't so anxious to fergive him neither. I reckon I'm done with them now, jest like they's done with me. If'n I'm becomin' a burden on ye though, I—I'll hunt me some other place to go."

"Nonsense, girl," Ellen said, "don't you know you're part of our family now? Why, I'd no more send you away than I would any of my other children."

Cassie put her arms around Ellen and laid her head on her shoulder. Ellen patted her and then said gruffly, "Well, just listen to us, cluckin' like two old hens. You'd think we didn't have anything better to do than stand around and jaw at each other."

She took the corner of her apron and tenderly wiped the tears from Cassie's eyes and then wiped her own as she said brusquely, "We'd best get busy now and get some vittles on the table before all these hungry young'uns descend on us."

Joshua Perkins had returned to his family in Tennessee at the close of the spring school session. All of his overtures to Cassie had been met with a studied indifference on her part, and he left very discouraged. He could not understand why she was so indifferent to him. When he tried to discuss Cassie with anyone, they became very closemouthed and noncommital. He put it down to mountain people's distrust of outsiders.

In August, during a lull in the harvest season, the men of the community met at the site that had been selected for the schoolmaster's cabin and, with three days of diligent work, raised a log cabin for Joshua. It was only a two-room cabin, but there was room to add a loft, if needed. Joshua was to return at the end of August to begin the next term of school. Cassie pretended little interest in his affairs, but Nola noticed she was always close by when his name was mentioned, listening for word of his plans.

"For somebody that don't care nothing about the schoolmaster, you sure do perk up when his name is mentioned, Cassie," teased Nola. "If you hadn't told me a thousand times how you can't stand him, I might think you were struck on him."

"Nola Johnston, ye'd just better hush yore mouth a'fore I put a hex on ye," threatened Cassie darkly. "Ye must be outta yore mind to think I'd be interested in a old stringbean like Joshua Perkins. 'Sides, why would the likes of me think any man would be interested in them, 'specially one with a fine education like him."

"Oh, Cassie, don't be mad. I was just teasing you. There isn't a prettier girl in this valley than you. I heard Mr. Perkins tell Sam McGinty one day that your hair put him in mind of a sunset in the summertime, it was so pretty."

"He did?" Cassie asked, unable to hide her excitement. "He truly said that? But you know what yore Ma allus says, 'purty is as purty does,' and I guess that leaves me out fer shore. I bet Sam thought they's somebody else that had purtier hair than me though. His eyes jest plumb bugs out ever time he looks at you, Nola. And that old John, he falls all over hisself when he gits close to you. Ye'd better be kerful or else ye're goin' to have them brothers warrin' over you one of these days."

"Oh, Cassie," Nola blushed, "you're just trying to get even with me for what I told about Mr. Perkins. But it's the truth, I swear."

When Joshua returned late in August, the community set aside one evening to give him a pounding. Each family contributed food items they could spare and deposited them at his door. Ellen and Will took him a sack of grain and a plentiful supply of canned goods that Ellen and the girls had preserved during the summer. Ellen also invited him to Sunday dinner.

Cassie spent an unusual amount of time washing and brushing her hair on Saturday night. She flitted from one task to another until Will declared to Ellen she was acting "as skittish as a colt."

During the meal the next day, she kept her head down and had little to say. The children were all eager to share what had happened to them during the summer. Nola recited the different books she had read, and Martha and Willie told him all about the cabin raising.

When everyone had finished their tales, Joshua looked directly at Cassie and asked, "Now, Cassie, I've heard from everyone but you. What have you been doing this summer?"

Cassie looked up, flustered, and stammered, "Why I reckon I ain't done nothin' special, jist the usual cannin' and preservin'. I leave all that book stuff to Nola. I ain't got time fer sich foolishments."

She ducked her head and tried to dismiss him, but he was not going to be put off so easily this time. He persisted. "Well, I would certainly be interested in hearing about some of the canning and preserving you have done. Did you can any of the food Brother Johnston brought to me?"

"Why, I suppose I did," she mumbled. "I can't remember ever jar of food I put up."

"Why, Cassie," exclaimed Willie, "you know how particular you was that Mama should put in one of your special jars of wild strawberry preserves, and you like to of took a fit till she got some of them pickled beans to take."

Cassie flushed angrily and glared at Willie. "I disremember any sich a thing."

Ellen, seeing that things were about to get out of hand, rose from the table and said, "Come, Nola and Cassie, let's be clearin' off the table so I can serve Mr. Perkins some of this blackberry cobbler."

Gratefully, Cassie rose and fled to the kitchen. When Nola and Ellen came in with the plates she told them, "I'm goin' to tan that Willie's hide when I catch up to him. He ain't got the sense God gave a goose. I vow, his tongue is loose at both ends."

Ellen looked at her in amazement and said, "Well, Cassie, maybe you'd best let sleepin' dogs lie. As I remember, what Willie said was the truth. Perhaps you'd better examine your own feelings a little closer. It seems to me you're mighty quick to let everybody think you don't care for Joshua. Maybe you'd best start bein' more honest with yourself. I've seen you lookin' at him on Sundays at preachin' when you thought nobody would notice. You looked fit to be tied at the Phillips's quiltin' party when Lon Severs's girl was moonin' over him."

"Oh, Mrs. Johnston," Cassie said miserably, "how on earth could I ever expect anybody as fine as Joshua is to look at the likes of me? I ain't fit to wipe the feet of a good man like him. He could have his pick of any girl in the holler. I wouldn't dast think he'd care about me."

Ellen was distressed when she realized how poorly Cassie thought of herself and regretted her teasing remarks. She put her arms around Cassie and told her, "You are a fine, good girl, Cassie, and I'd better not hear you or anybody else say different. You're just foolin' yourself if you think Joshua is not interested in you. He seeks you out everywhere he can. If you truly like him, you'd better give him some sign of encouragement before it's too late."

"I jist don't know what to do," Cassie said, bursting into tears. "What I done was a terrible thing, and I don't know if I can ever git past hit."

"You let Joshua be the judge of whether or not you're good enough for him," Ellen said, "and stop puttin' yourself down. It seems to me, the first thing you need to do is to forgive yourself. The Bible says that if we truly repent, God will surely forgive us. If He can forgive you, don't you think it's about time you forgave yourself?"

"Maybe if I pray on it like Brother McGinty told us at preachin' Sunday, I can find the answer. I promise to try anyways," Cassie said as she wiped her eyes on her apron.

"Well, we'd best get this cobbler to the table before they come a' lookin' for us," Ellen said brusquely.

The rest of the evening passed uneventfully, but just before Joshua left for his cabin he approached Cassie and said, "Cassie, I'd sure like to be your friend and get to know you better. I don't know why you dislike me so, but if you'd just give me a chance, you might find out I'm not such a bad fellow. Can't we be friends?"

Looking him straight in the eyes, Cassie said, "I'd like to be yore friend, but I guess 'afore you say ye'd like to be mine, ye'd better know more about me. 'Afore we meet again, maybe I'll have somethin' to tell ye that'll change yore mind about me. Anyhow, I got to think on hit some more."

"I'll wait for your answer, Cassie," Joshua said eagerly.

"Somethin' else ye'd best know about me is I ain't sich a good reader neither. I never read a book nor wrote my name till Nola learned me how. I ain't no edjicated person like you are."

Gently Joshua lifted Cassie's chin and looked deep into her eyes. "Oh, Cassie, don't you know there are other things just as important as book learning? I'm a teacher and if everyone were born knowing how to read and write, I wouldn't be able to earn a livelihood. I would never look down on you because you couldn't read."

Cassie flushed with pleasure and, giving him a happy smile, turned and ran back to the house. She slipped out the back door and went down the path to the springhouse. She lay under the big walnut tree and pondered all that had happened to her that day. She took from her heart each word that Joshua had spoken to her and examined them as reverently as if they were the finest jewels on earth.

TWENTY-THREE

The next two weeks were busy ones for Joshua as he settled into his new home and prepared for a new school year. On the morning of the first day of the fall session, he was delighted to see Cassie slip quietly into the schoolroom with the Johnston children. It took all of his will power to keep his eyes off her and to get through the day with some semblance of normality. As the students left that afternoon, he managed a moment alone with Cassie.

"I can't tell you how happy I am you decided to come with the others," he told her. "I hope you have thought about our last conversation. I have thought of nothing else."

"I have been a' thinkin' about it," Cassie answered, "and I've decided that I want to tell ye all about myself and then ye kin decide if ye want to be my friend or not. If'n ye've a mind to, I reckon we could meet at the rock come Saturday after I'm done with my chores. We kin talk there without no big-eared Willie a listenin' to us."

"I'll be there, Cassie," he responded eagerly.

Cassie was up earlier than usual that Saturday and fairly flew through her chores. "Slow down, Cassie," Nola pleaded, "you're about to work me to death. I've never seen you in such a snit to get through. A body'd think you were going to a dance or something."

"Oh, Nola, I jist got to tell somebody and if ye tell hit, I'll never tell ye nothin' again. I'm a' goin' to meet Joshua at the rock as soon as I git through my chores. If he hates me after I tell him what happened to me, I'll jist die."

"Oh, Cassie, promise me you'll tell me everything when you get home. I'm so happy for you. I just know everything will be all right with Joshua."

"I promise, Nola. I'll tell ye good ur bad," Cassie replied.

As soon as the noon meal was over and the dishes put away, Cassie slipped out and hastened up the mountain trail to the rock. She wondered what she would do if Joshua were not there, but she could have saved herself the worry. He had been there for nearly an hour, pacing back and forth impatiently. When he saw her, his face lit up, and he rushed to meet her. Taking her hands in his, he tried to draw her into his arms, but she held him off and shook her head.

"There's things that's got to be said first, Joshua," she told him firmly, "and when I'm done, ye might not want to touch me."

"Very well, Cassie, tell me if you must. I can't think of anything that would ever make me feel that way toward you, but say it and be done."

"I ain't no Johnston, ye know," began Cassie, "but I shore wisht I was. If'n I had a' been, there wouldn't be nothin' standin' between us. I don't know if ye've heard it or not, but when I come here I was a' huntin' fer a place to—to hide. I's a' gonna have a baby. I don't know what I'd a' done if Mrs. Johnston hadn't took pity on me and took me in. I guess I'd a' ended up dead, jist like my baby."

Joshua paled visibly, but waited quietly for Cassie to continue. She looked him straight in the eyes and said, "In case ye're a' wonderin', Joshua, I warn't married. Hit's took me a long time to be able to talk about what happened to me, but I guess like Mrs. Johnston says, if'n the good Lord can fergive me, then I think hit's time I fergive myself. I ain't never told a soul who the daddy of that baby was, not even Nola, but I figger you've got a right to know, that is if'n ye still want to."

Joshua nodded stiffly, and Cassie continued. "Ever since I first started turnin' womanly, my pa started a'pesterin' after me. I knowed hit were wrong, but he jist wouldn't leave me alone. At first I jist thought he was a' bein' lovin' to me and I was happy, 'cause he never did seem to like me much afore that. Hit was jist all of a sudden like that he's always a' tryin' to git me to set on his lap and was a' huggin' on me.

"When I finally seen that he had more'n jist a daddy's love on his mind, I tried to tell Ma what he's a' doin', but she's so scared of him, she let on like she never believed me. Ye see, he warn't my real blood pappy. My real pa died when I 'us jist a baby, and my Ma married him after that.

"When he seen he'd got me in a family way, he let on like I's some kind of bad woman and said I'd disgraced him and run me off. I 'us glad to leave and git away from him, but it shore hurt some when my ma never tried to git him to let me stay. I guess she 'us a' scared he'd run her off too if she said anything.

"Well, that's the whole honest to goodness truth, Joshua, and now I'll understand if'n ye don' want to see me no more. I know now that what happened to me warn't my fault, but hit's a powerful hard thing to expect ye to fergit somethin' like this. I won't hold hit agin ye if'n ye want to jist go on home now," she finished with a sob.

Joshua stared at her for several moments, not trusting himself to speak. The story had shocked him, but now he understood some of the remarks that Mary Severs had made to him. Cassie, mistaking his silence for disapproval, sadly turned away and started for home.

"Cassie, wait," Joshua called. "Don't go, Cassie! My Lord, girl, do you think I'm that shallow?"

Rushing after her, he took her in his arms and turned her tear-filled eyes up to his. Gently, he brushed the tears away and kissed her. Then he held her close.

"Don't you know that what happened to you didn't touch the real Cassie? That's who I've fallen in love with—the beautiful person I see when I look into your eyes."

"Air ye a' tellin' me true, Joshua?" Cassie asked timidly.

"Yes, I'm telling you true. The girl I see and love is pure and innocent and the most honest person I have ever met."

"Then ye think ye can fergive me?"

"Forgive you? It isn't you that has anything to be forgiven for. I'm going to need forgiveness if I ever meet that beast who did this to you, because I think I would strangle him with my bare hands."

"Don't think on him no more, Joshua. He ain't worth a minute of yore time. I guess what Mrs. Johnston said is true. What happened to me is finally over and done with, and there ain't no reason to keep on frettin' about hit."

"Cassie, I love you. Will you be my wife? If you will, I'll be the happiest man on the face of this earth."

"Oh, Joshua, if'n ye can put up with the likes of me, I'd be right honored to marry up with you, I do love you, but I got to say one more thing, though."

"Say it, Cassie, and then we'll never speak of this again."

"I never grieved fer that pore little baby, 'cause I knowed hit were jist saved from a life of shame. But I hope the Lord sees fit to give me lots of babies fer you."

"So do I, Cassie," laughed Joshua. "Come on now, let's go tell the Johnstons our good news. I am an impatient man, and I don't plan to wait very long to marry you."

TWENTY-FOUR

One look at Cassie's and Joshua's faces told the whole story to Ellen, and she put her arms around them both. "I don't reckon you need to say a word, neither one of you," she said. "Your eyes says it all, except maybe the date, and I guess that depends on when we can catch a preacher here to tie the knot."

The younger children looked on big-eyed at all the excitement. Willie, never at a loss for words, said, "Mr. Perkins, does this mean you sure enough mean to marry up with Cassie? What on earth possessed you to do such a fool thing? Girls ain't nothin' but a big pain. I shore thought you had better sense than that!"

"Willie, I would bet that in about three more years you would never admit to making such a statement as that," laughed Joshua. "Just you wait a little while, and I won't have to explain it to you."

Will entered in the midst of the excitement and, when told what had happened, he offered his congratulations to Joshua. "I must make a trip to the Shook's and see when a preacher will be coming through so we can make the arrangements. It seems like we just got that cabin raised in time. Ellen, we must see what we can do to help these young folks get started. I'm sure, knowing you, that you can get a wedding quilt put in and took out in time for the marriage day," he chuckled.

"It just so happens that I do have a real pretty Honeycomb top just about ready to go in the frame. Besides that, we'll have to look to some other plunder for them. You can't start housekeepin' with one quilt."

There was some gossip in the community from mothers who were disgruntled that an outsider like Cassie had captured such an eligible bachelor over their own daughters. When they tried to criticize Cassie to Joshua, he cut the conversation short with a curt, "Whatever it is you have in mind to tell me, I already know. Cassie and I have no secrets from each other."

If they were persistent in their efforts, he cut them off by tipping his hat politely and walking away. Ellen also treated would-be informers in a like manner, telling them, "I reckon it's like the Bible says, 'them that's without sins can cast the first stone.'"

Nola and Cassie, with Martha's help, began making a mattress for the bed, using the corn shucks saved from last year's crop. Ellen promised to save feathers enough as soon as she could to replace it, but until then the shucks would have to do. Will and Joshua built a very creditable bed from some chestnut wood that Will had cured out to replace the narrow bunk that was in the cabin.

As word of the impending marriage spread, various household items appeared from the people of the community until, as Cassie put it, "We'uns has got enough plunder to make our cabin look right peart."

Cassie worried about what she would wear for the wedding. Looking over the dresses Nola had given her or that Ellen had made, she told Nola, "I can't make up my mind. I guess it ain't important what you got on you as much as it is what you got in yore heart anyways."

From her chest Ellen took her own wedding dress that she had carefully wrapped and stored away and offered it to Cassie. It was a soft blue muslin edged in fine tatted lace that her mother had made for her.

"It would make me right proud, Cassie, if you would wear this dress on your marryin' day. I've been savin' it for the time Nola or Martha might need it, but we talked it over, and the girls both agree that they want you to wear it. You've become as close to them both as a sister."

Tears filled Cassie's eyes. "Why ma'm, I'd shore be much obliged to ye, and to Nola and Martha, too, if'n they're shore they don't mind me a' wearin' hit. Hit's jest about the purtiest dress I ever seen, and I'd be honored to think ye'd let me wear hit."

"Oh, Cassie, nothing would make me any happier," Nola exclaimed. "I just know you and Joshua will be happy, and it can't do anything but bring me good luck when . . . or that is, if I ever get to wear it. Anyhow, that takes care of your something blue. Now we have to find something old, something new, and something borrowed. I know what your something borrowed will be! I will loan you my very prettiest handkerchief to carry."

"And you can wear my mother's comb in your hair," said Ellen. "I wore it when me and Will married. Mama said it belonged to her mother and was one of the things she brought with her from Ireland. Now all we need is somethin' new."

"I reckon this feelin' I got in my heart fer Joshua is about all the somethin' new I need," said Cassie shyly. "Sometimes I feel like I'll bust wide open I'm so happy. I don't know as I'll ever be able to say enough thanks to you'uns fer all ye've done fer me, and now all this! Hit jest plumb makes me think the good Lord shore was a' watchin' over me the night I hid in yore springhouse. I reckon that's jest about the smartest thing I ever did do."

The Reverend McPeters arrived on October 12th, and on the 14th, standing before the great fireplace in the Johnston's home, he united Cassie and Joshua in marriage. As Joshua slipped a small gold wedding band on Cassie's finger, she turned to Nola and said, "Why looky here, Nola, here's my somethin' new!"

Everyone laughed and exchanged hugs and good wishes for the new couple. They rode proudly to their new home in the buggy that Joshua had borrowed from Jacob McGinty to begin their new life together.

That was not the only new life begun that night. During the night Ellen gave birth to her sixth child, another son, whom they named Joseph.

TWENTY-FIVE

Cassie's marriage left a distinct void in the Johnston household. Ellen told Will, "I didn't realize how much a part of the family Cassie had become. I wouldn't be any lonesomer for her if she was my own flesh and blood."

Fortunately, the new baby filled most of Ellen's time, and she did not have much leisure to dwell on Cassie's absence. Nola missed her more than anyone. She had come to look upon Cassie as her confidante, as well as her good right arm with the housekeeping chores. Martha tried to fill Cassie's place, but try as she would, she could not please Nola.

"Nothin' I do is right as far as Nola is concerned," she complained to Ellen. "I try my best to do things just like she tells me, but it's never as good as when Cassie did it. I tell you, Mama, I'm gettin' sick and tired of hearin', 'Cassie did it like this.'"

"Be patient with her, Martha. She's missin' Cassie right bad, but she'll get over it in time. Just remember when she's short with you and you're tempted to answer her back that 'a soft answer turneth away wrath.'"

Fortunately, the weather was mild up into late November; so Nola had her schoolwork to occupy her, and in time the loss of Cassie eased up somewhat for her. Also, Joshua had suggested a project for Nola that helped tremendously. He had always been interested in the poems and chants that Ellen composed, and he suggested to Nola that it would be a nice surprise for Ellen if Nola would put them down in a book. Nola labored many hours, writing down as many of them as she could remember. She enlisted Martha's aid in getting Ellen to recite them if she could not remember all the words. The shared secret drew them closer, and Nola began turning to Martha for the companionship she had enjoyed with Cassie. The girls were surprised to find that they had recorded nearly fifty poems and chants when they finished.

"The only trouble," Nola grumbled, "is before you get through writing one down, Mama has made up a new one. I think my favorite one is the poem she wrote about the quilts, but I like her new one nearly as well. See if I have the words right, Martha."

> *I looked into my mother's eyes,*
> *And much to my surprise,*
> *I saw myself reflected there,*
> *My every thought laid raw and bare.*
>
> *I listened to her voice that day*
> *And seemed to hear my own lips say*
> *The very words she said to me,*
> *'Twas quite a shock, these things to see.*
>
> *I thought it was a marvelous thing,*
> *That such a moment could bring*
> *A glimpse of life ahead for me,*
> *And things that had been and were yet to be.*
>
> *I sometimes wonder as I see these things,*
> *What time and life someday will bring*
> *If my daughters ever look at me*
> *And let my eyes, their mirror be.*

"That's it," Martha said excitedly, "you have every word just perfect, Nola. Now when we get this one wrote down, that will be all of them, and Papa can send it off to get it bound. Oh, I can hardly wait till Christmas time. Won't she be took back?"

"I guess she will at that," Nola answered. "I just hope she will be pleased. Let's hide it till Papa can send it off."

Will was as excited over the book as Nola and Martha, and he sent it to a friend in Raleigh who promised to have it bound and covered.

When it was completed and returned, the girls carefully hid it away. They were sorely put to contain their excitement until Christmas arrived.

Ellen always went to great pains to be sure each child had something special at Christmas, whether it was a dress sewn painstakingly with her own hands or a toy carved during the winter evenings by Will. For this Christmas, she had obtained a book of poetry for Nola and made both her and Martha new Sunday dresses. For Willie and the twins she made new linsey-woolsey shirts with cloth woven on her own loom. Will also had a squirrel rifle for Willie and carved identical sets of soldiers for the twins. Martha, who loved jewelry, would have Ellen's prized brooch handed down from her grandmother Cunnigan. Baby Joseph would get a new apron and a clever set of animals Will had carved.

The Christmas Eve ritual at the Johnston's was always the same. After a special evening meal of the best Ellen could offer from her pantry, the family gathered in the great room to decorate the tree Will and Willie had cut and brought in from the woods. They all worked diligently, stringing popcorn and red berries to drape around the tree. Then Ellen carefully took the decorations out of the chest and each child in turn hung them on the tree. Most of the decorations had been carved by Will or sewn by Ellen. Each year they added new ones, and Ellen could recite when and how each piece had been made.

"This here star was the first one your papa made for our tree," she told the children as she carefully took out a smoothly carved piece. "He worked many a night on it smoothin' it up so that it'd be ready that first Christmas. The next year he had four of these here little animals all carved and fixed for the tree. Nola, you loved the little bear best of all when we hung 'em up that year. I'd made these little crocheted pieces that looks like snowflakes, and we thought that was the prettiest tree ever was that year."

"What makes 'em stand out so stiff, Mama?" asked Martha.

"That's sugar water that does that. These little angels I made out of cornhusks was your papa's favorites. He thought I was mighty clever to fashion them," Ellen laughed.

"Still do too," Will declared. "I remember how you had to soak the cornhusks and work with them to make them look right. Never thought an old corn husk could be so pretty."

"These candleholders we're puttin' on now was made by your papa, too. He spent many a night whittlin' by lamp light before he got all these done."

After all the decorations were hung, Will and Ellen placed the candles on the tree, too, and lit them. Then, standing back with only the fireplace adding flickering lights to the scene, each declared in turn, "This is the prettiest tree we've ever had."

"Where did you get the candles, Mama?" asked Nola. "They look different from our other candles. I've watched you make ours, but these are a different color and they don't smoke as bad."

"My sister Kate sent me some bayberries that she'd got a hold of from some friends, and I made them out of the oil from the berries," Ellen replied. "It's the same method for makin' regular candles, but usually I make them from the tallow I render from beef and sheep fat. With the bayberries, you just skim off the green lookin' oil that rises to the top when you boil them."

"How do you get them little wicks inside them?" asked Willie.

Ellen laughed, "I think I'd better let you come watch the next time I make candles. You have to soak your cotton yarn in salt water and boric acid all day, and then when they're dry, you plait three strands together. Then you take your wicks and dip 'em in your hot oil or tallow till they're as thick as you want 'em. While they're still warm and soft, you roll them so they'll be nice and round."

"That's enough talkin' about candles, Mama," said Martha. "I want Papa to put up the manger pieces."

Will carefully unwrapped a wooden nativity scene he had carved and laid the pieces on the table.

"Please Papa," Nola begged, "is it time for the story now?"

"Yes Papa, the story," echoed the others.

As the children and Ellen gathered around the dancing light of the fire, Will told the familiar story of the birth of the Christ child, using simple terms so the twins could understand. As the story progressed, he placed the pieces of the nativity scene on the mantle.

"Now children, this story comes from the Bible, from a book named Luke. It tells why we have Christmas and about the most wonderful gift that was ever given to man.

"In a country far away, there was a girl about Nola's age, or maybe a year or two older. One night in a dream an angel appeared to her and told her she was to have a special honor. She would have a baby, who would be the son of God, and she should call him Jesus. Just before time for the baby to be born, the girl, Mary, and her husband, Joseph, had to go to a town called Bethlehem to pay their taxes. While they was there, the baby Jesus was born. Now the town was real full and there was nowhere for them to sleep except in a stable, so that's where they went and that's where Jesus was born. His mother wrapped him in some soft cloths and laid him in a manger on some clean straw."

"What's a manger, Papa?" asked James.

"Why, that's a trough like thing that the cows eat out of," Will smiled. "See, here's what it looks like."

He held up a tiny carved manger, placed a bit of straw in it, and then placed the baby in its bed.

"Well, out in the pasture above the town," Will continued, "there were some farmers called shepherds watching their sheep, when all at once the heaven was full of angels singing and praising God and telling the men about Jesus' birth and where they could find him. Well, they went at once to the stable and knelt down in front of the manger where the baby was and worshipped him."

Will placed three shepherds and two sheep by the stable and then picked up three figures to add to the scene.

"Now in another country, way, far away, three wise men were looking at the stars, and they saw the brightest star they'd ever seen. They knew from what they'd learned that this was the star that would show them where Jesus was. They followed the star for a long time, and finally they came and found the baby, too. They brought him gifts to show how much they thanked God for what he had done for the world. These were the first Christmas gifts.

"Now Nola, if you'll get your guitar and play for us, we'll sing some Christmas songs."

At Ellen's request, they began with "Silent Night," and each person added a favorite until they had sung all the carols they knew.

"Mama, what did you do at Christmas time when you was a little girl?" asked Martha. "Did you gets lots of presents and have a big tree?"

"Well, we always had a tree," Ellen smiled, "but we never got but one present. It was usually something Mama or Papa had made for us. We didn't get no toys or play things usually. Mostly it was a new apron or socks that Mama had knit. I do recollect one year, though, that Mama spent every night for months makin' me and my sisters dolls out of her scraps. We thought them was the finest dolls ever was. I drug mine around till it plumb wore out."

"What did your brothers get?" asked Willie.

"Mostly clothes, like the girls. A new shirt or socks. Papa wasn't clever with his hands like your papa is, so they wasn't no fine carved pieces for them. One year he made the boys slingshots, though, and they was sure proud of them."

"Did they kill anything with 'em?" Willie asked.

"As well as I remember, the animals didn't suffer too much danger," laughed Ellen. "One of my brothers, Matthew, got right good with his though. We had a right smart of rabbit stew that winter."

"Well, this is enough talk for one night," Will said, "better get to bed. The twins have done gone, it looks like. Morning will be here before we know it."

Nola and Willie each picked up a sleeping twin and carried him to bed. That night Nola dreamed of fine gowns and strange travelers bringing gifts.

Christmas morning dawned clear and cold. The early morning sunlight fell across the fresh snowfall, and it sparkled and shone like diamonds in the sun's rays. As the children tumbled down the stairs wide-eyed and expectant, Ellen and Will stood before the freshly laid fire and shouted, "Christmas gift!" They watched happily as the children exclaimed over their gifts.

When everything had been looked at and admired, Nola slipped out and got Ellen's gift. She and Martha had wrapped it carefully and had tied it with one of Martha's ribbons. Nola laid it in Ellen's lap and stood back, watching with shining eyes.

"What is this?" Ellen asked curiously.

"Well, why don't you just open it and find out," Will suggested.

Puzzled, Ellen unwrapped the package as six pairs of eyes watched her face expectantly. They were not disappointed. The expression on Ellen's face turned from curiosity to awe as she held the book in her hands. The cover was fine walnut-colored leather with the words, "*Mountain Poems* by Ellen C. Johnston" engraved on the front. Opening the book she turned the pages, unable to believe her eyes.

"Who? How?" she asked dazedly as she looked from one to the other.

"Nola is the 'who,' with Martha's help," replied Will, "and the 'how' is with a lot of love and pride from us all."

"I don't believe my eyes," Ellen said. "Why all these foolish little rhymes I've made up are in here—how in the world did you remember them all?"

"Oh Mama, they're not foolish, they're wonderful," Nola exclaimed. "We love your poems, and we wanted them all set down so we could keep them forever! Please say you like it."

"Like it? Of course I like it. Never in my wildest dreams did I ever think I'd see my words wrote down in a real book."

"Read some of them, Mama," begged Martha.

For the next while Ellen turned the pages of the book and read aloud the poems so painstakingly written by Nola. Then with a twinkle in her eyes, she looked up and said, "This has made me want to write a new one, so how would you like to hear it?"

"Oh yes," they chorused, and Ellen recited the following words:

> *"There once was an old woman called Ellen,*
> *Who made silly poems for the tellin'.*
> *Till her daughters one day*
> *Took her breath quite away,*
> *By writin' all of the poems of Ellen."*

They all laughed at Ellen's latest offering. Even baby Joseph, sensing the festivity of the occasion, clapped his hands and smiled.

A loud knock on the door quieted them momentarily until Will opened the door to Joshua and Cassie. They entered, stomping snow from their boots and shouting, "Merry Christmas, Merry Christmas!"

Ellen beamed with happiness and said, "Now don't this just make everything perfect, a' havin' you two here. Come on in, I think there might even be a present or two under the tree for you."

"Oh, Mrs. Johnston, I never seen such a purty sight as yore tree is. I couldn't wait to git here this mornin' a' thinkin' about havin' Christmas with you'uns."

"Yes," laughed Joshua, "she had me up before daylight rushing to get ready."

The friends spent the day together, sharing their news and catching up on all that had happened to each other since they had last parted.

When the day was over and the last piece of sweet potato pie eaten, Nola told her mother, "I'll never forget this Christmas, Mama. Everything was just perfect. I hope that we'll always be this happy."

"Well, I'd like to think we would be, but life just ain't like that, I'm afraid. Times like these gives us somethin' to remember when times ain't so happy. I hope you will remember today and other happy times when you're older and have a family of your own."

"I never want to leave you and Papa," Nola said. "I can't imagine ever living anywhere but here with you."

"Well, we'll see about that," laughed Ellen. "I expect before many more years you'll be thinkin' about makin' your own home. Not yet, though, not yet. I'm not ready for that yet."

TWENTY-SIX

The second year that Joshua and Cassie were married, he received word that his father had died suddenly. Since he was the eldest of eight children, he felt it was his duty to return to his home and help his mother raise the family. It was with heavy hearts that Cassie and he gave up their first home and bid farewell to the friends that had meant so much to them.

"I jest don't know what I'll do without you and Nola," Cassie told Ellen. "If they's any other way, we'd spend the rest of our lives here. But Joshua says he has to go and help his ma."

"Of course he does," Ellen replied sadly, "and you won't miss us any worse than we'll miss you. I do wish you could've stayed until the baby come, though. I was lookin' forward to bein' there and helpin' you out."

"I wisht we was too," Cassie said, patting her swelling stomach. "This time will be different from the other, thanks to you and yore family. This time I know everything will be jest right. I want ye to know, if'n hits a girl, I'm a' gonna name her Ellen. That is, if hits alright with you."

"Oh Cassie, I'd be honored," said Ellen happily. "You just take care and be happy. That's what all of us want."

Before he left, Joshua suggested to the parents of his students, "I think you could look a long time and go a far piece before you found a teacher for your children that would do a better job than Nola Johnston. She's been my strong right arm these three years I've been here, and this last year she's done as much teaching as I have. She has a good command of grammar and surpasses me in Latin. I know she's young, but she's dependable and commands the respect of her pupils. Furthermore, she has a personal interest in the school, like you do. It's not usual to have a female teacher, but I urge you to consider offering her the position."

"How old is Nola, Will?" asked Jesse Cole.

"She'll be eighteen on her next birthday. I think I'll excuse myself from this debate. I don't think it'd be proper for me to take part. I know you will do what you think is best for the school."

"I reckon you got as much say, or more'n the rest of us," Jacob McGinty said. "I think we ought to go ahead and ask Nola to be the teacher, and I doubt anybody would object."

A chorus of "yeses" greeted Jacob's proposal, and so it was decided that Nola Johnston would be the new teacher. Since she would not need the house they had built for the schoolmaster, the group also decided to raise the salary to $12.00 a month.

Nola was thrilled at the opportunity and accepted with great enthusiasm. The whole Johnston family was happy for Nola, with the possible exception of Willie, who grumbled, "Now I got to be bossed by Nola at school, too. It's bad enough puttin' up with her sass at home. Papa, couldn't I quit school now? I've learned all I need to know."

"No indeed, Willie. Not only will you complete another year of school here at home, but I have been inquiring into the possibility of enrolling you in an academy over in Buncombe County. They have a fine Presbyterian school there called the Newton Academy."

Willie paled at the thought of spending more years in school, but he decided not to push the issue right then. He had inherited a love for the land and wanted nothing more than to own his own farm.

Nola's transition from helper to teacher did not prove difficult. Female teachers were almost unheard of, but because the children all knew her, she had no difficulty being accepted by most of the students. Sam McGinty was the one exception.

"I'll not set in the room and be treated like a boy by her," he told John. "I'm a grown man, not a schoolboy. I reckon I'm done with schools. Think I'll just take my fiddle and make a little music till somethin' better comes along."

When Sam did not appear at school for several days, Nola inquired of John if Sam were sick.

"Well, you might say so," John replied with a twinkle in his eye. "He just seems to have got sick of the whole business of schoolin'.

Says he ain't comin' no more. Says he's just gonna take his fiddle and make music for a spell."

Nola stormed home that day and said to Ellen, "I have never been so all-fired mad in all my life. That Sam McGinty! He's just going to fritter away his life sawing on that fiddle of his. I know what's wrong. He just can't stand the thoughts of a female teacher. Thinks he's too high and mighty to listen to anything a woman can teach him. Well, just let him go. See if I care!"

Ellen listened to her in amusement and said, "Well, for someone who don't care, you sure are kickin' up a big fuss. Maybe there's more to Sam's reluctance to attend school than a female teacher."

Nola looked at her in amazement and asked, "What other reason could there be? Why, Sam's as smart as I am. He could maybe be smarter if he'd ever study a little. What are you talking about?"

"Did it ever occur to you that it might not be just the fact that there's a female teacher, but it might be who the female teacher is?"

"Why, Sam has always liked me," Nola replied in astonishment. "At least I always thought he did. You know how many times he used to come over to get me to help him with his Latin, and just last week at the Meeting House he told me he thought I was the smartest girl in the class. He even gave Zac a whipping that time he put that nasty old frog in my lunch bucket."

"Nola, you're a grown woman. Hasn't it ever occurred to you that Sam might care more for you than just as a friend? I think Sam is sufferin' from somethin' called male pride. I think he probably wants you to see him as a man and not as a schoolboy."

As the meaning of Ellen's words sank in on Nola, she blushed and dashed from the room. She ran out the door and up the mountain path, not stopping until she reached the haven of the rock. There she sank down, out of breath. She lay there for a long time, trying to sort out the new feelings crowding in on her. As she thought back to her recent encounters with Sam, she began to remember seemingly accidental touches of his hand on hers. A new wave of heat suffused her body.

What a baby he must think I am, she thought. *I never one time thought of him except as a friend. What makes me feel differently about him now? Is this the way you're supposed to feel when you're a woman? If it is, I don't like it—feeling all hot and sweaty like this. Oh, I hate you, Sam McGinty! I'm not ready to grow up yet.*

Nola lay for some time before she felt like she was ready to return home. Guilty thoughts of Ellen who was expecting her baby within the month, struggling with supper by herself made her decide to go home. Nola hurried back down the mountain.

As Nola entered the kitchen, she glanced at Ellen, expecting rebuke for her abrupt flight. Ellen continued her supper preparations and said mildly, "You can set the table now, Nola. Your papa will be home soon, and he'll be hungry for his supper. Martha should be through with her churnin' by now, and she can help you."

Grateful that she was not going to have to discuss Sam with her mother, Nola busied herself in the kitchen. She was so preoccupied with her own thoughts that she failed to notice that Ellen was moving slower than usual until she heard her gasp, then cry out in pain. Nola rushed to her, and all other thoughts left her as she saw her mother standing at the table, gripping it and hanging on for dear life. Her face was ashen, and great beads of sweat stood out on her forehead.

"Get your Papa," she gasped. "My time has come."

Nola pulled a chair up and helped Ellen seat herself before she ran outside and called to Martha, "Run quick and get Papa. Tell him to hurry. It's Mama."

She rushed back to her mother in time to see her sliding to the floor in a faint. She eased her down on the floor and raised her feet on a low stool as her father had taught her to do. Then she ran for a quilt to cover her. She dipped a cloth in the bucket of water by the back door, wrung it out, and pressed it to Ellen's forehead. She was alarmed to see how pale Ellen was and was ready to run for Will herself when Ellen moaned.

"Mama, Mama, can you hear me? Oh please, Mama, wake up."

Ellen slowly regained consciousness and opened her eyes. "Don't look so scared, Nola. I just fainted for a minute. Help me up to the bed. I don't want to have this baby a' layin' on the kitchen floor."

With Nola half carrying her, they made their way to Ellen's bed. Nola helped her mother remove her clothes and slip a gown over her head. Ellen lay back and involuntarily cried out as another pain wrenched her body.

Will came through the door, taking the situation in at a glance as he told Nola, "Get my bag for me, and then set some water to boil. Get a clean sheet from the closet, and then you and Martha keep the little ones out. You stay close by, though, because I'm

going to need your help. The baby is early, and we won't have
time to send for Aunt Addie. It will be just you and me, girl. Do
you think you can do it?"

"Yes, Papa, I'll do my best. You know I helped Mama with Cassie's baby."

"Yes, I remember, and she said you did a fine job, too. Now do
what I told you, and then get back in here as quickly as you can.
Be sure Martha gets a blanket ready for the baby. Tell her to have it
warm, and have Willie bring the cradle down from the loft. I was
going to get it down tomorrow, but it looks like I delayed too
long."

The labor was not simple for Ellen this time, and she struggled
all night long and well up into the next evening before the baby
was born. During the last month the baby had turned and was
wedged bottom first in her pelvis. Try as he could, Will had not
been able to turn it. Ellen became weaker with each passing hour,
and Will began to fear for her life as well as the baby's. Finally, in
desperation he took a knife, boiled it thoroughly, and cut Ellen
enough to allow the baby to emerge.

Nola took the baby boy from Will and wrapped him in the
warmed blanket. She carefully wiped his face and cleared his
throat and mouth as Will told her. The baby hesitated a moment
and then gave a loud, lusty cry. Nola looked at her father and
smiled tearfully.

"Come take the baby, Martha," she called. "Papa needs me to
help him with Mama."

Ellen was bleeding profusely and Will packed her to try and
stop the flow. He sewed up the area he had cut and then tried to
get her to take some sweetgum tea. She was so weak she could
swallow only a few drops. All that night and the next day he and
Nola took turns sitting with Ellen, trying to get some nourish-
ment into her. Finally, three days after the baby was born, she
began to improve. The baby was big and healthy and was beginning to tire of the sugar water Nola had fixed for him. When Will
laid him at Ellen's breast, he nursed hungrily.

"What shall we name this little man, Ellen?" Will asked her.
"From the size of him, perhaps we should call him Goliath."

"I think not, Will," Ellen replied softly. "Instead, let's call him
for the giant slayer. Let's call him David."

"Very well, David it is," said Will, "but I'm of a mind to put the
name of Elisha, my great-grandfather's name, with it. Welcome to
this family, David Elisha Johnston."

Ellen was slow recovering from the birth of this baby, and for the first time in her life she was not back up doing her own housekeeping within a week. It was almost a month before she was able to do anything other than care for herself and the baby.

David Elisha Johnston was the last child born to Ellen and Will.

TWENTY-SEVEN

Nola had found her niche in life. She settled down to the routine of school as if she were born to it. Her days were divided between teaching and helping Martha with the household chores. Ellen was regaining her strength slowly, and it took all their efforts to help with the younger children and keep the household running.

Social opportunities were rare, and unless there was a cabin or barn raising, the only other place young couples could meet was the Sunday gatherings at the meeting house.

John McGinty had begun to pay quiet, but consistent, court to Nola. John was almost the antithesis of his brother Sam, quiet and steady where Sam was brash and given to wanderlust. Since completing his schooling, he had taken over the majority of the work from his father. He seemed as content with his role in life as Nola was with hers.

John had admired Nola for a long time, but had never dared approach her because of his painful shyness. When he finally summoned up enough courage to ask Nola if he could call on her, she quietly agreed to see him.

"He's so shy I was afraid if I refused to see him, he might get scared back in his hole and never come out again," she told Ellen. "I like John. He's easy to talk to, and I feel very comfortable with him."

"Not a very romantic beginning," remarked Will when Ellen related the conversation to him. "I remember how tongue-tied and downright scared I was every time I talked to you those first weeks we were seeing each other. I was so struck by you I didn't know what I was saying half the time. I sure wouldn't describe the way I felt about you as 'comfortable.'"

"Well, I always thought you was right bold," teased Ellen. "Maybe Nola's feelings will change toward John. Sometimes it takes awhile for love to grow. I'm sure glad it's John payin' her court instead of Sam. He's turned into a wild one."

"That young man can't seem to settle on what he wants to do," said Will, shaking his head. "He's jumped from one thing to another in the last two years. Half the time he's off gallivanting around the countryside making music with that fiddle of his. He's got quite a reputation with the women, too. He is a handsome looking man."

"Humph, red hair and a fancy handlebar moustache won't put food on the table," said Ellen. "I hear tell they call him 'Fiddlin' Sam.' John may not be as handsome, but he's sure steady. The woman that marries Sam might as well pack her a tent with her dowry."

John saw Nola as often as he could manage it, and they slipped into a quiet relationship. He often managed to drop by the schoolhouse about the time Nola finished up her day's work and gave her a ride home in his buggy.

The buggy was his one vanity. He had saved his money for a long time before he was able to buy it. The hood was fine black leather, and he spent many hours soaping and rubbing it until it gleamed. When he hooked it up to his black mare, he cut quite a handsome figure.

Sam occasionally teased John about loaning it to him, saying, "Brother John, with my looks and that black mare and buggy, there isn't a girl in this whole county that wouldn't give her eye teeth to go out with me."

John just grinned quietly and said, "Why, brother Sam, you don't need my buggy. All you need is that fiddle and your gift of gab. You better just leave the buggy to old slowpokes like me."

Nola had been teaching for almost two years and had seen Sam only at a distance since he left school. Thomas Mann asked for help to raise a new barn, and when it was finished he declared they would have a dance to put all others to shame. Sam was one of the music makers at the dance.

The Johnston family came to the dance together, but it was understood that Nola would meet John there. As the evening progressed, Sam eyed Nola, speculating on whether or not she would dance with him. Several times he caught her looking at him, but when he tried to catch her eye, she became completely absorbed with what John was saying to her.

Sam did not lack for attention from the girls. He was usually surrounded by several vying for his attention. He did nothing to discourage their interest. This evening though, he felt himself drawn more and more to the dark-eyed, slender girl with his brother.

Nola had arranged her dark chestnut brown hair in a bun on top of her head, with tendrils of curls escaping to frame her face. The blue calico dress she wore emphasized her tiny waist as it flared out from the fitted bodice into a full gathered skirt.

"If she wasn't with John, I'd just steal that little old school teacher," he told his friend Jim Andrews. "Don't reckon he's got no official claim on her, though. What do you say, Jim? Will you take the next set for me? I think I'll see if she'll dance with me."

"Sure, go ahead, Sam. She can't do anything worse than say no," Andrews laughed.

Sam approached John and Nola and said, "How about dancing the next set with me, *teacher?* I'll show you how a master dancer does it. Old John here can't hold a candle to me when it comes to promenadin' and sashayin' around the garden gate. That is, if John will let you."

Nola flushed and laughed at Sam's brashness. "Well, maybe a little old school teacher might not be able to keep up with you. I guess I could try, though."

Giving John a mock bow, Sam drew Nola's arm through his and led her to the middle of the floor where the dancers were forming a circle.

John flushed angrily but said nothing. He was a study in black, from his black hair and beard to the dark scowl on his face. He stared darkly at his brother as he whirled Nola off into the square dance.

The band struck up "Shady Grove," and the couples began a complicated set of dance steps. When the set was completed, John started out to claim Nola, but Sam pulled her with him up to the platform where the band was playing. He leaned over and whispered something to Jim Andrews, then drew Nola back out onto the floor.

The band began playing, "Over the River Charley." This was a half dance, half kissing game. Sam entered into it with whole-hearted abandon, singing the words and punctuating them with kisses to Nola's flaming cheeks.

Hit's over the river to feed my sheep,
Hit's over the river, Charley;
Hit's over the river to feed my sheep,
And see my lonesome darling.

You stole my partner, to my dislike,
You stole my partner, to my dislike,
You stole my partner, to my dislike,
And also my dear darling.

I'll have her back before daylight,
I'll have her back before daylight,
I'll have her back before daylight,
And kiss my own dear darling.

Barely pausing for breath, the players launched into another tune which was a mock game of marriage:

All around the ring so straight,
Go choose the one to be your mate.

Law, law, law, what a choice you've made!
Better in the grave you had a-been laid.

Kiss the bride and kiss her sweet;
Now you rise upon your feet.

A furious John snatched Nola from Sam and propelled her off the floor and out the door before she realized what was happening. Once outside, he shook her and said, "How dare you embarrass me like that in front of everybody! Makin' a spectacle of yourself a' flouncin' around and a' showin' your ankles to anybody that wanted to look. You understand right now, Missy, that no wife of mine is goin' to act so unseemly!"

"John McGinty," exclaimed Nola, "how dare you talk to me that way. And what do you mean 'no wife of yours?' What ever made you think I'd consent to be the wife of such a mean hateful man like you? Besides, I couldn't help myself—it was that Sam throwing me around like that. Why didn't you put a stop to it if you was so all-fired jealous?"

"Jealous? Me? I tell you right now, Nola, I'll have no woman that I have to be jealous of. And as for that Sam—I'll settle with him later, never you fear."

Nola drew herself up to her full five feet and told John coldly, "It appears to me that you've been putting the cart before the horse, Mr. McGinty, assuming that I'd be interested in marrying you. I think that before we both say things we'll regret, you had better leave me be. When you have had time to control your temper, maybe I will discuss this with you. Until then, I do not think I wish to see you."

Nola turned and went back inside, looking for Martha and Willie. Ellen and Will had left earlier with the younger children and had not witnessed Nola's embarrassment. Grabbing her brother and sister, Nola beat a hasty retreat for home. Willie and Martha were hard put to keep up with her as she half ran along the path home.

When she and Martha were in bed that night, she told Martha, "Men—I hate them! You'd have thought I had asked that old Sam to dance instead of him asking me. I'm a good notion to never speak to either one of them again."

"Well, I don't know about you, but I sure do think that Sam cuts a fine figure on the dance floor. And, oh, Nola, you did make the handsomest couple that ever I did see."

"Humph," Nola snorted, "pretty is as pretty does, and there wasn't nothing pretty about either one of the McGinty boys tonight. Anyhow, let's forget it and go to sleep. I've got to get up early tomorrow."

Martha sighed and rolled over to dream of flying skirts and singing fiddles interspersed with handsome young men with red hair and handlebar moustaches fighting with dark-haired men with long black beards.

Nola was a long time wooing sleep that night, and when she did sleep, it was fitful and disquieting. The faces of Sam and John insinuated themselves into her dreams. One looking disapproving and angry and the other mocking and laughing, singing:

"Kiss the bride and kiss her sweet;
Now you rise upon your feet."

Sam's hands kept haunting her dreams as she saw them drawing the bow across his fiddle. She felt his hands on her waist and holding her hand as they danced, hands that were smooth and soft with long delicate fingers. Then she saw John's hands, rough and callused from the weather and hard work. She turned first to one and then the other as they both reached out to her, beckoning her.

TWENTY-EIGHT

Nola got through the next few days on nervous energy and sheer determination. She heard nothing from John or Sam, except for the gossip eagerly relayed to Martha by the other girls. Sam realized it would be foolish of him to confront John before he had a chance to cool off and went to Asheville for a few days with his friend Jim Andrews to inquire about a job.

John's sister Mary told Martha, "Nobody dasts to speak to John. He's like a big old thunderhead ready to break open. He's up and gone to the fields before anybody else gets up and don't come in till we're all in bed."

Nola was almost as bad as she went about her work, tight-lipped and with none of her usual good temper. The children in her classes soon learned to tend strictly to their schoolwork, as she used her paddle liberally.

Ellen questioned Willie about what had happened, but for once he was reluctant to talk. After she suggested that maybe he'd better "speak" with his Papa, he told her the whole story.

She told Will, "I don't know what to say to Nola. Maybe I'd better not say anything. If I tell her how I really feel about Sam, it might just push her over to his side. On the other hand, I'm disappointed in John. He should know Nola better by now than to think she encouraged Sam."

"Seems to me you'd better wait till she asks for your advice," Will replied. "If either of them two comes around here, though, they're going to have to answer to me. I won't have Nola's good name jeopardized by their behavior."

Two days later a near tragedy overshadowed the situation between Nola and John. Ellen had taken the younger children to the mountain behind the rock to gather chestnuts and black walnuts. She cautioned James and John several times to keep a sharp eye on David, but they found a grapevine to swing on and soon forgot to watch him.

When Ellen called them to gather their bags up and get ready to go home, they could find David nowhere. They called and searched until Ellen began to fear the dark would catch them all. With sinking heart, she headed for home as fast as she could. When she got within shouting distance, she began to call for Will.

"It's David," she sobbed, throwing herself in Will's arms, "we looked and looked and we couldn't find him anywhere. I'm a' feared he's lost. Oh Will, what will I do? I can't lose another one of my babies. I just couldn't stand it."

"Hush, Ellen. I'll find him, don't you worry. He's a sturdy little fellow. He'll be all right. Go to the house now and send Willie to help me. Send Nola and Martha to the neighbors for help. Tell them to come to the rock, and we'll spread out from there. Tell them to hurry; there's not much daylight left. Have Nola tell Jacob McGinty to bring some torches in case we don't find him before dark."

Ellen did as Will bid her and sent Martha and Nola to the McGinty's. The first person they encountered was John. He paled when he saw her, but she gave him no time to say anything.

Brushing past him, she rushed into the room where the family was just sitting down to their evening meal. "Papa says to come quick. David's lost on the mountain. Bring torches and hurry to the rock as fast as you can. Please!"

Without hesitation, Jacob began preparing torches to go to Will's aid. John, Thomas, and Sam, who had just that day returned, also grabbed coats and hats to join him.

"You go on home to your mama, Nola. I'll go tell the Manns to come," Pearl said.

By the time Will reached the rock, there were thirty men and boys on their way to join in the search. Starting from the point where the twins had last seen David, they fanned out in six search parties, trying to cover every inch of the area.

As the temperature began to fall and the light faded, Will's hopes sunk lower and lower. There were so many precipices and streams where a child could fall that it began to look hopeless that he could survive in the dark. Only Ellen's frantic tears kept Will searching long past dark.

Finally Jacob told him, "Will, I'm afraid somebody will get hurt if we keep on. I think it's best if we make camp and rise early in the morning."

They returned to the rock and built a fire to ward off the night's chill. Will began a long vigil. He could not sleep. Every time he closed his eyes, he saw the face of his youngest child and heard Ellen's frantic pleas to find her baby. The more uncomfortable he became, the more he agonized over the child stumbling around in the cold in his thin jacket. By morning the temperature had fallen to freezing.

At first light they were up and ready to go again, tired but determined, their hearts aching for this man who had always been the first to help in time of sickness or need. There was one exception. Sam McGinty had slipped away during the night to the comfort of his own bed.

The fall fogs of the mountains cast an eerie light as the men began their search that morning. In some places they were forced to drop to their knees as they searched and called for the child. The laurel thickets were almost impenetrable in many places. Had it not been for a small piece of cloth torn from his trousers, they might not have found David.

John was combing a steep hillside along with his search group when a piece of brown homespun stuck on a bramble caught his eye. On further examination, he could see signs of where something or someone had tunneled through the undergrowth. He dropped to his knees and pushed through the opening. He found David curled up sound asleep. The child was scratched on every exposed area, and his face was streaked with tears that had washed rivulets through the dirt and grime on his face. He was curled up in a tight ball and had found what comfort he could through the thumb stuck in his mouth.

John woke him as gently as he could calling, "David, David, wake up, boy. I've come to take you home to your mama."

David looked into the face of Nola's friend and silently extended his arms to him.

John backed out of the bushes and shouted, "I've found him! Glory be, I've found him, and he's safe."

Will rushed to them and, with tears streaming down his face, took him from John. David wrapped his arms around his neck and said, "Papa? I hungry."

Laughing and crying at the same time, Will started home. The neighbors followed, slapping each other on the back and congratulating John for finding the boy.

Ellen had neither slept nor stopped her pacing during the long night. The twins had finally cried themselves to sleep. Nola and Martha were both asleep in chairs near their mother, finally yielding to exhaustion.

Ellen had begun the night by bargaining with God. "Oh God, if you'll just spare him, I promise I won't never have another bad thought nor say another cross word to nobody. Just take me instead. Let me die, but let my little David live."

After a time she began pleading with him, "Please God, please don't take my David, too. You done took Tildy, ain't that enough? Ain't I paid enough? Why do you have to take this baby, too? God, you know I can't stand it if you take him. You can save him. You can do anything, so just send him back to me, please."

Finally, in the early hours just before dawn, she reached a quiet acceptance. She fell to her knees and bowed her head, praying, "Lord, we've walked together these many years now, and it's took me all this time to admit I'm just a pore human bein' that don't know what's good for me and mine. I got to rely on you. I got to believe that whatever comes my way, I only got to ask and you'll be there for me. We both know I never could've got through that awful time after Tildy died if you hadn't of helped me. Now I got to ask you to help me again. I ain't makin' no more promises nor makin' no more threats. I ain't beggin', just askin' you humble as I know how for your strength to bear whatever is comin'. If David don't make it through this, then I got to ask you to let me lean on you again. I got to ask you to give me the wisdom to help Will and the children through it, too. You know me, Lord, and you know how weak I am without you."

After her prayer, Ellen felt an inner serenity. She knew that the burden had been lifted from her shoulders and placed on stronger ones. She rose and opened the front door just as Will came down the mountain trail triumphantly bearing David on his shoulders. He looked at her in amazement. He had expected to find her hysterical, but instead she was serene and calm. She took her child from him and raised her eyes to the heaven, thanking God for his goodness.

Ellen called Nola and Martha, "Get up, girls, and cook up some breakfast for these men who have found our David and brought him home safe."

David looked at her with solemn eyes and said, "Mama, I hungry."

She laughed joyfully and hugged him to her breast. "Yes, my baby, I know you're hungry, and you're gonna be fed. I'm gonna feed you the biggest breakfast you ever saw."

David was none the worse for his experience, although he did show a tendency to cling to his mother's skirts for a time. Will would remember with gratitude the way his neighbors rallied around him but, try as he would, he could not forget that Sam McGinty had not stuck out the long night with the rest of them.

Nola stirred and opened her eyes, staring into those of her great-grand-daughter's. "I should have known then that he couldn't be counted on," she said. "It was there as plain as the nose on my face and I just ignored it. Serves me right for being so blind!"

"What on earth are you talking about, Grandma?" asked Cindy. "Who is it you can't count on? You know we're all here for you anytime you need us. What do you want?"

"Nothing that's not long gone, honey," replied the old woman.

TWENTY-NINE

Amonth went by before John got up enough nerve to call on Nola again. He appeared one snowy Sunday afternoon while she was sitting by the window piecing a new quilt with Martha. The day had been overcast, but in the early afternoon the sun broke through and they were taking advantage of the light streaming in through the windows. The pattern, called Flying Geese, was complicated, and Nola and Martha were both absorbed in fitting the pieces together and did not see John as he approached. His knock startled them.

Nola opened the door to a shamefaced John. "Won't you come in, John?" she asked quietly.

"No, I wondered if you would walk a ways with me, Nola. Just where yore pa has cleared the path to the barn. There's somethin' I need to say to you."

Nola picked up her shawl and wrapped it around her. The snow made everything seem warmer somehow after the gray iciness of the skies of the past few days. Everything was still coated in snow, and large chunks were only now beginning to fall from the tree limbs.

John kicked snow out of the path as they walked and began to speak hesitantly, "Nola, I know I was wrong thinkin' you'd be anything less than a lady. I come to beg you to forgive me. I'm mighty ashamed of the way I acted."

"Oh, John, of course I forgive you. We've been friends too long to let one silly quarrel make a difference," Nola answered quickly.

"It's not your friendship I'm askin' for, Nola," John said earnestly. "'Course I want to be your friend too, but I'm hopin' you

163

feel more for me than friendship. I didn't mean for it to come out the way it did that night, but I guess it ain't no secret that I want you to be my wife. I'm hopin' you feel the same about me."

Nola stopped and looked up at John. The words he had spoken should have made her happy. Instead, she felt a deep sense of sadness. She waited a long moment before she answered him.

"John, I do love you. It's not a marryin' kind of love, though. I love you like a friend, and I wouldn't ever want to do anything to change that. You're a fine man, John, and any woman ought to be proud to be your wife, but I'm just not the right one for you. I'd be miserable, and soon I'd make you miserable, too, if we married. To tell the truth, I don't know who or what I want right now except to teach my children."

"I can wait, Nola, if it's time you want. You said you love me like a friend, and that's a start. Let me come callin' on you again. We always had a good time, and I am a very patient man. I can wait as long as I have to."

"No, John. It wouldn't be fair of me to give you any false hopes. I want to be your friend again, but I don't think you should come calling on me anymore except as a friend."

She looked steadily into his eyes, not wavering in her decision.

"Ah, Nola," he cried, "are you sure? Ain't there no hope at all?"

Sadly she shook her head. She reached one hand out and laid it gently on his. With a cry, he wrenched away and turned back across the snowy field. Her heart ached for him, and her eyes filled with tears as she watched him walk away, his shoulders slumped in dejection.

Nola returned slowly to the house, sad that their friendship had ended this way. Martha took one look at her face and decided it was not the time for questions. Nola went to their room and threw herself across the bed.

Why does somebody always have to get hurt? she thought bitterly. *Oh how I hate that Sam McGinty for causing all of this. I hope I never see him again.*

But the thought of never seeing Sam again brought an unhappy frown to her face.

THIRTY

Sam lounged against the wagon, one shiny, booted foot propped on the spokes of the wheel. His wide-brimmed hat was pushed rakishly on the back of his head, and he was chewing on a straw dangling from the corner of his mouth. His black string tie was arranged carefully in a neat bow against the white of his soft linsey shirt. He idly twisted the ends of his handlebar moustache as he watched Nola approach the wagon. His gaze took in the slender shape of her body as the wind whipped her dress around her. He observed how the pleated dress front emphasized her high-breasted figure. Soft, brown tendrils framed her oval-shaped face, making a perfect setting for the dark eyes, pointed chin, and small cupid's bow mouth.

They had been seeing each other for nearly three months. Sam had never asked John what transpired between him and Nola, and John never volunteered any information. When it became obvious that John was no longer calling on Nola, Sam began to appear periodically at the school when it was time for Nola to go home.

The first afternoon he came, he used the pretext of looking for some good-sized locust trees to cut for his father. After that, he made no excuses but just appeared with horse and wagon to drive Nola home.

Ellen watched the progress of the romance in tight-lipped silence, hoping that Nola's common sense would prevail before she became too deeply involved with Sam.

"In my heart I know he won't bring her nothin' but grief," she lamented to Will. "Why can't she see through him?"

"Well, he does appear to have settled down some," Will said. "I guess she's hoping he's changed. Don't worry, though, his kind will slip again. If we oppose him now, it might just make her more determined to see him. Let's just bide our time, and eventually she'll wake up to his faults. She won't go against our wishes, and she sure knows how I feel about him after the cowardly way he acted when David got lost."

"I hope you're right," Ellen sighed. "I just don't think Sam's a man Nola could depend on. He's here one minute and gone the next. A dependable man don't act like that. He's shore a charmer, though. Sometimes I think he knows just what you want to hear."

"I know, but if a man isn't as good as his word, there's not much to him."

This was the last day of the school year, and as Nola closed up the classroom for the last time, she had a sudden feeling of sadness. *Why, I think this is the last time I'm going to be in this room as the teacher,* she thought. She impatiently brushed away the tears that welled up in her eyes.

"End of the year blues," she told herself as she closed and locked the doors. When she saw Sam waiting for her by the wagon, all unhappy thoughts left her and she rushed eagerly to him.

"Well, little teacher, are you glad school's out and all the young'uns are gone?" he drawled.

"Yes and no," she said. "In a way I'm glad the year's over, but in another way I'm sad, too. There's nothing I'd rather do than teach, but I am kind of tired. I had the funniest feeling I'd never be back again when I closed the door."

"I'd get tired real quick tryin' to teach a bunch of long-headed young'uns," he teased. "Ain't you glad I quit so's you wouldn't have to try to teach me? You'd really be tired!"

"Maybe I'm getting spring fever," she laughed. "Don't you dare tell Mama I said that. She'd probably give me a dose of sulphur and molasses."

"Forget about school for a while. Let's ride up the mountain a' ways. It's too pretty a day to be settin' in a schoolroom or anywheres else."

"Oh, Sam, nobody else I know makes me feel as good as you do. I can be lower than a snake's belly and you always come up with something to make me laugh," Nola said.

"That's me! Old fiddlin' Sam, your funnin' man," he teased her. "And you're my sweet Nola, my little schoolmarm. I know what you need. You need for me to sing you one of my guaranteed, bona-fide, never fail, cheerin' up songs."

He began singing one of their favorite tunes, "Cindy," and substituting Nola for Cindy in the song. Soon he had Nola laughing and singing with him.

They came to a secluded spot where they had picnicked the previous week, and Sam pulled the horse off the trail into the grove.

"Come on Nola, let's walk for a piece," he said.

"All out of songs, Sam?" she teased him.

"Well, there's one more I'd like to sing to you," he said smiling. "I've never sung it to a girl before. I think it's an old Scottish ballad. Leastways that's where Pa said it come from."

Taking both of her hands in his, he sang tenderly in his deep clear voice:

> *I've been gatherin' flowers in the meadow*
> *To wreathe around your head,*
> *But so long you have kept me a-waitin',*
> *They're all withered and dead.*
>
> *I've been gatherin' flowers on the hillside*
> *To bind them on your brow,*
> *But so long you have kept me waitin',*
> *The flowers are faded now.*
>
> *O many a mile with you I've wandered,*
> *And many an hour with you I've spent,*
> *Till I thought your heart was mine forever,*
> *But now I know it was only lent.*
>
> *Now I will seek some distant river,*
> *And there I'll spend my days and years;*
> *I'll eat no food but the green willow,*
> *And drink no water but my tears.*

"Oh, Sam, that was beautiful. I've never heard it before."

"I meant them words, Nola," he told her earnestly. "If you keep me waitin' much longer, I'll just wither up and die like the flowers. I've stood all this courtin' business about as long as I can. I want us to get married. I want you to be mine forever."

"Why, Sam McGinty, do you mean to tell me you're ready to give up your fiddlin' and dancin' and settle down?"

"I'm serious, Nola," Sam said. "Ever since we were young'uns in school together, I've wanted you for my own. I nearly went out of my mind with jealousy when you was keepin' company with John. Tell me you love me as much as I love you."

"I do love you, Sam, with all my heart. I know now why I couldn't love John the way he wanted me to. It's always been you, Sam. Ever since you stood up for me when Zac beat me in that spelling match."

"Does this mean you'll marry me then?"

"Yes, I'll marry you, Sam, and I'll have your children and be your wife for the rest of my life. It's what I want, more than anything!"

He drew her into his arms and kissed her, caressing her and pulling her body tightly against his. Then he picked her up and carried her back to the wagon where he sat her up on the seat.

"Whoopee!" he yelled, climbing in beside her. "Let's go tell your folks and mine. I want everybody to know you're promised to me."

"Wait, Sam," she said, "I think you'd better let me tell Mama first. Papa will expect you to ask him for my hand—it's the way he thinks things should be done. I'll talk to Mama tonight, and then when you come after preaching Sunday, you can talk to Papa."

"Alright, we'll do it your way," he replied, "but I'm tellin' you now, nothin' or nobody will keep me from marryin' you."

"Oh, Sam, I'm so happy. Just think, we'll be together forever. Just like it says in the Bible, till death alone parts us. I've given my heart to you for good. You feel the same way about me, don't you?"

"Of course, darlin'. I wouldn't have it any other way. You're the only girl I'll ever love," he assured her.

They parted at the gate and Nola was hard put to contain her happiness. She wanted to shout to everyone that she would soon be Sam McGinty's wife.

"That's all I ever wanted," Nola told Alma. "I just wanted him to keep his promise. I was always his—even after he left. That other one wasn't any better than a whore, I tell you. He could have said all the words to her he wanted to, and it still wouldn't have set aside his promises to me. Till death us do part!' That's what we both promised, and I kept my vows. He's the one who broke them, not me!"

"Please, Grandma, don't upset yourself," Alma begged. "Forget sad memories today and enjoy your party."

She fluffed up Nola's pillows and straightened the ribbons on her gown, shaking her head in helplessness at Cindy.

THIRTY-ONE

The next night Nola went to Ellen, planning to pave the way for Sam's talk with her father. She found it difficult to broach the subject, and talked of many things before she got up the nerve to say what was on her mind.

Finally, she swallowed hard and with the words tumbling over each other said, "I have something very important to tell you, Mama. Yesterday Sam asked me to marry him, and tomorrow after preaching he wants to ask Papa for my hand. I—I hope you'll speak to Papa for us."

"Oh, Nola," Ellen exclaimed unhappily, "surely you don't mean this!"

"I know Papa holds it against Sam because he left the mountain that night when David was lost, but Sam told me he had to leave to tend some business. Besides, he meant to come back early the next day and help hunt again, but they found David before he got there. Please, Mama, I love him so much! Won't you please speak to Papa?"

Ellen looked sadly at Nola, shaking her head. "Why do you choose this man over his brother, Nola? You've never been a flighty girl, and yet here you choose this flighty man. John is a good steady man, and Sam hops from one crazy scheme to another. How can I ask your papa to give you permission to do somethin' that will only bring you heartache and misery? What on earth can you be thinkin' of, girl?"

"Oh, Mama," Nola cried, "how can marrying the man you love bring you heartache? My heart will break if Papa won't let us marry. I'll never love anybody else. If I can't have Sam, I don't want anybody else. He makes me so happy. John is a fine man, but he's always so serious about everything. Sam makes me see the happy side of things, and he makes me laugh. He makes me feel so special, too. He makes me feel like the most beautiful woman in the world. I could never marry any man but Sam."

"I can tell you're determined, Nola," Ellen said sadly. "I'll speak to your papa, but Sam will have to plead his own case. Your papa only sees right and wrong, and what Sam done that night was wrong. He'll have to convince Will himself."

That night Ellen told Will about her conversation with Nola. The news brought an explosion from Will that left no doubt about how he felt about Sam McGinty marrying Nola.

"Give my Nola to Sam McGinty?" Will shouted. "Not while I've got a breath left in my body! Why that low-down good-for-nothing fiddler! How dare he have the nerve to think he's good enough to ask for my girl's hand. He's not even fit to clean the dirt off her shoes! No—and that's final, woman. I will not hear any more of this, and if I catch him sneaking around here again, I'll give him a good load of buckshot in the seat of his britches! What could Nola be thinking of to even consider such a thing? I should have put my foot down before now."

Ellen listened to Will's tirade, and when he had finished, she laid her hand on his and said, "I'm not happy about this either, Will, but if Nola thinks she wants Sam for her husband, we're goin' to have to at least hear him out. After all, if she sets her mind to it, what can we do? She's of age to do as she pleases."

"No! I say no, and that's my final word. Nola would never defy me. She loves me and respects my opinions. You know we've always had a special bond between us. She likes the things I like, my medicine and my herbs and the feeling I have for this land. If I hadn't had her when you were so sick after Tildy died, I don't know what I'd have done. Why, she's my first born, Ellen! Nothing . . . nobody can come between a man and his first born. I tell you, the first time she wrapped those tiny fingers around mine, it was the same as wrapping a chain around my heart. We're bound together as sure as God made these mountains. I'll hear no more about this. That man will not have my Nola."

When Ellen told Nola the next day what Will had said, she burst into tears. "Oh, Mama, how could Papa be so cruel? I tell you Sam is good, and I love him. It's not fair of Papa—the least he could do is talk to Sam. I will marry him. I'd rather have your blessings, but if you won't give them, then I guess it'll just have to be without them."

"Oh, Nola, you know you don't mean that," Ellen exclaimed. "It would break your Papa's heart and mine too if you went against us. Is this what this man has done to you?"

Nola flounced away in silence, and a time of unhappiness began that Ellen had never thought would have been possible in their home. The atmosphere became tense and unhappy, with Nola sulking and moping around teary-eyed all day and Will vacillating between anger and hurt at the rift between Nola and himself. Ellen was caught between the two, trying to talk Will into being more reasonable and begging Nola to have patience. Will Johnston was a man who needed peace and order in his life, and a week of turmoil was more than he could bear. He finally weakened.

"Every time I look at Nola, I remember the night when she was born and I held her in my arms for the first time," he told Ellen. "It seemed a miracle when I realized that I was looking at a little part of myself all wrapped up in that little life. It would purely tear my heart out to lose her. I know she could just run off and marry, and I don't want that. Tell her I'll listen to what Sam has to say, but I'm making no promises."

After services on the following Sunday, Sam pled his case to a stern-faced Will. Sam had thought long and hard about what he could say to win Will over. He knew Nola said she would marry him without her family's blessing, but he also knew things would be easier if he could bring Will around. Too, he had met with unexpected opposition from his own father.

Jacob told him, "Sam, I'll not help you in any way if you go against Will Johnston's wishes. I owe him too big a debt to see him hurt like this. You know if it wasn't for him, I'd a' died from that fall or at best been hoppin' around on one leg. You better make things right or else. You'll be on your own in this."

Sam planned very carefully what he could say to get around Will's opposition. He approached Will respectfully and with none of his usual cockiness.

"Mr. Johnston, first of all I want to tell you I know now what a mistake I made leavin' the night David was lost. What seemed important to me then, don't seem so important now, so I'm offerin' no excuses. I'm just tellin' you if I had it to do over, I'd never act that way again. I can't change what happened. I can only learn from it and tell you I regret it more than anything I've ever done. Next I want you to know that if you won't give your consent for us to marry, I'll leave and never see Nola again. It would tear my heart out, but I won't put myself between Nola and her family. I know we could go ahead and marry, but I also know how much Nola treasures her family, and I know that some day she'd regret what she'd had to give up for me. If you do consent for us to marry, I promise you I'll love and honor her the rest of my life."

Will was surprised at Sam's speech. He had expected defiance, not penitence. He had remained silent during Sam's speech, and he gazed intently at Sam for a time before he replied. Sam returned his look steadily.

"I'll take your words under advisement, Sam, and when I've reached a decision, I'll give you my answer. I want you to know that, although it don't change what you've done, I do believe you're sorry for it. If you learned from it, maybe some good will come of it."

Sam nodded his head grimly.

"I also want you to know there's other reasons Ellen and I object to this match. You have not shown yourself to be dependable and the kind of man that will make a good home for Nola. She's used to having food on the table and people she can depend on. I want to know if you're ready to be that kind of man, or do you think you can still fritter away your time making music?"

"Mr. Johnston, I'm ready to make Nola a home. I've already spoke to my pa about a piece of land, and he says if I get your consent, it's mine. I understand that I've got to earn your trust, and I stand ready to do that. I love Nola with all my heart, and it's my dearest wish to make a home for her."

"Very well, Sam. I'll let you know my decision."

A pale and shaken Sam left without a backward glance. Nola watched from her bedroom window as he got in his buggy and drove away.

Will put on his hat and, without a word to anyone, strode off into the woods. He stayed there most of the afternoon, returning late to a silent evening meal. He did not mention his conversation with Sam to Ellen, and she dared not question him. Neither of the three slept much that night as Will wrestled with his decision.

The next morning he called Nola to him and said, "You know that you are more precious to me and your mother than anything on earth, and if I have seemed harsh or unfair, it is only because we do love you so much. I won't pretend that I'm happy about this match, but if you are still determined, then I will consent to you marrying Sam. I can tell you now that if he had defied me and threatened to run off, I'd have sent him packing right then. However, his promise to abide by my decision says to me that he does love you, and I've got to believe that if you love him, there has to be some worth to the man. I hope I've made the right decision, Nola, for your sake. Now, let's put all of this behind us and get busy. I know your mama well enough to know she's going to have a heap of things for us all to do. Just be happy, daughter, be happy."

Nola threw her arms around him and cried, "Oh, thank you, Papa. My heart has ached to think you were displeased with me. You know I love you and Mama, and I'd be miserable if you couldn't be happy for me now."

As the days passed, the whole household was caught up in Nola's excitement. They all became involved in her plans. Will found out when a preacher would be in the community, and a wedding date was set.

Will and Jacob agreed to give the couple an equal amount of acreage bordering the two properties to build themselves a cabin. Sam set about felling the trees to use and clearing a spot for their home.

Nola already had six quilts in her bridal chest, but Ellen had one more for her. She had made a Double Wedding Ring quilt the previous winter, planning to surprise her at Christmas. She had used scraps from all of Nola's dresses to piece the intricate interlocking rings.

As she looked at the quilt, she pondered over each piece and the different stages of Nola's life they represented.

This little blue calico was her very first apron, she thought to herself. *I recollect that I made her a bonnet to match, and Will said she was the most beautiful thing he'd ever seen.*

As she fingered a deep wine piece, she recalled the camp meeting at Shook's. *This served as her "best dress" for a long time*, she mused. *She was so proud of it. I let it down for two years before she'd give it up. These next prints come from her first school dresses. Law, she was proud of herself that first mornin' her and her papa went up the trail to school. And her papa was proud of her too. Thought she's the smartest one in the class. Never thought then that she'd be the teacher herself some day. That's where these scraps come from. Her first teachin' dress. Oh*

*Lord, where has the time gone? Yesterday she's just a babe stumblin'
around after me. Now she's a growed woman startin' out in her own
home. It's gone too fast.*

Will was doing his own reminiscing as he worked on furniture
for Nola and Sam. He selected his finest piece of oak for the head-
board of the bed. As he pondered what design to put on it, he
chuckled to himself.

*Don't know why I'm wondering, long as it's a mountain flower on it
Nola will be happy,* he thought. *My, but that girl is fond of these wild
flowers growing in the mountains. Bet she's asked me five thousand questions about them. It's hard to pick a favorite, but I bet if I roll the top and
put dogwood blossoms along it she'll be tickled pink. I guess me and her
has tramped hundreds of miles in these hills searching for herbs. She
always managed to come home with a handful of flowers, too.*

He pulled out a piece of red maple left from making Ellen's new
spinning wheel. *Now don't that beat all. I didn't think when I put this
back I'd be using it so soon.*

He sighed and thought, *Just yesterday I was whittling out play-
things for her. I sure wasn't thinking about the day I'd be making spinning wheels.*

Sam's family also was busy helping the couple. Sam was working on chairs. He drilled holes in the green wood of the chair legs
and inserted seasoned hickory rounds in them. "When that green
wood dries, it'll shrink and make a good tight joint," he told his
sister.

"When you get finished," Pearl told him, "me and Mama and
Mary'll weave the bottoms out of them oak splits Mama's been
savin'. These'll look right pretty with that pine table Papa's
makin'. I reckon you and Nola's gonna be fixed up mighty fine.
Do you think she'll let you take yore fiddle with you?" she teased.

"I reckon that fiddle's the first thing I'll be takin'," he answered
her shortly. "I'm just gettin' married, Pearl, not dyin'."

John grudgingly offered to help Sam and his father cut down
the trees for the cabin, but he made no comment about the up-
coming marriage. When the subject came up, he managed to find
somewhere to go.

The days passed swiftly, and almost before she realized it,
Nola's wedding day was there. Ellen's wedding dress, stored in
the chest after Cassie's wedding, had been taken out and carefully
washed and ironed for Nola.

The morning of the wedding Will came in with a special gift for
her. "Nola, I've managed to get you a pair of new-fashioned high

button shoes. They told me these are the latest style for ladies. I hope you'll like them."

"Oh Papa, they're beautiful. What pretty black shiny leather, and they're as soft as kitten's fur. Oh thank you, Papa," Nola said, throwing her arms around his neck.

When she put on the lavender brooch encircled with tiny pearls that Sam had given her and placed the circlet of wild clematis around her dark coronet of braids, Will declared, "Next to your mother, you are the most beautiful bride I have ever laid eyes on. Sam McGinty had better be good to you, or he will answer to me. I know we're supposed to raise our children to make homes of their own some day, but it's a hard thing for a man to give up his daughter. No matter how far you travel from our hearth, a part of you will always belong to us. Be happy, Nola, but do not forget your home."

"Oh, Papa," Nola cried, "no one ever had such a kind and good Papa as I have. I could never forget you and Mama. I just hope I can make as good a home for my family as you and Mama made for us."

When it was Ellen's turn to embrace her, she said, "Daughter, if there's love and respect in your home, it will be happy. You've been a good faithful daughter to us, and now you have to be a good and faithful wife to Sam. In our hearts, you'll always belong to us, but in your heart, now you have to belong to him."

With these words ringing in her ears, Nola stepped forth to the waiting arms of her groom and a new life separate from Ellen and Will. The ceremony was simple, and it seemed to Nola that it only took an instant to step over the threshold from girlhood to womanhood. Sam bundled her into the wagon along with the rest of her belongings that had not been moved to the cabin, and they jolted off down the rough trail to their new home.

Ellen had packed them a supper, but they barely touched it. They carried in their things, and Nola tidied up after the brief meal. The moment Nola had waited for, partly in anticipation and partly in fear, arrived. The moment when she would truly be Sam's wife. She undressed quickly and put on the white cotton gown she and Ellen had made. It was trimmed with lace Ellen had made herself. She stood before him trembling, her eyes glowing with love. Sam looked at her in wonder as she stood framed by the lamplight, her dark chestnut hair streaming down her back.

Sam doused the lamp and tenderly took Nola in his arms. They kissed, and he lifted her in his arms and carried her to bed. At

that moment, all hell broke loose. There was the sound of shriek-
ing and caterwauling, accompanied by the clanging of cow bells
and the banging of pots and pans.

"Sam, what on earth is it?" Nola cried as she threw her arms
around his neck.

"Tarnation and d _____ n!" Sam exclaimed. "I'll kill that no-
good Jim Andrews. He promised me he'd leave us be tonight. I'll
get even with him for this if it takes the rest of my life."

"I don't understand," Nola said. "Who is it and what are they
doing?"

"My poor innocent," Sam laughed, "it's a shivaree—an infare.
Just old Jim and some of my so-called friends' way of celebratin'
our weddin'. They're just yellin' and beatin' on some pots to liven
things up. I don't know why I thought they'd leave me alone,
Lord knows I've been in on my share of 'em. Just lie still, and
maybe they'll get tired and leave when their whiskey runs out."

But this was not to be. When they got no response to their calls
of "Sam, oh Sam, come on out and take your medicine like a
man!" the crowd of boisterous young men forced the door open
and unceremoniously lifted Sam out of his bed. Nola sat big-eyed
and helpless with the bedclothes pulled up to her chin as they
hauled her groom off.

"What are you going to do to him?"

"Why, we're just goin' to take him down the road a piece and
git him all ready fer his weddin' night," laughed Andrews.

With that, they left as noisily as they had arrived, carrying the
protesting Sam with them.

Nola spent an uneasy night, alternating between worrying
about Sam and being mad at him because her wedding night had
been spoiled. When they finally brought him back, the first rays
of the morning light were breaking over the mountain peaks.

"Here's yore groom, Miss Nola," laughed Andrews. "We figger
he's jest about ready fer ye now."

They dumped him roughly on the bed and left amid much
laughter and rough joking. Sam rolled over, gave a sigh, smiled
drunkenly at Nola, and passed out cold.

Nola shook him furiously, but he was too drunk to wake up.
She dropped her face in her hands and sobbed. All the happy
anticipation of the last few days had been ruined, and she felt
cheated and hurt. She cried for a time and then sat up and glared
at the drunken form of her husband snoring in the bed.

"Well, Sam McGinty, this is a fine wedding night. I'm not going to sleep in the bed with a drunk, and I'm sure not going to spend the night on the floor.

She jerked the quilt under him, rolling him off onto the floor. Then she pulled the cover down, crawled into bed, and cried herself to sleep.

THIRTY-TWO

Nola rose around mid-morning. For a moment she forgot where she was, and then memories of the previous night washed over her. She sat up and looked at Sam, still sprawled out on the floor sleeping.

She set her jaw, stepped over his immobile form, and went into the kitchen where she poured water into a pan and rinsed the night's tears from her face.

"If it wasn't so humiliating, I'd just walk off right now and let you wonder where I was, Sam McGinty," she muttered to herself. "I can just hear that Willie now, though, making fun of me for being treated like this on my wedding night. He'd tell everybody in the cove."

She dressed quickly and tied an apron over her dress. She lit the fire they had laid the night before and set a kettle of water over the flame to heat and began preparations for breakfast for herself. She slammed the pots down furiously, not caring that Sam still slept on in the bedroom. Before long she heard him beginning to rouse.

There was a deep moan and then a fit of coughing before he finally stood unsteadily and looked around, trying to remember where he was and what had happened. He staggered into the next room where the ear-splitting, head-thundering sounds were coming from. He was confronted by the cold, rigid back of his bride.

"Oh my G ____ ," he moaned holding his head in both hands as Nola slammed the skillet down on the hearth. "Do you have to shake the rafters every time you set a pot down? My head's a' splittin'."

She turned on him like a cornered mountain bobcat, fire and vengeance shooting from her dark eyes. "I am not shaking the rafters. You must have a hangover from all of your drinking and gallivanting last night. What would you have me do? Maybe you'd rather I just left and went back home, and then you could have it as nice and quiet as you wanted it to be."

He looked at her in disbelief, and then as the events of the night came back to him, with a look of chagrin and shame. "Surely you don't think I wanted to go with them, do you? You saw what they did. They carried me out. I didn't have nothin' to say about it. Oh, Nola, darlin', you know I couldn't help myself. You . . . you ain't mad at me are you, sweetheart?"

"Mad at you?" she asked icily. "Now why would I ever be mad at you for treating me to such a fine wedding night? I'm sure that's what every girl longs for after all the months she's spent getting ready for her wedding. Mad? Me? You can bet your bottom dollar I'm mad at you. If I live to be a hundred, I'll never be any madder than I am right this minute."

"Oh come on now, darlin', let's not get started off like this. I'm sorry. Let's not let it spoil things for us."

"Spoil things? I'm not sure there's going to be any 'things' to spoil between us," she said furiously. "I'm fixing me some of this ham and a biscuit for my breakfast. If you're hungry, you can fix for yourself."

The mention of food caused his stomach to lurch dangerously. "No thanks," he muttered. "I think I'll just walk outside for a minute and get me a little air."

He made a hasty exit, and she smiled tightly as she heard him retching. When he returned later, she had cleaned up the remnants of her breakfast and was furiously scrubbing the kitchen floor.

"Guess I'll work on that garden patch I'm tryin' to clear," he muttered. She did not look up as he left, taking his bushaxe with him.

When Sam returned to the cabin that evening, Nola had put away all of their belongings and was setting the table for supper. They ate a quiet meal, his attempts at conversation having been met with short yeses or nos.

When Nola had washed and put away all of the dishes and run out of excuses for avoiding him, she finally settled across the table from him and picked up her bobbins and began working on a piece of lace.

Sam was strumming softly on his guitar and watching her face as the lamplight played across it.

"I wrote a song for you," he said softly. "I'm not much good with words, but sometimes I can sing what I can't say. Can I sing it to you?"

She shrugged her shoulders, trying to look indifferent.

He strummed several chords lightly and then sang in a soft, plaintive voice,

> *"Now there was a poor mountain lad,*
> *Whose life was truly so sad,*
> *Till he met a fair lady*
> *Whose face and whose form*
> *Was all that he'd ever desired.*
>
> *Now he courted and won her,*
> *this unworthy man,*
> *And he promised he'd love her*
> *Again and again.*
> *But alas, a foul villain*
> *A man of low mien,*
> *Took him away from his love.*
>
> *She spurned him, despised him,*
> *She took back her love.*
> *He pleaded in vain*
> *To God up above,*
> *For mercy, for pity, for one tiny smile,*
> *To heal his poor broken heart.*
>
> *Now Sam, this poor mountain lad,*
> *Has gone back to his life*
> *Ah—so sad.*
> *He loves only Nola and she alone*
> *Can save him from misery if she will let him atone.*

As the sound of the guitar faded, Sam knelt by Nola's chair and took her hands in his, looking up into her face.

She looked at him a moment and then burst into laughter. "Sam, that's the worse song I've ever heard. Is that what you've been doing all day long? I feel sorry for the critters in the forest if they've had to listen to that caterwauling."

He put his hand over his heart in mock pain. "Nola, I've poured out my heart to you, and you've flung it back in my face. Can't you tell a heartbroken man when you see him?"

"Don't think you're going to get around me with a bunch of sweet talking. I sewed my fingers to the bone making that gown for our wedding night, and then you spent the night with that bunch of no-good drunkards."

"Hush," he said laying his fingers against her lips, "can't you see that ain't important? What's important is I love you and you love me, and it's our weddin' night. Now stop this talkin', and go put that pretty gown on. And let your hair down, I want to see it layin' on your shoulders and down your back like a rich brown river."

She rose as he pulled her toward him and reached up and pulled the pins from her hair. He ran his fingers through it as it fell around her, then buried his face in it, pulling her tightly against him. He lifted her and carried her to their bed where all thoughts of gowns and lace and anger were wiped from her mind as they sealed their marriage vows with his whispered promise, "With my body, I thee worship."

THIRTY-THREE

Ellen missed Nola terribly. For the first time, Ellen had to admit to herself that she was getting older. She didn't like the feeling.

"Humph, old enough to have a grown, married daughter," she said to herself. "Why, I don't feel any different from the day Will brought me here practically a bride with a new baby. Guess it won't be long till Nola and Sam will make me a grandmother. Then I guess I will be gettin' old. Grandma—wonder how that will feel?"

She caught herself many times in the next weeks starting to show Nola something or tell her a bit of news, then realizing that Nola was gone. Martha preferred playing with the twins and tending David and Joseph to housework, so Ellen was left alone much of the time.

The first Sunday that Nola and Sam came to take dinner with them, she found herself talking incessantly. Words tumbled over the top of each other as they tried to catch up with all the news they had been saving.

As they left that afternoon, Nola put her arms around Ellen. "Mama, Sam and I are happy, but I can't help missing the good talks you and I had. Sometimes I catch myself starting to tell you something, and you're not even there. I miss you."

Fighting back the tears, Ellen said, "I know what you mean, Nola, I do the same thing. It makes the times we do have together more precious, though."

Time did help ease Nola's absence for Ellen, time and her determination not to give in to self-pity. "I'm not goin' to turn into one

of them weepy self-pityin' women," she told Will. "I've got too
many other people dependin' on me to molly-coddle myself. Nola
and Sam seem to be real happy, and I'm grateful for that."

The next time Nola and Sam came for a visit the glow on Nola's
face was all Ellen needed to see to know that they were expecting a
baby.

"I'm so happy, Mama," Nola told her, "I feel like I am doing
what I was meant to do. Will you mind very much being a
grandma?"

"Mind? Course I won't! My goodness, this is the way it's supposed to be. You'll make a fine mother, and Sam acts like he's as
pleased as punch."

One year after Nola married Sam, she gave birth to their first
child, a son. They named him William Jacob after their fathers, but
they soon shortened his name to Jake.

In spite of her positive words to Nola, Ellen had some misgiv-
ings about how she would feel about becoming a grandmother.
She experienced a myriad of feelings the first time she held Jake in
her arms. Any resentment she had felt was erased when she felt
the warmth of the little body against her breast.

"There's just no other feeling in the whole world as that of a
new little baby cuddlin' up to you," she told Will. "Sometimes I
just pure ache for the feel of another baby in my arms. I guess I'll
just have to content myself with my grandchildren now, though.
Oh what pleasure Nola has ahead of her. Sometimes I wish we
could start all over again."

"Well, when I look back and remember some of the colic and
mumps and measles, I think I can be content with where we are
now," Will answered her. "I think I'll be perfectly happy to let
someone else walk the floor at night. I find I am beginning to need
my rest more and more."

Jake flourished under the love and attention showered on him
from his parents and grandparents. He was the only grandchild
in both families for a time.

John McGinty had begun a quiet courtship with Martha, and
before either family realized what was happening, he asked Will
for her hand in marriage. Martha glowed with happiness, and
Will and Ellen were delighted with the match.

"We're goin' to live with John's folks," Martha told Ellen. "Mr.
McGinty's leg bothers him a lot, and he really needs John there to

take care of the farm. Since Pearl and Mary married, there'll just be me and Mother McGinty, and we get along fine. Oh, we're goin' to be so happy!"

Ellen and Will had barely recovered from Martha's wedding when a suddenly shy Willie announced that he had asked Nancy Cole to marry him. "We want to marry as soon as the preacher makes his rounds again," Willie told them. "We want to build a cabin on that piece of land in the valley between our land and the Cole's. Nancy's pa says he'll give us some acreage if you'd be willin' to give some."

"Of course we will, Willie," Will replied. "Well now, think of that, you and little Nancy Cole. She was one of 'my babies.' Never thought when I was delivering her she'd be part of our family. Our family is surely growing. I am disappointed that you're not going to continue your education. I hoped you'd decide to go to the Academy. The new schoolmaster says you could do it if you wanted to, but if your mind is made up, then I won't press you about it."

"Papa, you know all I've ever wanted to do was farm. Maybe James and John will decide to go. They've got more talent for school work than I have."

Within the next year, James and John did decide to enroll in the Newton Academy, and Ellen felt as if her nest had really been deserted. This would leave only David and Joseph at home. Will was so proud that the boys wanted to further their education that he started making arrangements at once.

"They will attend as boarding students," he told Ellen. "With what they can earn as part-time help at the boarding house, I will be able to manage the rest of their tuition. Part of their duties are to furnish firewood to cook and heat with. When we go this fall, I'll take a wagon load to get them started."

"I know we're gonna miss them more than they'll miss us," Ellen said, smiling pensively. "They've always been so content with each other's company, they've never seemed to need anybody else. I've figured out why they don't talk much. It's because they read each other's minds. I declare, one starts a sentence, and the other one finishes it for him."

The letters they wrote home were as noncommittal as the boys themselves, giving only the barest information. The reports from the headmaster were good though, and Will was content that they were doing well.

Although Ellen missed her children, she found that she enjoyed the extra freedom she had now that there were not so many to care for. She began to spend more time working on her quilt pieces.

"I wonder how many different quilts I've made or seen in my lifetime," she said to Will one evening. "I'm just of a good notion to make me one big quilt and use every pattern I've ever made in it. If I framed each one in the same color, it seems to me I'd have a right pretty sampler."

When Nola saw the quilt, she said, "Mama, I hope when you're done with that quilt, you'll give it to me. Maybe I'll have a daughter some day, and I could pass it down to her. I'd be proud to tell her what a fine quiltmaker her Grandma Ellen is."

Ellen flushed with pleasure at Nola's praise. "This quilt is like a history book in a way," she said. "There's a Log Cabin, Rail Frence, Double Wedding Ring, Dutch Girl and Dutch Boy, Jacob's Ladder, Grandmother's Flower Garden, Bear's Paw, Ohio Star, Drunkard's Path, Wild Geese Flying, Turkey Track and Job's Tears just to name a few. I can think of a story to go with every one of 'em."

Nola's request had given Ellen another idea, and she began setting down some of the stories that her mother and grandmother had told her about their lives before they came to America and some of the things that happened to them as they grew up. When she finished writing the stories down, she wrote down all of the poems she had composed since Nola and Martha compiled the book of her writings. After they were complete, she wrapped them and stored them in her chest.

She told Will, "Maybe some day some of our great-great grandchildren will read them and learn somethin' about the history of their family. I'd hate for them to never know where their folks came from."

The visitors began to say their goodbyes. Nola listened impatiently to their remarks, anxious to talk to her great-grandaughter alone. When all but Cindy and her mother had left, she motioned the girl to come closer.

"Listen, girl," she said, "I want you to promise me something. I want you to go to my big chest and take out my sampler quilt and unfold it. Wrapped up in the middle of it is my mother's poems and stories. I want you to promise me you'll take care of them and see that nothing happens to them. Someday I want you to read these stories to your children just like I

read them to mine. And the quilt—the quilt must be yours someday. You treasure it now, you hear? It's a whole lifetime of work, and a whole lifetime of memories. You do like I say now!"

"Yes, Grandma," Cindy answered, *"I promise I'll take good care of everything and I'll treasure it too."*

"You be a good girl now," Nola admonished her. *"Remember, pretty is as pretty does, and don't you forget it!"*

Having finished what she wanted to say, Nola turned her back on the two and pulled her quilt up around her chin, shutting them out once again.

Alma and Cindy looked at each other and shook their heads. "She's never let that quilt out of her sight before," Alma said. *"I wonder what brought all that on?"*

THIRTY-FOUR

Nola was pregnant with her second child. This time she was experiencing miserable bouts of nausea. Instead of abating after the first few months, they continued throughout her pregnancy. It left her tired and with little energy, so Ellen did all she could to help her. She took Jake home with her often, trying to relieve Nola of some of her responsibilities.

This baby was a girl, and Nola named her Samantha Ellen McGinty. Sam was as proud as he had been at the birth of Jake. It gave him special pleasure that Nola wanted the baby to have his name. She was blonde and blue-eyed and knew from the beginning that a smile would get her anything she wanted from her father.

Samantha had bouts of colic for the first six months, and Nola spent most of her nights walking the floor with the screaming child. She was tired most of the time, often short-tempered from loss of sleep.

Ellen helped Nola as often as she could. When Ellen came, Sam usually found some reason that he needed to look up his friend Jim Andrews or help out with a dance. Nola seemed unconcerned with his frequent absences as she became increasingly preoccupied with the children.

Ellen kept her silence as long as she could, but finally she could hold her tongue no longer. "Nola, don't you think Sam should be at home tending to things a little closer? Seems to me he spends too much time with his music makin' when there's other more important things for him to be seein' after."

"Now, Mama, don't fault Sam," Nola said hastily. "He's just trying to find a little extra for us with another mouth to feed. He's been playing all the dances he can for whatever they will give him. Just last week a man over at the next settlement gave him half a bushel of corn. It helps out."

Married life with two children in the house was somewhat different than Sam had anticipated. He loved the children, but sometimes the noise and confusion was too much for him.

"Couldn't you just put the children to bed early tonight and let's me and you have some time to ourselves?" he asked Nola one night. "Seems like we don't never get any time alone anymore. You're jumpin' up and down with Samantha all night long, and you're always too tired to pay any attention to me."

"Sam, I do the best I can," Nola answered him shortly. "If you'd help me a little more, maybe I wouldn't be so tired."

"I ain't doin' woman's work," he told her stubbornly. "Oh come on, honey, let the kitchen go tonight, and while they're both quiet for a change, come on to bed. Where's that pretty gown of yours? I can't remember when you've wore it lately."

Nola looked at him and thought guiltily that she couldn't remember the last time she'd worn it either. "Oh all right, I guess nobody ever heard of dirty dishes running away," she laughed.

She had just washed her face and brushed out her hair, with Sam lying back on the bed watching her, when Samantha began crying. "Let her cry for a change," Sam told her when she started for the baby. "You spoil her takin' her up everytime she whimpers."

"Sam, how can you be so cruel? You know she gets the colic if she cries too long."

Sam rose from the bed and grabbed her wrist as she started out the door. "I said let her cry for awhile. It won't hurt her. Come on to bed. I need you now."

Nola jerked her wrist out of his hand. "What's got into you, Sam McGinty? You're acting more like a baby than Samantha is. I'm not going to let that baby lay and cry. I'll be back as soon as I get her quiet."

For almost two hours Samantha cried and Nola walked and patted and tried to quiet her. When she finally got her settled down, she returned to bed to find Sam asleep, with his back turned to her. Nola shrugged tiredly, crawled into bed and fell asleep.

The next morning Sam left after feeding the animals. He was gone for three days on what he tersely described to her as a part business and part fun trip for a change.

The cow dropped a calf that spring, and the mare foaled. The sow produced ten babies, and Nola told Sam, "I declare, we are about overrun with babies around here, between our two and every animal on the farm having little ones. It seems that everywhere you turn there is a baby underfoot."

"Yes," Sam replied somberly. "Sometimes it's just more than a body can stand. I tell you, Nola, I hope we've had all the babies we're a' goin' to for awhile. It near drives me out of my mind when Jake and Samantha both get to cryin' at once. I thought this cabin was plenty big enough for us, but sometimes I feel like the walls are closin' in on me."

"Why, Sam McGinty, how can you say that about your own dear children? Shame on you! Besides, I don't make babies by myself, you know."

Sam slammed out of the house and went to the barn. He picked up the reins of the mules which he had thrown down in disgust when he came in from the field that afternoon and hung them across the top of the barn stall. He winced as the rough leather scraped the top off the blister in the palm of his hand.

"D ____ mules," he muttered. "D ____ cornfield. D ____ farm!" Then as the wailing of the children fell on his ears, he unconsciously muttered, "D ____ young'uns!"

He looked guiltily over his shoulder toward the cabin, fearful that Nola might have heard him. He left the barn and reluctantly started toward the cabin. He thought longingly of his bachelor days when the most important decision he had to make was what tune to play at the dance on Saturday night.

He stopped at the back stoop and reach for the gourd dipper to pour some water in the pan with which to wash his face and hands. The dipper made a dull thud as it hit the bottom of the empty bucket.

"Is that you, Sam?" Nola called. "Where have you been? You'll have to fetch me a bucket of water. I haven't had time to carry any today. And can you hurry, please? The children both need washing, and I need some for my cooking."

Sam grabbed the bucket and threw it as hard as he could into the yard, then sheepishly retrieved it and headed for the well.

The evening meal was silent that night, except for the chatter of the children. Sam sulked, brooding on Nola's preoccupation with the children and the new blisters on his hand. Even though he wore gloves when he plowed, the pull of the reins kept his hands tender.

I'm soon gonna get so I can't hold my fiddle, he thought to himself as he flexed his hand.

Nola knew that Sam was out of sorts with her, and that night when they went to bed, she ignored Samantha's cries and made love with him. Their third child was conceived that night.

Nola had known for almost two months that she was pregnant before she had enough courage to tell Sam. When she finally told him, he only looked at her bleakly, put on his hat and left the cabin. He was gone longer this time than ever before. It was almost a week before Nola saw him again.

When he finally came home, he gave her no explanation of where he had been but sullenly went about getting the fields ready for the spring planting. Nola was hurt and mad at Sam for his childishness and decided that she would not ask him any questions.

The atmosphere in their home became even more tense, and the only words they exchanged were sharp questions and short answers.

THIRTY-FIVE

Martha and John were expecting their first child, and Nola decided to give them some bootees she had crocheted for the baby. It was too far to walk with two little ones, so she took the wagon.

"I ought to go without telling him anything like he does me," she muttered. "I won't be as childish as he is, though. I'll leave him a note."

She wrote her note, packed food and supplies for both children and set out on her trip. The trail to Martha's was rough, and the mare was skittish. She had a new colt and resented being separated from it. It was all Nola could do to control her and keep the wagon on the trail. When they finally arrived, she was exhausted from her efforts.

"I declare that old mare just about pulled my arms out of the socket," she told Martha. "She didn't want to leave her baby, and she sure let me know about it. I expect she won't be so reluctant to go home though, so I probably won't have any trouble going back."

The sisters had a good visit, catching up on family news and talking about the baby that was coming. Nola thought to herself that Martha looked mighty big, and her still three months away from her time. *Maybe she'll have twins*, she thought to herself. *I remember when James and John were born that Mama looked awful big too. Guess Sam would have a conniption if I ever had two at a time.*

The thought of Sam caused her to frown as she remembered the terse note she had left him. The cold silence between them had begun to wear on her nerves, and she was ready to get their problems solved. She sighed deeply.

"What's wrong with you, Nola?" asked Martha. "You've acted like your mind was somewhere else all day long. Is something wrong with the children, or Sam?"

"Oh, it's nothing to worry yourself about," she told Martha. "Just a little spat between me and Sam. I expect it'll all be over in a day or two. The truth is, he just isn't too thrilled about us having another baby. Maybe I'm not all that thrilled myself, but if the Lord sees fit to send us another one, then I'm going to do my best for it."

"Of course you will. What in the world is wrong with Sam?"

"I don't know, Martha," Nola said miserably. "Sometimes I just don't think Sam was cut out to be a family man. I don't mean he doesn't love the children," she added hastily, "especially Samantha. She can twist him around her little finger anytime she wants by just smiling at him. It's just that sometimes he gets so restless. I guess a lot of it's my fault, too. I get so busy doing for the children that I know I haven't paid him as much attention as I should have."

"Don't worry, sister. I'm sure Sam will settle down before long. It just takes some men longer than others to get used to having a family. My John says he just can't wait till our baby is born. He says he wants a house full," she added smugly.

At that moment John came in from the field, and Nola realized with a start that it was later that she thought. She jumped up and began to hastily gather up her belongings.

"Now, Nola, why don't you just let this little fellow stay the night with us," asked John, who was dangling Jake on his knee. "Ma and Pa will be home from Pearl's directly, and they'll be fit to be tied 'cause they've missed you. I have to take a plow over to Sam tomorrow, and I'll bring him home then."

"Well," Nola said hesitantly, "I guess it would be all right. Be sure you bring him first thing in the morning, though. I don't think I can spare him any longer than that."

She hugged Jake, picked up Samantha, and settled her in the box in the wagon that she had fixed for traveling. She took up the reins and set out for home.

Nola soon found that it took all her strength to keep the mare from breaking into a run. The closer to home they came, the more unmanageable she became. Finally she broke into a full gallop despite Nola's efforts. The trail was rough, and it was all Nola could do to keep her balance in the seat. As they rounded a particularly sharp curve, the wheel struck a rock and flew off. The wagon overturned, throwing Nola out and tossing the box that Samantha was in to the ground. The horse ran wildly on, breaking free of the wagon and dragging the traces behind her, headed for home and her colt.

Sam was sitting in the cabin glumly eating a cold supper of biscuits and ham. He picked Nola's brief note up and read it again, then angrily wadded it up and threw it on the floor.

"D ___ this business anyhow," he said angrily. "I'm sick and tired of her silence and of this whole mess. A man can't even have no fun anymore without bein' made to feel guilty. I'll show her a thing or two. I'm goin' to make that trip over to Asheville with Jim and the boys tomorrow, and she can like it or lump it. Where in tarnation is she anyhow? It's gonna be dark pretty soon, and her not home yet. What does she mean takin' off like that anyhow?"

He opened the cabin door and peered out into the dusk. Just as he turned to go back in, the mare came galloping across the yard. Cold terror gripped his heart as he saw the wild-looking, sweat-lathered horse with no wagon behind her. He set out at a run down the trail to see what had happened.

"Oh G ___ , what has happened to them?" he cried. "Why didn't I tell Nola I was sorry for the way I acted? I wanted to tell her this mornin', but she was so cold I couldn't bring myself to. If somethin' has happened to them, I'll never forgive myself."

He ran for almost a mile before he found them, and he felt like his heart would burst when he saw Nola lying so pale and unmoving on the ground. He raised her head to his breast and pressed his face in her hair, fearing that she was dead. She stirred and moaned.

"Samantha, my baby," she said weakly.

"Nola, sweetheart," Sam cried. "Where is Samantha? Where is Jake? Can you hear me, dearest? Where are the babies?"

Nola opened her eyes. "Find Samantha—in the box—in the box—find Samantha."

Sam laid her gently back on the ground and looked around for the child. It took him several minutes to find the box, upside down where it had rolled. With his heart in his mouth, he lifted the box and under it lay Samantha. She was so still he thought she was surely dead.

"Oh G ___ , please, no!" he cried.

There was a large bruise on her forehead and a gash across her cheek that was oozing blood. He felt for her pulse and heaved a sigh of relief when he felt it beating weakly, but steadily. He picked her up carefully, cradling her in his arms, then turned back to Nola.

"She's alive," he said, "do you think you can walk if I help you? We have to get her home and get some help. She's got a bad bruise on her head. Oh G ___ , why didn't I think to bring that crazy horse? I'll kill her for this! Nola, where's Jake?"

"He stayed with Martha and John, thank God. She struggled to her feet, wincing at the sudden pain in her back. Gritting her teeth, she took a few painful steps, leaning on Sam for support.

"Nothing seems to be broken. Let's go, and I'll do the best I can. Let's just get her home, and then you go for Papa. He'll know what to do."

THIRTY-SIX

Sam carefully laid Samantha in her crib, then helped Nola make cold compresses to put on her head.

"Go quick and get Papa," Nola told him, "Oh, dear God, she's so pale. Hurry, Sam, hurry."

"Are you sure you'll be all right?" he asked her anxiously. "You don't look none too good yourself."

"Yes, yes, I'll be fine, just hurry."

He did not bother to saddle the mare, but just threw a blanket on her back. She had fed her colt and gave him no trouble. He urged her on as fast as he could over the ridge to Will's house.

Will and Ellen were getting ready for bed when they heard Sam's frantic yells as he came up the trail. Before he got to the house, Will had his trousers on and his bag in his hand. Ellen also dressed hastily and hurried out to where Will was already hitching up the buggy.

When Sam told her what had happened, she paled but asked quietly, "What about Nola? Is she hurt?"

"She's shook up some, but she made it back to the cabin all right. We were so worried about Samantha, I didn't have time to question her too close."

"Let's get started," Will said. "The sooner we get there, the sooner we'll know about them both."

"I heard Nola tell him two weeks ago that that wagon wheel was loose," Will told Ellen angrily as they rode off.

Sam rode the mare hard going back, beginning to worry as much about Nola as the baby, He left the buggy behind, kicking the horse in the sides when she slowed down.

He rode into the yard at a full gallop, less than an hour after he had left, dismounted and slapped the horse toward the barn. He ran on to the cabin and pushed open the door. Nola knelt by the crib, where he had left her, applying compresses to Samantha's head. She looked up in relief as he entered and spoke only one word, "Papa?"

Sam nodded his head and said, "Less than ten minutes behind me. Your Ma, too. How is she?"

Nola shook her head. "She still hasn't moved."

Will and Ellen arrived shortly, Will opening his bag as he entered. He went straight to the child, pulled up her eyelids, examined the bruise on her forehead then looked in her ears for signs of bleeding.

"She's got a bad bruise, that's for sure," he said. "Let's just pray there's no break in her skull. I see no signs of any bleeding, but her pupils are dilated, which means it's not good. All we can do now is watch her and keep her quiet. You did right to put the compresses on her, Nola. That will help keep the swelling down. Let your mother take over now. I want to have a look at you and clean up some of these scratches."

"Oh, I'm all right, Papa. I'm just so worried about Samantha. She so still and so pale," Nola said.

She stood up and took one step, then collapsed in Will's arms in a faint. Sam stepped to her side, lifted her and carried her to the bed.

Will rubbed her hands and laid a cool cloth on her head. She regained consciousness shortly, and Will began checking her injuries.

"Well, you are scratched and bruised, Nola, but otherwise you seem to be all right. Let's get your scratches washed and put some of that snakeroot ointment on them so they won't get infected. Sam said the wagon wheel fell off."

"Yes. The mare got to running and I couldn't hold her. We must have hit a rock or something."

"Sam, why on earth didn't you fix that wheel when Nola told you about it?" Will asked sharply. "Things like that need tending to at once."

Sam shook his head and turned away.

As Will started to rise, Nola grabbed his arm. "Papa," she said slowly, "I'm afraid I've hurt the baby I'm carrying. When I fell out of the wagon, I hit my stomach on the side, and it hurts something awful."

Will paled when he looked at the deep bruise on her abdomen. "You must lay still, Nola," he admonished. "Don't get out of this bed for anything. If you're going to lose this baby, there's nothing I can do about it. Your only hope is to be as still as possible. Don't worry about Samantha. Your mother and I will take good care of her and do what needs to be done. Right now you must think about yourself and this other baby. Now remember, don't move!"

Will called Sam aside and told him what he had just told Nola. "Go to her, Sam," he said. "She needs your support now."

Sam shook his head numbly. "How can I face her? It's all my fault. I knew that wheel was loose, and I should have fixed it. Instead I went off with Jim. If anything happens to Nola and Samantha, I'll never forgive myself."

"Get hold of yourself, man," Will said sternly. "This is no time for self-pity. Go and comfort your wife. She needs you."

"I can't," Sam said. "I'm no good for her. There's nothing I can do or say to make up for what I've done."

"Then go draw a bucket of cold water for Ellen to use for compresses," Will told him disgustedly. "Then build a fire and set some water on to boil in case I need it with Nola."

During the night Nola lost the baby. The blow had been too severe for the womb to absorb. Nola cried softly when Will told her, grieving for the child she would never hold in her arms.

For five days and nights Samantha lay as still as death. Then as the sun rose on the sixth day, she slowly opened her eyes and gave a soft whimper. Ellen spooned some milk into the child's mouth, and after a few swallows, she fell asleep again. This time it was a deep, natural sleep, and Will breathed a sigh of relief.

"I think she's going to make it now," he told Ellen. "Let her sleep, and when she wakes, feed her again. I was beginning to fear she would never open her eyes."

He went to tell Sam, who was in the barn feeding the stock. Sam burst into tears and buried his face in his hands. "Thank God, thank God," he cried.

Will patted him awkwardly and then said, "Sam, I don't know what's been going on between you and Nola, and it's no secret that I wasn't fond of the idea of her marrying you, but I don't want to see my daughter's marriage break up. If you don't go to her now and try to set things right between you, you might not ever have another chance."

"It's too late, Mr. Johnston," Sam said, shaking his head. "Too much has happened."

"Dad blast it, man! Trouble should make a marriage stronger, not pull it apart. The longer you let this thing fester, the harder it's going to be to resolve it. Don't let stubborn pride cost you your wife and family."

"It's not pride, Mr. Johnston," Sam said. "I'd crawl to Nola on my hands and knees if it would make things right. It's just me and the way I am. I'll never forgive myself for what I've done. All I've ever done is cause Nola pain. She'd be better off if I'd stayed out of it and let her marry John."

Will looked Sam in the eye and said, "That's a bunch of hogwash, Sam. If Nola had wanted John, she'd have chosen him. She chose you for better or worse. She meant her vows. Did you? If you did, you'd better put this thing behind you now."

Sam only shook his head stubbornly. Will finally sighed in disgust and left.

Samantha improved rapidly. Ellen was hard put to keep her quiet and had to call on all her store of tricks and stories to keep her quiet. Nola was still in bed, slow to heal from her bruises and the miscarriage.

Will had returned home after Samantha was out of danger, but Ellen stayed on to care for Nola and the children. Sam slept in the barn, giving up his half of the bed to Ellen. They barely saw him, except for the brief trips he made to check on Samantha and bring in their supplies.

"Do you want to talk about what's troublin' you and Sam?" Ellen asked Nola. "You're goin' to have to get things straightened out between you."

"There's nothing to talk about, Mama," Nola said. "Sam will just have to decide what he wants. Me and the children or that fiddle and his friends. I can't keep living like this anymore."

A week after Samantha's recovery, Will came to take Ellen home. When he went to look for Sam, he was nowhere to be found.

"Do you know where Sam is, Nola?" he asked. "I hate to leave without being sure that he's close by in case you need something."

"See if his fiddle is gone," Nola answered. "If it is, then you needn't look any further for him. He's gone off with his friends again."

Ellen had never seen Will so angry. "If I could lay my hands on him right now, I'd horsewhip him. It's a sorry excuse for a man that'll leave his wife and children to fend for themselves when they're well, let alone when they're sick. Pack up Nola's and the children's things and get them ready to go home with us. I will not have my daughter at the mercy of his selfish whims. If he knows what's good for him, he'd better keep out of my sight."

Nola did not protest when Ellen told her she wanted her to stay with them for awhile. She only said, "Send David to ask if John will help him look after our stock for a while. They can take turns about feeding them."

Nola helped Ellen pack in stony silence, and when they left the cabin she did not look back.

THIRTY-SEVEN

For three months Nola heard nothing from Sam. She had resumed her place in her mother's household, helping with the cooking and cleaning and caring for her babies. For almost a month she refused to go to the meeting house on Sunday, fearing the questions she might have to face.

"Nola, you have done nothing to be ashamed of," Will told her one Sunday morning. "Sooner or later you are going to have to get out among your friends again, and the longer you put it off, the harder it will be. I want you to dress my two handsome grandchildren and go to preaching with us today. I think it will be easier than you think. Just remember, these people are your friends."

"Yes, Papa," she told him meekly. "I know you're right. It's just so hard."

"I know it is, but you will be surrounded by people who love you. Now what better help could you have?"

After the first time it was easier for Nola to resume her life, and she was soon taking part in community activities again. It was at a quilting session at Martha's house that she overheard a conversation that made her realize her marriage probably was over.

She had gone to the kitchen to fetch a stool for Martha to prop her feet on. When she couldn't find it, she came back to ask Martha where it was and overheard Mary Cole saying, "That Sam McGinty has shore shamed pore Nola. My boy said he saw him over at the Pless's barn dance last week with that redheaded Pruitt gal, and they was shore doin' more than a little square dancin'. He said her Daddy was about to get his shotgun after Sam. Pore Nola, I feel so sorry for her."

Nola turned and fled from the house, running as hard as she could and wanting to shut out the hateful words. When she could run no more, she flung herself on the ground and cried until she was exhausted. When she returned home that day, she shut herself up in her room with Jake and Samantha. It was only the children's hunger that finally brought her out.

The next day Nola packed her belongings, and with her two children, went back to her cabin. She told Will and Ellen, "I've got to look after myself for a change. I've just been fooling myself that Sam would come and get me and take me home and everything would be all right again. I can't depend on him. That's obvious. I am a grown woman, and I will not be a burden on you."

Will started to protest, but she held up her hand and continued, "I've got a good piece of land, and I'm going to tend it. I'll get one of the Mann boys to help me with the plowing, and if I need you, I'll send for you. You warned me about Sam, Papa, and I was too headstrong to listen to you. I let his sweet talk and his handsome looks blind me to his faults. Maybe he can't help doing like he does, but I can't live like this any more, hoping for something that isn't going to happen."

"Don't say that, Nola," Ellen said. "Don't make any hasty decisions. Maybe when he's had time to think things out, he'll change."

"I'll never forgive him for what he's done to me and my babies. He's made me the object of everybody's pity, and I can't stand that. He's betrayed me, and he's been false to the vows he made to me."

Ellen and Will tried to persuade Nola to stay with them, but nothing they could say would change her mind. All she would let them do was pack up provisions for the little family and send them on their way.

As they left, Will told Ellen, "I am beyond anger at what has happened to Nola. I am heartsick. If thrashing Sam would help, I would find him and beat him into the ground, but that wouldn't help her or us. I blame myself for this, I should have followed my instincts and forbidden her to marry him."

He slumped down in a chair and buried his face in his hands, shaking with the sobs that engulfed his body. Ellen put her arms around him, alarmed at the depth of his grief.

"Will, oh my poor Will," she cried, "you're no more to blame for this than I am or anybody else is. You know that there was no stoppin' Nola from marryin' him. You couldn't have stopped her if you'd tried. All you'd have done was drove her away from us. At least we can help her now. Please don't carry on so; she's strong like her Papa is. She'll be all right. You wait and see."

They sat for a long time with their arms around each other, trying to ease their pain and make some sense out of what had happened to their child.

Nola worked from dawn to dusk each day, filling the hours so she wouldn't have time to think. As days blended into weeks and weeks into months, she hardened her heart against Sam. When his name was mentioned, her only answer was a cold stare. Almost six months passed before he came home again.

Nola had just finished milking the cow and throwing hay down to the horses when she heard a buggy drive up into the yard. She was dirty, with perspiration streaming down her face. She hastily picked up the corner of her apron to wipe her face as she strode from the barn. She stopped short when she saw that it was Sam. He stood gazing at the cabin, his back to her. Jake cried out, "Papa, Papa, you've come home!"

He whirled, taking in the scene before him. Jake ran to him and flung his arms around his legs. He stooped and scooped him up in his arms, hiding his face in the child's chest momentarily.

He knelt down and held his arms out to Samantha. "There's my pretty girl," he said. "Look how big you've grown. And just as pretty as ever."

Samantha toddled to him, and he picked her up in his other arm, hugging both children tightly. He looked over their heads at Nola standing silently, milk pail in her hand.

"Hello, Nola," he said. "How are you? You look just fine."

"Do I?" she asked. "Well, I reckon I'm all right. Just a mite tired from trying to take care of everything by myself. I must say, you're looking prosperous though."

He looked guiltily at his shiny boots and stylish pants. "Oh, I guess I'm makin' it all right," he replied defensively.

"What was it you wanted?" she asked coldly.

"Why I wanted to see my babies, and you too. I wanted to see how you're gettin' along and if you need anything. You know I've always loved our babies, Nola. You know that, don't you?"

"Love doesn't come free, Sam," she retorted. "Love has responsibilities attached to it."

She walked past him and went into the cabin. Her heart was pounding furiously, and she felt as if she would faint if she didn't sit down soon. She put the milk down and sat down abruptly at the table. The sight of Sam with the children in his arms had moved her as she had never thought he could move her again. She remembered achingly how he had loved the children, how she had thought he loved her. She gripped her hands tightly in her lap and looked up as he entered the room. She reached up and smoothed her hair back from her face, resenting that he had caught her at such a disadvantage.

"Nola, could we talk to each other for a few minutes? I told Jake to keep Samantha out in the yard for a little while. It's took me a long time to get up enough courage to face you again, and I need to say this while I've still got enough nerve."

"What is there to talk about? You made your choice, and it didn't include me and your children. What is it that you want from me, Sam? Forgiveness? Is that it? You want me to say I forgive you so your conscience won't bother you any more?"

"Yes, I want your forgiveness, and I want your understanding," he answered hotly. "I want you to understand why I did what I did. It's took me a long time to understand it, and now I want you to understand too."

"I'd like to understand Sam, I really would. I'd like to understand how a man could walk off and leave his wife and children with never a backward glance or a thought about what would happen to them. You make me understand that, Sam!"

"Nola, you got to understand. I just couldn't get used to bein' tied down. I couldn't stand the farmin' and the workin' from daylight to dark and never havin' any fun. I felt like my life was over, and I just wasn't ready for that. I know now that I can never be a farmer. I just ain't cut out for it."

"And just what is it you're cut out for, Sam?"

"Why, I got two or three deals I'm workin' on with Jim," he answered. "Any day now one of 'em is goin' to work out, and then I'll be on my way."

He fell to his knee in front of her and reached for her hands, wincing as he felt the hard calluses and roughness of them. He kissed them and held them against his face. She steeled herself as she strove to keep from responding to his touch.

"I want to come home, Nola. I want you and the children with me, and I want us to be a family again. We can sell this farm when things work out for me. It's good land, and we won't have no trouble gettin' rid of it. Ah, Nola, I've never quit lovin' you. You still love me don't you? Say you'll forgive me and let me come back."

"How long do you want to come home for, Sam?" she asked him, pulling her hands away. "Do you want to come home for a week, or a month, or a year? How long? Do you think I don't know about your other women? Don't you know how it's pleasured some of my 'friends' to tell me about all the times you've been untrue to me? What kind of fool do you take me for?"

"Ah, Sweetheart, you know them other women didn't mean nothin' to me. I was just lonesome for you, that's all. You got so wrapped up with Jake and Samantha, you acted like you didn't have time for me no more. I was hurt, too, you know."

"When we married, Sam, I told you I expected you to be true to me and the vows you made to me. You broke the vows that you made in front of my family and yours and before God. You've made a mockery of our marriage, and you've shamed me before my people. My Papa has had to look after me and your children, and I've had to face people knowing they feel nothing but pity for me for the way you've dishonored me and your children."

"Nola, don't you feel anything for me any more? Don't you remember how it was with us? It was always so good for me. You can't tell me it wasn't good for you, too."

"I try not to remember how it was with us, Sam. I try every day of my life not to remember, because it hurts too much to remember. I couldn't stand to be hurt like that again, Sam. To take you back and then have you walk out on us again. I'm never going to let myself get hurt that way again."

"Does this mean you won't forgive me?" he cried, jumping up and pacing back and forth. "Does this mean you don't want our children to ever know their papa? Think what it'll be like tryin' to raise them by yourself."

"I already know what it's like, Sam. It's hard, but it's not as hard as getting my heart stepped on every time you get bored with responsibility. No," she said slowly, "no, Sam, I won't take you back. I have nothing left but my pride now, and I won't lose that. I know in my heart that you would never stay with us. You know it too. It's best to end it now."

"I'm warnin' you, Nola, I won't ask you again! You don't know what it took for me to ask you to take me back. It wasn't easy, and if you turn me away, I won't come back no more."

"You better go now, Sam," she said coldly. "My Papa is coming over to help me mend my fences today, and I don't think you'd want to face him. He's sworn that he'll take a horsewhip to you if he ever sees you again. I don't think you want your children to remember you that way."

Sam gave her one last anguished look and then turned and left. He picked up the children once again and hugged them, then climbed up into the buggy where he slumped dejectedly. Finally he picked up the reins and clucked the horse into motion.

Jake and Samantha went to Nola where she sat at the table.

"Ain't Papa going to stay, Mama?" asked Jake.

"Don't say ain't, Jake," she said automatically. "No, he's not going to stay."

She put her arms around her children and pulled them to her. "It's just me and you now, and we might just as well get used to it. Your papa has chosen another way of life. I guess we'll just have to look after each other from now on."

"Don't worry, Mama," Jake said stoutly, "Grandpa will look after us, and I'll look after us, too. I'm strong enough!"

Nola buried her head in Jake's shoulder and cried. She cried as she had never cried before, great soul-wrenching sobs. The child patted her and begged, "Please, Mama, please don't cry."

After a time Nola straightened up and smoothed her hair back. She took the corner of her apron and wiped the tears from her face and from the face of her child.

"That's enough of that," she said firmly. "Come on, Jake, let's go finish our chores. You watch Samantha for me. You're right, Grandpa will help look after us, and with a big, strong boy like you, we'll be just fine."

"You—you won't cry no more will you, Mama?"

"No, son, I'm done with tears."

THIRTY-EIGHT

Will and Ellen sat by the fire enjoying the last of the embers before they went to bed. Ellen had pulled her rocker up close to the firelight and the lamp, trying to finish up a bit of lace she was working on. Will had his knife out whittling on a piece of wood, not making anything but just enjoying the sight of the long pale curls of wood as they fell from the stick.

"I hope you're plannin' on cleanin' up that mess you're makin' before bedtime," Ellen said mildly.

"Yes, I thought I'd add them to the kindling I've set aside for morning. Nothing on earth is prettier than the way wood curls if you shave it just right. What's that bit of lace you're making for? As if I couldn't guess!"

"You know as well as I do I'm working on a christening dress for Lucinda. I've made one for Charles too, but I was forbidden to put any lace on his."

"My, my, but those twins of Martha's are growing. Seems like they've gained a pound and an inch evertime we see them. John's going to bust his britches with pride if he's not careful."

"I never saw a man so proud of anything as that man is over them babies." Ellen smiled. "He sure worships them. I miss that for Nola."

"Yes, but she's going to be fine. Joseph is a big help to her. He stays there about as much as he stays at home. If she's sorry she didn't take Sam back, she never lets on. I know it must be lonesome for her, though. I've tried talking to her about divorcing him, but she won't hear to it. I hope she doesn't let pride keep her from some kind of happiness."

"Yes, I hope so too," Ellen sighed, "but I found out a long time ago that you can only suggest so far with Nola, and then you might as well stop wastin' your breath. Jake is so fine, though, he stands up like a little man for his mama. And that Samantha, ah me, she's so much like her daddy. The good qualities he had, that is. I think her hair is goin' to be red, and she can just melt my heart when she smiles at me."

"All our grandchildren are pretty special, and I say that without one ounce of prejudice," Will laughed.

"I heard you, Will Johnston. I heard what you told Willie when he come over last Sunday to tell us his Nancy is expectin'. 'Has to be beautiful, my grandchildren comes from such good stock.' The good Lord will get you for such vanity."

"Why, I was talking about you, of course. I knew when I married you that we'd have the prettiest children and the finest grandchildren that could be had. You won't deny that we have, will you?"

"I know we sure are a' multiplyin' lately. And if what the headmaster wrote about James and John is true, we may be a' multiplyin' even more soon."

"Wouldn't you know those two would court sisters?" Will chuckled. "they sure want to guarantee they'll not have to stray far from each other. If what he wrote is true, their father has offered them jobs in one of his banks. How do you feel about that, old woman? Having two bankers in the family?"

"Well, for one thing I'm not no old woman. And for another, if that's what makes them happy, then that's fine by me. Humph, old woman, indeed!"

"Now that's what I like to see, some sparks in those blue eyes. Here, put that thread down for a minute. Your hands are always busy with something."

"Why, what on earth is wrong with you?" she asked as he took her tatting from her. "What am I supposed to do with my hands, just sit here and hold them?"

"That wasn't exactly what I had in mind," he said, pulling his chair next to hers. "I thought maybe I might hold them for a while. I can remember when we used to spend an awful lot of time holding each other's hands. I remember once your pa almost caught us when we were holding hands under the quilting frame."

"Yes," she laughed, "and there was that time in church services when you pretended to be listening so close to Brother Caldwell, and all the time you was about to squeeze my fingers off under the folds of my dress."

They sat quietly for a time, smiling and reminiscing, hands clasped companionably. "Where have the years gone, Will? It must have been just yesterday that we topped that ridge and looked down into this cove. We never dreamed of all the things that would happen to us, did we? Have you regretted any of them? I mean, of course, except for little Tildy."

"Not one minute, dear Ellen," he answered tenderly. "You have given me more happiness than I ever deserved. I wouldn't trade places with any man on the face of this earth. I've been blessed with the most beautiful and wonderful wife any man could ever have and seven wonderful children. And I've been allowed to help my neighbors when they need me. What more could any man want?"

"My goodness, what's got into us?" Ellen said. "You'd think we was gettin' old talkin' like this!"

"I'll never feel old as long as I can still remember how you looked that day I saw you peeking out from under that poke bonnet at me. You captured my heart right then and there, and I haven't ever wanted to be free again."

"Will Johnston, you'll make this 'old woman' blush if you keep up that blarney. Be ashamed of yourself, tryin' to turn my head, and me nearly five times a grandma."

They laughed together and went about their nightly rituals, closing up the house.

Will left early the next morning and went to the upper pasture where he planned to cut a tree for firewood. A strange blight had struck the black oaks, and many of the huge trees were dying. He would cut this one down now so that it would dry by wintertime.

He had worked for some time when he looked up to see Jesse Cole approaching. "Well howdy, neighbor," Will said, "what brings you up here today?"

"Heard the sound of your axe and thought I'd stop by and howdy you. Been out since daybreak lookin' for old Bess. That old cow is gettin' plumb flighty of late and wanders off at the drop of a hat. 'Pears like you're a' layin' by yore winter store of wood."

"Yes, I thought I'd cut this one out and let it be drying. Makes me feel sad somehow, cutting down a majestic old tree like this. It's a pity it's took the blight—must be near two hundred years old. It's sure weathered a heap of summers and winters. Stood in silent witness to a lot of changes in its day too. Guess when it comes right down to it, we're a lot alike, trees and man, that is. His acorns has sired a lot of descendants I bet. We all live on this old earth for a little while and then depart, leaving our children and grandchildren behind to mark the place we've been."

"That's true for shore," Jesse agreed. "Well, I best get on and find that ornery cow. Bring the missus and come when you can!"

Will toiled all morning cutting the tree, his axe biting deep within the thick trunk. He calculated where it would fall, but the old tree seemed to have a mind of its own. It reversed itself in mid-air and fell toward Will instead of away from him. He almost escaped, running desperately to his right, but a vine tripped him, and as he fell, he knew the tree would get him. One of the huge limbs caught him across his back and crushed the life from him. His last thought was of Ellen, and his last sensation was the odor of the thick rich earth as it rose up to receive him.

The sound of the falling tree reverberated through the forest, and Ellen, feeding her chicks in the barnyard, paused and looked up as she heard the distant thud. She shivered as a sudden chill wind swept around the house.

When the sun began to set and Will had not returned, Ellen called for David, and together they set out up the trail, expecting to meet Will at each turn and be chided for their worry. As they traveled farther with no sign of him, Ellen became more and more alarmed. She was running when she came to the place where the tree had fallen. At first they saw no sign of Will, but then David spotted the blue of his shirt against the dark earth. They ran to him, sure he was only caught and would be laughing at himself for getting into such a predicament. One glance told Ellen the whole story. She had no need to feel his pulse to tell her that he was dead.

"Go across the ridge and get Jesse Cole," she told David. "It's closer to their house than it is to home. Tell him to bring his mules and a sled. It's goin' to take a lot of strength to get this limb off him. Go quick now. Be the man your papa expects you to be."

Once David left, Ellen gave in to her grief and flung herself on the ground by Will. She clawed at the tree limb, beating it until her hands were raw, cursing it, and pleading with it to give her Will back to her. When she had exhausted herself, she lay down on the ground as near to him as she could. They found her there when they came back with the mules and sled.

THIRTY-NINE

Word of Will Johnston's death spread rapidly through the community. A steady stream of people traveled to the little farm home to pay their respects to Ellen and her children. Jesse Cole, Jacob McGinty, Thomas Mann and Elisha Phillips selected their best pieces of chestnut and set about building a coffin for Will. As they labored over it, they reminisced about the many times Will had tended a neighbor in his or her last illness, then joined with the others to make a coffin for the burial.

Jesse Cole said. "I recollect one time that Will come on one of the Vinson boys that had been mauled by a bear and findin' him still with breath in his body, carried him on his back to his home. He done what he could in the way of patchin' him up and set for two days with him till he died. Then he helped his pa build him a coffin and dig his grave. Then since they wasn't no preacher thereabouts, he read from the Bible at the grave and spoke his buryin' words. After he helped fill in the grave, he went on back home to his own family. I don't know what more a man could do for a neighbor than he done for that boy."

The friends solemnly nodded their heads and silently pondered the loss of their friend. "Yessir, that sounds like Will," declared Thomas Mann. "I never knowed a man so willin' to share what he had with others. Me and mine will always be beholdin' to him for helpin' us out that winter I was laid up with the 'new monies.' Not only did he doctor me with his yarbs and poultices, but he kept us in firewood and rations all winter, too!"

Elisha Phillips laughed suddenly, "Jacob, do you recall that time you and him decided to visit them outlanders that moved into the cove and invite 'em to the Sunday meetin'? They had the meanest old hound dog I ever recollect runnin' into. Well sir, Will come up on the cabin and hailed them, but instead of gettin' a howdy from the folks, he got a bite from their dog. Fool dog snuck up behind him and nipped him right on his setter. Will said he'd had some good conversations in his day, but none quite as 'bitin' as that one. Didn't slow him down none, though, he went right on in and spoke his piece for the Lord just like nothin' had happened!"

Jacob chuckled softly and said, "I remember that well—we kept a sharp eye out for that old hound as we left that day. As I recall, Will didn't just talk about the Lord to them folks though. They was the porest lookin' bunch I ever seen. The old man was so pore, he looked like a tramp that had robbed a scarecrow. They had eight puny lookin' little young'uns and not a mouthful of food on the place. When Will seen how things stood, he went home and got Ellen, and they gathered up some rations and come back with 'em. Will told me, 'It's hard to feed a man's soul when his stomach's a' rumblin' so loud he can't hear you.' Yes sir, I reckon he lived his faith as true as any man I ever knowed. You all know what I owe him."

When they had finished, they carried the coffin into the house and gently placed his body in it. Ellen had insisted on washing and dressing Will herself, with the help of Sarah Cole and Louisa McGinty. She dressed him in his good black Sunday suit, placed two silver coins on his eyes, and then sat with folded hands, knowing this was the last act she would ever perform for her beloved Will. They had spent twenty-eight years together, raising seven children, burying one, and building three homes. Ellen knew the tree had severed her life as surely as it had Will's.

When Nola first heard the tolling of the church bell, she had a premonition that it was someone near to her. She told Joseph, "Run home and see if Papa and Mama are all right. The bell means somebody has died. I feel uneasy about them for some reason."

One look at Joseph's face when he returned confirmed her fears. "It's Papa," he gasped through his tears, "Mama says you're to come quick as you can. A tree fell on him, and they wasn't nothin' could be done."

Nola felt as if the life's breath had been knocked from her. For awhile she could only sit and cry over and over, "Papa, oh, Papa." Finally she was able to rise and put together the few things she could think of for the children and her. Numbly, she and Joseph loaded the children in the wagon and began the sad trip home.

By the time Nola got there, the house was already filling with neighbors offering help. Thomas Mann had already set out for Asheville to bring James and John home, and other neighbors had gone to tell Willie and Martha. Nola put her arms around her mother as they grieved for Will.

That night nearly fifty neighbors "set up" with the corpse of Will Johnston. They spent the night talking about the man who had lived so unselfishly among them and recounting stories of special acts of kindness he had rendered to them. Throughout the night they sang softly the old hymns of faith and promise of life eternal.

Willie, James, John, Joseph, David and John McGinty dug Will's grave next to the grave of little Tildy and Cassie's baby on the mountainside near their first home. They took his body to the meeting house he had helped build, and Jacob McGinty read from the Bible and spoke quietly of the life of Will Johnston and what he had meant to the community and his family. He concluded the service by saying, "Friends, take comfort in the words Saint Paul spoke. He said for us to 'be not sorrowful for those who are departed,' and there's no reason for us to be sorrowful for Will today. Will lived his beliefs, and I know that now he's with our Lord in paradise. Will Johnston's life is an example of a man who lived a life of companionship with God every day of his earthly life. Now I know he's reapin' his reward."

At the conclusion of the service, the neighbors filed one by one past the casket for one last look, then the family went for their final farewell to the father and husband who had been the mainstay in their lives.

They placed his coffin on a wagon and took it to its final resting place in the mountain. After it had been lowered into the earth and the dirt filled in over the top, they brought their simple homemade wreaths of hemlock and cedar twined with flowers from the mountain forests that Will had loved so well, and laid them on the grave.

Ellen stared at the grave, unable to believe that he was gone. She had insisted on lining his coffin with his Freedom Quilt made for him by his mother as his bridegroom's quilt. It seemed fitting that he should be buried with this quilt that had covered their marital bed. Wearily she turned from the grave and began making her way back down the mountainside. She felt the years weighing on her soul, and her shoulders sagged as she slowly plodded home.

Jacob McGinty and Jesse Cole set in place the rock upon which Jacob had carved the words, *William B. Johnston, Father—Husband—Friend to His Fellowman.*

FORTY

*C*indy unwrapped the yellowed quilt and took out the book and papers that had been carefully wrapped and tied with ribbons.

"I feel like I'm unfolding a history book," she told her mother. "These stories cover our family for nearly seven generations. Did you know that some of our people came from Ireland and some from England and France?"

"Yes, I remember my mother tellin' me about them. I guess I never paid much attention to that kind of story. I sure did like to hear the story about the mountain Boojum though."

"This must all be in great-great grandmother Ellen's writing. Look at all the poems she wrote and this quaint old book. Why it says 'Mountain Poems by Ellen C. Johnston.' Oh, I can't wait to read them! Oh look! What's this?"

"Let me see," Alma said. "Why, it's a document of divorce. It says here that Samuel McGinty divorced Nola Johnston McGinty."

"I didn't know they divorced. I thought he just went off and was never heard from again. I don't ever remember hearing Grandma say they were divorced."

"Oh yes, they were divorced all right. Or at least he was," said Alma. "She never considered herself divorced. Doesn't believe in it. He'd been gone about five years when she got this in the mail. Mama said nobody ever dared ask her about it."

"What did his folks say about it? Did they believe in divorce?"

"His sister told Uncle Willie that he'd married again and was living in Florida. I think he raised another family. Anyhow, they disowned him, and I never heard his name mentioned till word came that he'd died."

"Oh, how sad," Cindy said. "She never did forgive him then, did she?"

"Nobody knows but her," Alma said, shaking her head. "Mama said after she heard he'd died, she got on the train and went to where he'd been living and hunted up his grave. Then she came back home."

"What did she say when she came back?"

"Nothing. Never mentioned it again. 'Cept for one time when I heard her tell a neighbor that she was a widow, I don't reckon she ever talked about it again."

"What a hard life she must have had, raising two children by herself."

"It was hard for her. After her Papa died, she went to live with her mother and took care of her as long as she lived. Then she moved to town and ran a boarding house and took in sewing for people. There weren't many ways for a woman to earn a living in those days."

Cindy spread the stories and poems around her, quickly becoming absorbed in them. She was familiar with many of the stories, recalling the times her grandmother had told them to her and her brothers when they were children.

Even more fascinating to her was the account of the family tree, which Ellen had carefully set down. It included both Will's and Ellen's side of the family. She read Ellen's explanation for the recording of these events:

> "I set this down for the eyes of them who come after me. So that they will know where their people come from and know what good strong Christian people they were. I put the stories down so they'd know that we was human beings with human failings."

Cindy fingered the document of divorce, thinking how humiliated and rejected Nola must have felt. At the same time, she felt a sympathetic twinge for Sam. She thought about the many lonely years Nola must have spent nursing her hurt pride. Then she thought about Sam—rejected by his wife and his family. Doomed to live out his life in an alien place. She cried for both of them.

A noise from the bedroom interrupted the spell the past had woven around Cindy, and she and Alma both rushed to Nola's side. The old lady was trying to sit up in the bed and was calling out, "Sam, Sam!"

"What's that you said, Grandma?" asked Cindy. "Who do you want?"

"Why, I want Sam, I said," she replied impatiently. "Tell Sam to have Papa come and get me. I'm ready to go home now. Tell him to have Papa bring the wagon and come on. It must be getting on toward dark, and I need to get home and tend to Jake and Samantha. They'll be getting hungry and nobody there to fix for them."

"Oh dear," Alma said, "she's talking about her children again. I don't know what to do when she gets like this. There, there, Grandma, you just lie back and rest awhile. They'll all be along directly. Don't fret yourself so."

"Come down here, girl," Nola said suddenly, her voice taking on an unexpected strength. "I want to ask you something. Have you seen my children today? And where's Sam gone to? I bet he's off somewhere playing that fiddle of his and making music when he ought to be at home tending the crops. Hurry and get me out of here. It must be past sunup. My Mama always said 'it's as big a sin laying in the bed after daylight as it is to be loafing abroad after dark!'"

She fell back on her pillow, exhausted from the unusual excitement of the day. The years rolled over her as she closed her eyes and ignored Alma and Cindy.

Memories crowded through her mind like a parade down Main Street, pushing and rushing at her, one after the other. Mama and Papa and sister Martha playing with her on the mountainside. Willie teasing them and James and John looking at her with their big solemn eyes. Joseph and David running on fat baby legs through the grass, half hidden in the clumps of black-eyed Susans. And Sam—and her own two little ones and the sweet little baby that died before it ever had a chance to live. Cassie and little Tildy, all calling to her, beckoning, calling.

A kaleidoscope of sounds and voices tore at her—"Grandma, Mama, Nola!" And over all of them the deep dulcet tones of Sam, the fiddlin' man, calling to her, luring her, entreating her, "Nola, Nola! Hurry up, come on, Nola!"

Then she was caught up in a myriad of colors as bits and pieces of her life blended together in a patchwork of love. She gave herself to it, reaching out her arms and pulling it around her until she was engulfed in the warmth. Then she knew that this was where she belonged.

CHRISTIAN HERALD
People Making A Difference

Christian Herald is a family of dedicated, Christ-centered ministries that reaches out to deprived children in need, and to homeless men who are lost in alcoholism and drug addiction. Christian Herald also offers the finest in family and evangelical literature through its book clubs and publishes a popular, dynamic magazine for today's Christians.

Our Ministries

Family Bookshelf and **Christian Bookshelf** provide a wide selection of inspirational reading and Christian literature written by best-selling authors. All books are recommended by an Advisory Board of distinguished writers and editors.

Christian Herald magazine is contemporary, a dynamic publication that addresses the vital concerns of today's Christian. Each monthly issue contains a sharing of true personal stories written by people who have found in Christ the strength to make a difference in the world around them.

Christian Herald Children. The door of God's grace opens wide to give impoverished youngsters a breath of fresh air, away from the evils of the streets. Every summer, hundreds of youngsters are welcomed at the Christian Herald Mont Lawn Camp located in the Poconos at Bushkill, Pennsylvania. Year-round assistance is also provided, including teen programs, tutoring in reading and writing, family counseling, career guidance and college scholarship programs.

The Bowery Mission. Located in New York City, the Bowery Mission offers hope and Gospel strength to the downtrodden and homeless. Here, the men of Skid Row are fed, clothed, ministered to. Many voluntarily enter a 6-month discipleship program of spiritual guidance, nutrition therapy and Bible study.

Our Father's House. Located in rural Pennsylvania, Our Father's House is a discipleship and job training center. Alcoholics and drug addicts are given an opportunity to recover, away from the temptations of city streets.

Christian Herald ministries, founded in 1878, are supported by the voluntary contributions of individuals and by legacies and bequests. Contributions are tax deductible. Checks should be made out to Christian Herald Children, The Bowery Mission, or to Christian Herald Association.

Administrative Office: 40 Overlook Drive, Chappaqua, New York 10514
Telephone: (914) 769-9000

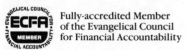 Fully-accredited Member
of the Evangelical Council
for Financial Accountability